A TALE OF
TWO KITTIES

A MAGICAL CATS MYSTERY

SOFIE KELLY

BERKLEY PRIME CRIME
New York

BERKLEY PRIME CRIME
Published by Berkley
An imprint of Penguin Random House LLC
375 Hudson Street, New York, New York 10014

ISBN: 9780399585593

Berkley Prime Crime hardcover edition / September 2017
Berkley Prime Crime mass-market edition / August 2018

Printed in the United States of America
3 5 7 9 10 8 6 4 2

Cover design by Rita Frangie
Cover art by Tristan Elwell

Titles by Sofie Kelly

For Patrick

ACKNOWLEDGMENTS

There are so many people working behind the scenes at Berkley Prime Crime that I never talk to directly, who helped put together this book. Thanks to each one of you. A special thank-you goes to my editor, Jessica Wade; her assistant, Miranda Hill; and PR whiz, Roxanne Jones. I'm so glad we're on the same team.

Thanks as well are due to my agent, Kim Lionetti, and the entire staff at Bookends Literary Agency. I don't tell you nearly enough how much I appreciate your hard work and unfailing good humor.

To all the readers, bloggers, reviewers and booksellers who have embraced Kathleen, Owen and Hercules, thank you from the bottom of my heart.

And, as always, thanks to Patrick and Lauren. Love you both!

A TALE OF
TWO KITTIES

1

You'd think by now it wouldn't bother me to step on a body in the middle of the kitchen floor, but I was in my sock feet and the body—missing its head, no surprise—was damp.

With cat slobber.

"Owen!" I yelled, hopping on one foot while I rubbed the other against my pant leg.

The cat stuck his gray tabby head around the living room doorway and looked at me, face tipped quizzically to one side.

"Come and get this," I said, pointing at the headless yellow catnip chicken, aka Fred the Funky Chicken, I'd just stepped on.

He craned his neck to see what I was referring to, then gave a murp of recognition almost as though he were saying, "So that's where I left it." He came across the floor, picked up the chicken body in his mouth and deposited it next to his food dish beside the refrigerator, nudging it out of the way with one paw. Then he turned to look at me.

"Thank you," I said. I leaned down to pick up the few bits of catnip that had fallen out of the mangled cat toy. Owen had a thing for catnip in general, and neon-yellow chickens stuffed with it in particular, and I had friends who bought them for him just about as fast as he could chew them apart.

I dumped the bits of dried catnip in the garbage and reached for my shoes on the mat near the back door.

"Mrr?" Owen said.

"I have a meeting at the library."

He immediately raised his paw and took a couple of passes at his face with it. Then he crossed to sit in front of the kitchen door.

I knew what that meant. "No, you can't come with me," I said.

He glanced over his shoulder at me. "Mrr," he said again.

I shook my head. "You can't come. Cats don't belong at the library." They didn't belong at the library, but both of mine had ended up there more than once. "Just because I'm the head librarian doesn't mean that you and your brother get special privileges."

Owen narrowed his golden eyes. His whiskers twitched, and then he disappeared.

Literally. It was his superpower, so to speak, the way the Flash could run faster than anyone else on the planet, although I was pretty sure Owen hadn't gotten his ability due to the explosion of a particle accelerator during a thunderstorm.

I'd gotten very blasé about Owen's ability to just vanish whenever he wanted to. I remembered how it had made me think I was losing my mind the first few times I'd seen it happen, and then the stomach-churning fear I'd felt when I realized what could happen to him and his brother, Hercules, if anyone found out about my cats' unbelievable abilities. Hercules couldn't become invisible at will; he could walk through walls. Both cats also had a seemingly uncanny ability to understand what was said to them. And now, to make things ten times more complicated, I was almost positive that Marcus's little ginger tabby, Micah, had the same vanishing skill as Owen.

My Marcus. Detective Marcus Gordon, who only believed in the facts, in things he could see and touch. If I was right about Micah there was a lot I'd need to explain. Not that I had any explanation. All three cats came from the old Henderson estate, Wisteria Hill. That had to have something to do with their abilities. I just had no idea what.

I'd sold my car when I'd moved to Mayville Heights from Boston two and a half years ago to supervise the renovations at the library. I spent my first few weeks in town exploring, walking for miles, which is how I'd stumbled on Wisteria Hill. At the time the property was abandoned. Now my friend Roma owned it, and the old farmhouse was full of life again. Back then it had seemed lonely and forgotten.

Owen and Hercules had peeked at me from a tangle of raspberry canes, two tiny balls of fur, and then trailed me while I explored the overgrown English country garden behind the old house. When I left, they'd followed me down the rutted gravel driveway. Twice I'd picked them up and carried them back to the empty house, but they were undeterred. They were so tiny and so determined to come with me that in the end I'd given up and brought them home. They were affectionate with me, but I'd quickly learned that because they had been feral they didn't tolerate anyone else touching them.

I stepped into my red Keds and bent down to tie the laces. "You're wasting your time," I said in the general direction of the last place I'd seen Owen. "You can't go with me in the truck because I'm going to walk."

I counted silently to three and he appeared again.

"I'm sorry," I said. "I'm going to a meeting. You'd be bored."

Owen made grumbling noises in the back of his throat and turned his head, pointedly looking away from me.

"I think you left a Funky Chicken in my closet," I said.

One gray ear twitched but he still didn't look at me.

"Look in my black pumps."

Owen shook himself and started across the kitchen floor. "Mrr," he said softly when he got to the living room doorway.

"You have a good day, too," I said.

It was a gorgeous morning as I started down Mountain Road. The sun was high in the sky over Lake Pepin and it was already warmer than the typical high for a day in early November.

It had been a while since I'd walked to the library. It was something I used to do every day. When I'd discovered everything I wanted to do was within walking distance, I hadn't bought a car. Eventually, Harrison Taylor had gifted me with a truck that could make it through even the worst Minnesota snow, a thank-you because I'd discovered some papers that had helped him find his daughter. Harrison's son, Harry Junior, took care of the yard work at my small house. The old man and I had met when he'd accompanied his son one day. I'd stepped into my backyard and for a moment thought Santa Claus was sitting on one of my Adirondack chairs. Harrison and I had quickly become good friends.

Mountain Road curves in toward the center of town, so as I headed down the hill the roof of the library building came into view. The library sits just about at the midpoint of a curve of shoreline, protected from the water by a rock wall. The two-story brick building has an original stained-glass window at one end and a copper-roofed cupola, complete with the restored wrought-iron weather vane that had been placed on the roof when the library had been completed more than a hundred years ago.

The Mayville Heights Free Public Library is a Carnegie library, built in 1912 with money donated by philanthropist Andrew Carnegie. I'd originally come to town to supervise the restoration of the building for its centenary, as well as update the collections and set up Internet access for the library's patrons. Very quickly the town and its people began to feel like home and when I'd been offered the chance to stay I'd said yes.

At the bottom of the hill I waited for two cars to pass and then crossed over to the same side of the street as the library. My friend Maggie, who was an artist, had created a collage map of the hiking trails in the area for the new Tourism Coalition that would be ready to hand out in the spring. Now Everett Henderson had her working on some ideas for a similar map of Mayville Heights. Everett had financed the repairs to the library as a gift to the town. The self-made businessman knew how to get things done and I felt confident that we'd have a town map by spring.

Ella King drove past me, waving when she caught sight of me. I waved back. I was guessing that she had just dropped her husband, Keith, at the library for the same meeting I was headed to.

Several weeks previous, a crew working on renovations to the main post office had torn down a wall and discovered a small cache of photos and undelivered mail. No one had any idea how it had all ended up there. Based on the postmarks, the mail had been behind the wall a bit more than twenty years. Some of the photos were of the same vintage; others were much older. The letters and cards had all been delivered, but no one was quite sure what to do with the photos, and before I knew what was happening the library board had offered to take them. Several days later a small cardboard box had been delivered to the library.

Mary Lowe and I had opened the box at the front

desk and looked through the photos. Mary was my most senior employee. I'd hoped she might recognize some of the people in the pictures. In the end she'd taken seven photos to give to, if not their original owners, a family who'd probably be happy to have them.

As far as the post office was concerned the photos were now the property of the library. I hated the thought of them sitting in a box on a shelf in our workroom. What I wanted to do was reunite the pictures with the people in them or at least a family member. I thought of how much fun my sister and brother and I had gotten from looking at old photos a friend of our parents had unearthed from early in their acting careers. I knew there had to be people who would treasure these images if I could just find them. That's what this meeting was about.

Maggie was coming because I knew whatever we ended up doing would benefit from her artistic eye. Rebecca Henderson and Keith King were on the library board. Rebecca was a longtime member, while Keith was the newest addition, and I felt both of them would have some good suggestions. I'd also asked Sandra Godfrey, who was a mail carrier now but who had worked in the main post office at one time, to join us.

It looked like I was right about Ella having dropped off Keith. He was standing on the walkway in front of the building, talking to Abigail Pierce, another of my staff members. She was wearing a chocolate-brown sweater coat she'd knit herself, which went well with her red hair streaked with gray. Abigail was also an author and I was hearing lots of great buzz about her new children's book.

Keith caught sight of me and smiled. He was about average height, wiry and strong with dark hair and a pair of black-and-stainless-steel-framed glasses. The glasses were new in the last month. "Hey, Kathleen," he said, nudging one corner of the frames.

"Good morning," I said. I pulled my keys out of my pocket and started up the library steps. "Why don't you come wait inside?"

"You sure?" he asked.

I nodded. "You can have a cup of coffee before the meeting starts."

"I can't say no to that." He grinned.

I unlocked the doors, shut off the alarm system and we stepped inside.

Abigail had switched on the main floor lights. She started for the stairs. "I'll put the coffee on," she said over her shoulder.

"You mind if I take a look at the magazines?" Keith asked.

I shook my head. "Go ahead. I'll let you know when the coffee's ready."

I went upstairs and dropped my things in my office. It only took five minutes to get set up for the meeting since I'd gotten the room ready before I'd left the previous day.

"Napkins," Abigail said, poking her head around the doorway.

"Thanks," I said, taking them from her. I looked around the room. There were enough chairs around the long table, I'd brought down a whiteboard and there was a carafe of coffee along with another of hot water for tea.

Maggie arrived about five minutes after we opened. I was at the circulation desk sorting the books from the book drop when she walked in. She smiled when she saw me and walked across the mosaic tile floor to join me.

"Good morning. Is this really November?" she asked, unzipping her jacket. "I think it was colder in September than it is today."

"According to the forecast we could hit close to seventy this afternoon," I said.

"Global warming or something else?" Maggie cocked her head to one side and eyed me. "I know you know."

"A weak La Niña that developed in October," I said, feeling a little like that kid back in elementary school who had liked to read the encyclopedia for fun—which was exactly the kind of kid I had actually been.

Maggie grinned, playing with the fringe of the multicolored scarf she'd wrapped twice around her neck. "You're better than Google!"

I grinned back at her. "And I work even when there's no Wi-Fi!"

"Am I the first one here?" She looked around the main floor of the library.

"Keith's here," I said, gesturing in the direction of the meeting room.

Just then Harry Taylor walked into the building.

He looked around and when he saw us raised a hand to get my attention and headed over.

"Morning," he said, nodding at both of us.

Harry was in his late fifties. There were deep lines carved around his green eyes from years of working in the sun, and the fringe of salt-and-pepper hair peeking out from under his Twins baseball cap was pretty much the only hair he had left. He was a quiet, thoughtful man, and very well-read, I knew.

"I was hoping I'd catch you before it got busy, Kathleen," he said. "I've pretty much done all I can do on those shelves in the workshop. Next step is to get them put together here."

Harry was building a shelving unit to fit on one wall of our upstairs workroom. I was hoping that would help us finally get the space organized.

"I can get everything moved out of the way this afternoon," I said. "You can get started tomorrow if you want to."

"Sounds good," he said. "And I'll be back this afternoon to fix the broken seat in the gazebo."

"You're putting shelves in the workroom?" Maggie asked.

I nodded. "On the end wall that's common with my office. And not just shelves. Harry is making a cupboard we can lock with a drawer underneath. That whole wall will be storage."

Maggie turned to Harry. "Could you do something like that for me at my studio? I need a better way to organize supplies."

"What did you have in mind?" he asked, pulling a

small notebook and a pencil out of the pocket of his green quilted vest.

Maggie looked at me. "Do I have time to talk to Harry?" she asked.

I nodded. "Go ahead."

They started toward a nearby cluster of tables, Maggie's hands moving through the air as she talked.

I set the pile of books by my elbow on a cart as Susan came from the computer area, where she'd just booted up all of our public-access computers for the day.

"I have about half of the books from the book drop sorted," I told her. "It's almost time for the meeting to get started, so I'm just going to run up to my office for a minute."

"I'll finish this," she said, sliding into the chair behind the counter and reaching for the handle at the side to raise the seat.

Susan was tiny, barely five feet tall in her sock feet. She wore retro cat's-eye glasses that made her look like anything but a stereotypical bespectacled librarian, and her dark curly hair was always pulled up in a topknot secured with anything from a pencil to a chopstick. This morning her hair seemed to be held in place with two white golf tees.

"And if you need me—," I began.

"Don't worry," Susan said, pulling one of the rolling carts closer. "Abigail and I can handle things. If anyone gets out of line I can give them the Mom Look, and Mary taught Abigail some kind of one-legged takedown maneuver that kickboxers use."

Mary—who looked like the sweet grandmother she was—was also the state kickboxing champion for her age. I didn't want to think about what maneuver she'd taught to Abigail.

"Then I'll just leave things in your capable hands . . . and feet," I said, heading for the stairs.

Up in my office I grabbed a pen and a notebook. Then I stood for a moment by the wide window behind my desk and looked out over the water. For me, one of the most beautiful parts of Mayville Heights was the waterfront, with all the big elm and black walnut trees that lined the shore, and the Riverwalk trail that made its way from the old warehouses at the point, past the downtown shops and businesses, all the way out beyond the marina. I could see the barges and boats go by on the water just the way they had more than a hundred years ago.

As I headed back down the stairs Sandra Godfrey came into the building. Rebecca was with her. The latter was carrying a large, round metal cookie tin and I knew there would be something good inside.

"Are we late?" Sandra asked. Her sandy blond hair was parted in the middle and pulled back into a low ponytail. She wore jeans and a red cable-knit sweater with a navy quilted vest over the top. Even in flat sneakers she was several inches taller than my five foot six. Rebecca seemed very tiny beside her.

I shook my head. "You're right on time."

Rebecca handed me the cookie tin. "Mary's cinnamon rolls," she said. Her blue eyes twinkled. "She said the leftovers are for the staff."

"That's assuming there will be any leftovers," I said with a smile.

It turned out to be a productive meeting. Everyone liked the idea of returning the photos to the people in them, or at least to their families. Sandra asked about leaving the box of pictures at the circulation desk and encouraging people to look through them when they came in. I explained that many of the photos were dry and brittle and wouldn't stand up to a lot of handling. Keith suggested putting them on a large table and covering them with a piece of glass. I thought that idea had potential and he volunteered to price the glass for me. Rebecca and Sandra offered to stay behind and sort through the pictures again. Rebecca had spent her whole life in Mayville Heights and Sandra had been a mail carrier for years. Between the two of them they knew a lot of people in town and I was hopeful they would find some faces they recognized.

I walked Maggie to the front entrance. "You were quiet," I said.

She ran a hand over her blond curls. "I like Keith's idea to display the pictures," she said. "But I think we need a way to get more people in here to look at them."

"Any suggestions?" I asked.

She frowned. "I don't know yet. Do you think I could come back and take a look through the photos some other time?"

I nodded. "Of course. Just let me know what works for you."

She hugged me, promised she'd call about the photos and left.

I went back to the meeting room to tidy up. Rebecca and Sandra had taken the box of photos and moved to a table in the main part of the library. I tucked the chairs in against the table and opened the window blinds about halfway to let a little sun in. Abigail tapped me on the shoulder and when I turned around she handed me a coffee mug.

"Oh, thank you," I said. "You read my mind." I took a long drink.

"Dishes are done," she said, "and there are three cinnamon rolls left for our break."

I wrapped both hands around my cup. "Thank you," I said. The seniors' quilting group was set up in our other meeting room and I could see Susan through the open door, checking someone out at the circulation desk. It was going to be a busy day.

The temperature was in the high sixties by lunchtime, so I decided to go for a walk. Marcus was out of town taking a course on crisis negotiation. He'd left a message on my voice mail and when I called him back I'd had to settle for doing the same.

I walked down along the Riverwalk as far as the hotel before turning back. I knew that a month from now the wind would be coming in off the water and pulling at the tree branches, so I was glad to take advantage of the out-of-season warmth while it was here.

I had just turned the corner toward the library

when a man stopped me on the sidewalk. He looked to be in his late sixties or early seventies; a tourist, I was guessing, since his face didn't look familiar. "Excuse me," he said with a polite smile. "Could you tell me if I'm headed in the right direction for the library?"

"Yes, you are," I said. "I'm headed there myself. I can show you."

The man smiled. "Thank you," he said. He offered his hand. "I'm Victor Janes."

Victor Janes was maybe five foot nine, with salt-and-pepper hair. He was on the thin side, I noticed, and there were dark circles under his eyes, but his handshake was strong.

"I'm Kathleen Paulson," I said. "Are you related to Simon Janes?"

"Simon is my nephew," he said. "His father and I are brothers." We started walking. "Is Simon a friend of yours?"

Were Simon and I friends? I wasn't sure how to answer that. We'd met at a fundraiser for the library's Reading Buddies program. At the time his daughter, Mia, had been our student intern. Simon and I had gotten to know each other better over the past few weeks, working together to try to figure out if a proposed development out at Long Lake had had anything to do with the death of an environmentalist. Did that make us friends?

I settled for saying, "Mia works for me." I gestured at the library building. "I'm actually the librarian here."

"It's been a long time since I've been in the library,"

Victor said. "And I wasn't what you'd call the studious type back in the day." He smiled and looked up at the roof and the copper-topped cupola. "That can't be the original weather vane?"

"It is," I said. "It had a bit of a cant to one side, but we managed to get it straightened out. Rumor has it that happened one year at Homecoming, when a surprisingly lifelike effigy of the high school principal ended up on the roof."

"It was tied to the weather vane and it was a lot heavier than it looked." He shifted his gaze to my face. I was having a hard time keeping a grin in check. Victor Janes cleared his throat. "Or so I heard."

"I'm sure it was," I said.

I led him down the sidewalk to the main entrance. Inside he stopped and looked around, taking in everything from the wide plaster medallion on the ceiling over the circulation desk to the sun coming through the stained-glass window. "I heard the building had been restored, but I didn't expect anything like this," he said. "Very nice."

"Thank you," I said. I looked in the direction of the stacks. "Is there anything I can help you find?"

"Could you tell me where I could find whatever you have on vegan cooking?"

"The subject in general or cookbooks?"

"The subject in general," he said. "I've been following a vegan diet throughout some . . . health issues, but I left my books at home."

I wondered if those health issues were why he

seemed a little gaunt and pale. "They would be in the 613s." I pointed across the room. "Go down to the end of those shelves and turn right."

Victor smiled. "Thank you," he said. "It's been a pleasure to meet you. I'm sure I'll see you again."

"If you need any help please let one of us know," I said. He headed for the stacks and I turned and walked over to the front desk. Mary was there, staring unabashedly after Victor Janes.

She shook her head. "Lord love a duck, it can't be," she said, more to herself than to me, it seemed.

"Can't be what?" I asked.

"That can't be who I think it is." She was still staring after Victor, who had disappeared "I didn't really think he'd come."

"It's Simon's uncle."

She turned her attention to me then. "I know that. You might want to go get a fire extinguisher."

I frowned at her. "What on earth are you talking about?"

"If Victor Janes is back in town there's a good chance we're going to be struck by lightning." Mary made a face, two lines forming between her eyebrows. "Don't tell me no one told you?"

I stifled a sigh of frustration. "I think it's pretty clear no one did since I'm completely lost."

She patted her heavily hair-sprayed gray curls. "I don't want to be a gossiping old busybody but since darling little Mia works here you should probably understand the nuances." Her expression was serious.

"All right," I said.

"Like you said, Victor is Simon's uncle, his father—Leo's—twin. Victor had an affair with Simon's mother, Meredith. He convinced her to run off with him and shortly after she was killed in a car accident."

I didn't know what to say.

"Simon was about fourteen or fifteen. Leo was devastated and disowned his brother. No one in that family has spoken to Victor in more than twenty years."

"Why would he come back now, after all this time?" I said.

"He's sick," Mary said flatly.

I stared at her. I'd never heard so little compassion in her voice.

"Apparently he has cancer. I don't know what kind. Leo's here for the first time in years and I'd heard that he invited Victor to come for a visit, and maybe even for some kind of reconciliation." Her mouth twisted. "I guess blood is thicker than water."

Something of what I was thinking must have shown in my face.

"I must sound cold to you," Mary said. She was several inches shorter than I am and she cocked her head to one side and looked up at me. "Meredith was my friend, Kathleen. I haven't told Mia that because as far as I know Simon never talks about his mother and I didn't want to go stirring things up. I know Meredith wasn't blameless in what happened. But there was a rumor that she was on her way back to Leo and Simon when she was killed." She stared past me, at some memory maybe. "I didn't realize how much I still blame him. I guess I'm more judgmental than I thought." Her gaze came back to mine.

I reached over and touched her arm. "I don't think you're judgmental," I said. "I think you're a good friend."

The phone rang then and Mary reached for it. I headed up to my office.

I had just finished updating the public-access computers later that afternoon when Mia Janes came in—half an hour early—for her shift. I didn't need Mary or anyone else to tell me the man with her was her grandfather, Simon's father and Victor Janes's twin brother. I could see the resemblance.

As usual Mia was sedately dressed in a white shirt, gray jacket and dark pants with no holes or worn spots. Her hair was streaked a deep plum color, which looked good with her fair skin.

Leo Janes was smiling at Mary across the circulation desk as I joined them. "Mary, it's good to see you," he said.

"It's good to see you, too, Leo," she said.

Leo turned to his granddaughter. "Mary was friends with your grandmother."

"I didn't know that," Mia said.

"I probably have some pictures of us from high school," Mary said. "Would you like me to see if I can find them?"

Mia beamed at her. "Yes," she said. "I mean, if it's not too much trouble."

"It's not any trouble," Mary said. "You have to promise not to laugh at my clothes."

"I wouldn't do that," Mia said, looking a little puzzled.

"I have two words for you. Go-go boots."

Mia pressed her lips together in a valiant attempt not to laugh. I did laugh and then tried to disguise it into a cough. It didn't work.

Mary turned, pointing an accusing finger at me. "Are you laughing at the idea of me in a minidress and white patent-leather go-go boots, Kathleen?" she asked. I could see a hint of a smile lurking behind the mock frown she gave me.

"I am making every effort not to," I said as my shoulders shook with laughter.

Mia smiled. She was a serious young woman and it made me feel good to see her so clearly happy. She turned to her grandfather. "Grandpa, this is Kathleen Paulson, my boss."

He held out his hand and I shook it. "I'm Leo Janes," he said with a smile. "I've heard a lot about you from my granddaughter." He looked so much like his brother and yet he didn't. The color in Victor's hair and beard had been touched up, I suspected; Leo had more gray. He also had a few more lines in his face but also far more warmth. And he and Simon had the same smile.

"Sweetie, there's a tin of oatmeal-raisin cookies upstairs in the staff room for you. If you don't go get them now I can't promise they'll be there by the end of the night," Mary said. "Heaven knows the cinnamon rolls I sent over this morning with Rebecca seem to have disappeared." She eyed me and I tried to look innocent, hoping I didn't have any crumbs on my clothes to give me away.

Mia narrowed her eyes at Mary. "Are you going to talk about me while I'm gone?"

Mary put a hand on her chest in mock outrage. "I can't believe you'd ask that," she said. She paused for dramatic effect. "Of course we are!"

Mia laughed. "I'll be right back," she said to her grandfather.

"Thank you," Leo said to Mary. "She loves working here."

"We love having her," Mary said. She looked at me. "Kathleen, could you watch the desk for a minute?" She pointed at a man over at the card catalogue. "I don't think he understands that our computers don't have touch screens. He's going to poke his finger right through the monitor."

"Go ahead," I said.

She came around the desk. "It's good to see you," she said to Leo, patting his shoulder.

He nodded. "It's good to be back."

Mary hurried across the floor and I turned to Leo Janes. "Mia and Simon both speak highly of you," he said. He'd been studying me, I'd noticed, since I walked over to join them, watching me in much the same way I'd seen his son do. Something else they had in common.

"They're both special people," I said. "Simon probably didn't tell you that he made a very generous gift to our Reading Buddies program."

Leo gave his head a slight shake. "He didn't. But Mia told me." A smile pulled at the corners of his mouth. "She also told me she called him an ass."

I remembered how Simon had walked into the library several days after a disastrous fundraiser for the literacy program. He'd handed me an envelope with a very large check inside. When I'd thanked him, he'd told me the person I should be thanking was his daughter. She had pointed out that he could easily afford to help fund Reading Buddies and called him out because he hadn't.

I laughed. "She did. And yes, that probably had a lot to do with the first donation. But he's made two more since then."

I could see the gleam of approval in the older man's eyes.

"And Mia is so good with people. The little ones love her. She gets down on the floor with them at story time and when she reads she does all the voices." It had only taken a little encouragement to nudge Mia out of her shell. "She actually put orange streaks in the hair of a couple of the seniors from the quilting group for Halloween."

Leo smiled and once again I saw the resemblance with his son. "She thinks of you all as family and that means a great deal to me, Ms. Paulson. She only has Simon and me."

I noticed he didn't mention Victor.

"Please call me Kathleen," I said.

"Then you'll have to call me Leo," he countered.

I nodded. "I can do that."

A burly man in a dark overcoat and sunglasses came in the main entrance then. He stopped to remove the glasses and I automatically smiled in his direction. Leo followed my gaze and it seemed to me his expression hardened a little, his jaw tightening.

The man's eyes seemed to slide over Leo. He turned left and headed for the stacks. Mia's grandfather watched him go. "Is that someone you know?" I asked.

He shook his head. "No," he said. "The man just looked familiar for a moment. That's all."

Mia returned then, hugging the tin of Mary's cookies to her chest. "Grandpa, can I trust you to take these home and not eat them all?" she asked.

"I can't believe you're asking me that!" Leo said, echoing what Mary had said earlier, his eyes widening in surprise. "Of course you can't."

Mia made a face at her grandfather but I could see the sparkle in her eyes and I knew she wasn't really angry. "I'm serious," she said, frowning at him.

Leo gave her a guileless look. "So am I."

Mia shook her head and laughed. "You and Dad could at least save me one," she said, passing over the tin. She leaned forward and hugged her grandfather. Then she looked at me. "Kathleen, Grandpa is the reason I roll left. He's a lefty."

"That explains it," I said.

Leo looked uncertainly from his granddaughter to me. "Excuse me," he said. "What does 'roll left' mean and why am I being blamed for it?"

"It's not a bad thing," I said with a smile. "I promise. Yesterday Mia and I and someone from the fire station were teaching a group of kids to stop, drop and roll. Everyone rolled to the right, except Mia."

She laughed. "I told them you were the one who taught stop, drop and roll to me and I've always done it that way."

"You're left-handed," I said. "That's why you roll left and that's what you taught Mia. Most right-handed people will roll to the right."

Leo held out his hands. "I'm in here for five minutes and I've learned something new."

I grinned at him. "I should tell you the source of that information is my mother."

He smiled back at me. "I'm sure she's an unimpeachable source. However, in the interest of full disclosure I should tell you that I'm actually ambidextrous." He turned to his granddaughter and gave her a hug. "I'll see you later, kiddo," he said as Mary rejoined us. "It's good to see you again, Mary," he said to her. "It's been too long. I won't make that mistake again."

"Good to see you, too, Leo," Mary said.

He turned to me. "And it was a pleasure to meet you, Kathleen."

"You as well."

He raised one hand in good-bye, and with that he left.

Mia moved behind the circulation desk just as the phone started to ring.

"I'm going to start shelving," Mary said.

I nodded. "I'll be in my office."

I went upstairs and detoured into the staff room long enough to get yet another cup of coffee. In my office I turned on my laptop and then went to stand in front of the window behind my desk. I expected to see Harry Taylor out there, working on the broken gazebo seat.

Harry was outside at the gazebo but he wasn't repairing the broken seat. He was having a very heated conversation.

With Leo Janes.

2

As I watched, Leo said one last thing to Harry and walked away. Harry in turn slammed his hand down hard on the top of the rain barrel that sat next to the gazebo. I couldn't help wondering what the two men had been arguing about. Harry was easy to get along with and slow to anger, and although I'd just met Leo Janes he seemed like a pleasant man. So what had been going on? I turned away from the window and sat down at my desk.

I managed to get the staffing schedule finished up through the holidays and to make a start on going over the circulation stats for the various magazines we offered.

I did a circuit of the building before I left for the night. Mary was at the front desk going over what I was guessing was a reading list of some kind with a couple of teens I didn't remember ever seeing in the library before. I found Mia shelving books in the young adult section, humming softly to herself.

"I like your grandfather," I said.

"Grandpa's great, isn't he?" she said, her face lighting up. "I'm so happy he finally agreed to come here for Thanksgiving. Before, we always went to see him. My dad bugged him and bugged him and then suddenly one day he said yes."

I smiled. "I'm not surprised. It's pretty clear he loves you very much."

"I love him, too," she said. Her expression grew serious then. "He's not just here because of me. My uncle Victor—great-uncle, really—he's here, too." She picked at a bit of loose skin on one side of her thumb.

She didn't like the man, I realized. It was written all over her face, in the way her eyebrows knit together and her jaw tightened. "I met him," I said, "walking back here at lunchtime."

"What did you think of him?"

"I didn't really spend enough time with him to be able to say." It was the most diplomatic answer I could come up with.

"You didn't like him," Mia said flatly. She crossed her arms over her chest and studied me.

"Why do you think that?" I asked. I hadn't really formed an opinion about Victor Janes.

"You only spent a few minutes with my grandfather but you like him."

I nodded. "I do. But sometimes you need to spend more time with a person before you can make up your mind about them. At least I do."

"That's because you're terminally nice. That's what Mary says."

I couldn't help laughing. "I appreciate Mary's confidence in the way I try to treat people but I don't think it's true." And I wasn't sure Mary had meant the comment as a compliment. "Sometimes I'm mean and petty."

Mia shook her head. "No, you're not. You're nice to people who aren't nice to anyone else—who aren't nice to you. I'm not like that."

I reached over and straightened three books on the shelf next to my shoulder. "Yes, you are," I said. "You're thoughtful and kind and yes, nice." I held out both hands. "Sorry. You just are."

She didn't smile. She just shook her head again. "I'm not. Because I don't like my Uncle Victor. In fact I pretty much hate him. That's not what a nice person would do."

I wanted to wrap her in a hug, but I didn't want to overstep any boundaries.

Mia pushed a strand of plum-colored hair back off her face. "My uncle Victor had an affair with my dad's mom. He didn't care about them. My grandfather says everyone deserves a second chance but I don't see why I should give Uncle Victor one, even though Grandpa wants me to. You can't use the word 'sorry' like it's an eraser and it just takes away all the bad stuff you did." She let out a breath. "You probably don't get that."

"I get it better than you think," I said. "Someone hurt my dad once very, very much."

"Who?" Mia asked. She'd been reaching for the

books she'd set on the cart but she put them down again.

"My mother."

Her eyes widened. "I . . . I don't understand."

"When I was a bit younger than you are now my parents got divorced. My mom went to LA just for a couple of months to do a soap and I stayed with my dad in Boston." I remembered the anger that had seemed to eat a hole in my stomach because my mother had been the one to file for divorce. "Mia, I hated my mother for a while. Half the time I wouldn't talk to her when she called. Then, one day after an angry conversation with Mom on the phone in which I said she was selfish and actually knocked the phone onto the floor, my father came into my room and told me that my behavior toward my mother was selfish."

Mia frowned. "I don't understand."

I swiped a hand over my mouth as if I could somehow go back in time and wipe away all the hateful words I'd said to my mother. "Neither did I, but Dad said that the end of their marriage was between the two of them, that he loved me for caring about him but he didn't like the way I was treating Mom, who he knew loved me more than anyone or anything in the world." I still remembered his voice. He hadn't raised it but I'd had no doubt how he felt about the things I'd said to Mom. There had been a hard edge of anger in his tone although he'd spoken quietly. My father saved the dramatics in his life for the stage and the screen.

"He said, 'What's between your mother and me is

between us. Don't put it between the two of you.' Then he called her and they talked for about an hour, I figured about me." I gave Mia a wry smile. "A few months later they started secretly seeing each other and then suddenly I was going to be a big sister to twins and they were getting married. Again." I was probably never going to forget my teenage mortification at the undeniable evidence that my parents had been having sex.

"Are you serious?" Mia asked.

"Yes," I said. I didn't add that it *wasn't* the most embarrassing thing my family had ever done, either.

"Wow," she said.

I nodded.

"Are you going to tell me that I should give Uncle Victor another chance?"

"No," I said. "I'm going to tell you that families are messy. As far as anything else goes I know you'll figure it out." I put my arm around Mia's shoulders and gave her a squeeze. "I'll see you tomorrow," I said, and headed out to walk home.

After a bowl of turkey-rice soup and crackers—cracked pepper for me and sardine for Owen and Hercules—I grabbed my bag and went to pick up Rebecca for tai chi class. It was Rebecca who had originally invited me to try the class right after I'd moved to town. I sometimes wondered if I would have the circle of friends I had now if I hadn't said yes to her invitation.

When Everett and Rebecca had gotten married he

had moved into her small house just across my back-yard and sold Wisteria Hill to Roma. I'd been happy to know that I wasn't losing Rebecca as a neighbor. I was certain Owen and Hercules felt the same way. She kept them both in cat treats. In Owen's case that meant a steady supply of yellow Fred the Funky Chickens. For Herc it was little dishes of whitefish and the occasional bit of salmon. Everett had just hired Oren Kenyon to refinish the floors and the trim in the small farmhouse, so their furniture was in storage and they were living in Everett's downtown apartment—or as Rebecca laughingly liked to call it, their pied-à-terre.

Everett's former bachelor pad was in a two-story Georgian-style brick house that he owned, close to his downtown office in a neighborhood filled with similar, beautifully restored houses. It had crisp white trim and shutters and a wrought-iron fence around a small flower garden between the house and the sidewalk. The garden was one of Rebecca's touches, put to bed now for the winter.

I pushed open the wrought-iron gate and went down the narrow walkway between the house and its neighbor to the left of the entrance. At the top of the steps was a set of double six-panel doors painted with a gleaming black finish. They opened into a small entryway with another set of double doors. These were half-frosted glass. To the right were doorbells for the three apartments in the building. To the left were three mailboxes.

Everett and Rebecca had the entire second floor. One of the smaller main-floor units was kept for business associates of Everett's to stay in when they came to town and for family when they visited. Until recently the other had been rented to a cousin of Everett's assistant, Lita.

As I stepped into the entryway the second set of doors opened and a woman hurried out, pushing past me with a rushed apology. She was gone before I had a chance to say anything. I didn't recognize the woman. Her head had been down and she'd been pulling up the hood of her navy jacket over a tie-dyed silk scarf as she brushed past me, but I'd caught enough of her face to realize she wasn't someone I knew and she didn't look happy. Her lips were pulled together in a tight, thin line and her cheeks were flushed.

I caught the inside door and headed up the stairs. I knocked on the apartment door and Rebecca opened it right away. She had one arm in her jacket.

"Hello, dear," she said. These days she was wearing her silver hair in a short, layered cut, which showed off her neck and cheekbones.

"Hi," I said, reaching over to hold the front of the coat so she could get her other arm in. "I'm sorry I didn't ring the bell, but your visitor was just leaving so I just came up."

"I didn't have any visitor," Rebecca said, pulling down one of Ella King's scarves from the wooden coatrack and wrapping it twice around her neck. She frowned for a minute and then her expression cleared. "It must have been someone visiting Leo."

"Leo?" I said slowly. "You don't mean Leo Janes, do you?"

"Yes, I do," she said, smiling at me. "Simon's father. Have you met him?"

I nodded, reaching for the tote bag that I knew held her shoes for tai chi and a towel. "Just a little while ago. He drove Mia to work."

"He used to live here in Mayville Heights," Rebecca said. She stopped to lock the apartment door and we started down the stairs together. "He hasn't been back in—goodness, let me think—it must be more than twenty years." She adjusted the scarf at her neck. "When Everett heard that Leo was coming to spend some time with Simon and Mia he offered him the apartment." She made a gesture in the direction of the front unit.

I wasn't surprised. Everett may have been relentless when it came to business but he was a softie when it came to anything related to family. I remembered how he'd flown in Rebecca's son, Matthew, from a remote job site in the Canadian far north, where he was working as a geologist, to surprise her on their wedding day.

"Mary told me a little about the family," I said.

Rebecca glanced sideways at me. "So you know," she said, not phrasing her comment as a question.

I nodded. "Yes."

"The whole thing is just so sad."

I moved ahead of her to open the door to the entryway.

"Hold on a minute, dear," she said. "I need to check the clock." She moved to the left side of the stairs and I noticed there was a small mantel clock settled in a niche in the wall. She checked the clock face and then nodded. "It's still running. Good."

"I never noticed that before," I said.

"The clock came with the house," Rebecca said. "It's been there for a good fifty years, but it's temperamental."

I nodded, reaching for the door handle. "I know. My father has one just like it at home. Do you keep the key taped to the back?"

She nodded. "In a little envelope. Before I did that I misplaced the darned thing twice."

I held the door and we stepped into the entry. I waited while Rebecca locked up.

"Maybe if Meredith hadn't died things would have turned out differently," she continued as we headed down the walkway toward the truck. "Maybe Leo could have forgiven them both. That doesn't mean I'm excusing what she and Victor did. It's just that sometimes we don't get a do-over in life, a chance to fix our mistakes, but I think it would be nice if we could." She sighed softly.

I thought about what Mia had said to me about the word "sorry" not being an eraser.

When Rebecca and I got to tai chi Taylor King was waiting for her, sitting on the bench beneath the coat hooks, a brown paper shopping bag at her feet. Her long red hair was pulled back in a French braid and she was wearing a black T-shirt and black-and-gray-patterned leggings.

Rebecca smiled when she caught sight of the teen. "Look at your hair!" she exclaimed.

Taylor got to her feet, a huge smile spreading across her face.

Rebecca made a circular motion with her index finger. "Let me see the back."

Taylor obligingly turned around.

"Excellent," Rebecca said. "I knew you'd be able to do it."

The teenager looked at me, a flush of pink in her cheeks. "Rebecca taught me how to do a French braid. She's a hair ninja."

"That she is," I agreed, grinning at Rebecca as I slipped off my jacket. She'd been a hairdresser and she kept current as far as new styles and techniques went. She'd fixed an ill-advised pixie cut I'd gotten before I came to Mayville Heights and gotten me through the awkward growing-out stage fairly painlessly. Now my dark hair almost brushed my shoulders.

Rebecca gestured at the paper shopping bag. "You brought the bags," she said to Taylor, her smile widening.

The teen nodded. "I brought two and if you don't like either of these I have a couple of others that might work." Taylor collected and sold vintage purses. She'd turned a hobby into a little business that was going to help pay her way through college.

"A possible Christmas gift for Ami," Rebecca said to me. She sat down on the bench and set her own bag at her feet. Taylor joined her and pulled out a small, black lace evening bag with a gold clasp and black satin strap.

"That's pretty," I said.

"It came from an estate sale in Pucketville," Taylor said. "Oh, and Mom said to tell you she got the yarn for your scarf, so she'll probably start it this week."

"Tell her thank you," I said.

Ella King was a talented fiber artist. She was knitting a linen stitch scarf for my sister, Sara, for Christmas.

Rebecca was holding the evening bag on her lap. She looked up at us. "Do you think Ami would like this?" Ami was Everett's only grandchild. She was away at college studying voice and piano. Ami adored Rebecca, and I knew she would be happy with the paper shopping bag if it came from her.

"I think so," I said, stepping into the canvas shoes I wore for class.

Taylor pulled out another evening bag. This one was a beaded silver-tone clutch with a silver chain strap.

"That's beautiful, too," Rebecca said. "How on earth am I going to decide?"

I leaned down toward her. "We both know you're going to buy both of those bags," I whispered.

She winked at me. "Well, of course I am, but I want to be able to tell Everett that I tried to pick just one."

I smiled back at her. "Your secret is safe with me," I said, heading inside. I walked over to join Maggie at the small table she had set up for tea.

She smiled. "Hi. Did Rebecca and Sandra have any

luck figuring out who any of those photos might belong to?" Her hands were wrapped around a blue pottery mug and I could smell spices and oranges.

"Between the two of them they recognized the people in eight of the pictures," I said. "The only way we're going to figure out who's in all of the other ones is to somehow get people into the library to look at them."

She took a sip of her tea. It smelled so good I was almost tempted to make myself a cup. Almost.

"Hey, guess who I met?" she said. "Simon's father. He came into the shop and bought a tea set. He had such a warm energy around him."

"He drove Mia to work. He's a nice man." I glanced across the room. Roma had just come in with Eddie. I raised a hand in hello and they started over to us.

Maggie followed my gaze. "I love a happy ending," she said softly.

I nodded. "Me too."

It was wonderful to see Roma so happy. She was getting married. After insisting she was too old for hockey player Eddie Sweeney and ending their relationship, she'd realized that how she and Eddie felt about each other was more important than the number of years between them. So she'd proposed to him in the middle of my kitchen and he'd happily said yes.

"Hey, Eddie, are you going to stay for class?" Maggie asked.

Roma tipped her head to one side and smiled up at him, her dark eyes sparkling. "Are you?" she asked.

He made a face at her. Then turned to Maggie.

"Thank you for the invitation, but no. The hockey team has practice." Now that Eddie was retired and living in Mayville Heights he was helping coach the girls' hockey team. The girls' team because of a nudge from his daughter, Sydney.

Eddie's expression grew serious. "The strangest thing happened to us on the way down here," he said.

Roma's smile disappeared and she nodded.

"We were followed down the highway by a drone."

"Followed?" I said.

"For close to a mile," Roma said.

"It was definitely deliberate," Eddie added, running a hand over the stubble on his chin. "The road turned twice and the drone stayed with us."

Maggie set her mug on the table. "The same thing happened to Brady on the weekend."

"When?" Eddie asked.

"Where?" I said.

Maggie let out a breath. "Saturday evening, maybe seven o'clock. But he wasn't on the highway. He was out past the marina."

"And something similar happened?" Roma asked, her forehead creased into a frown.

"Very," Maggie said. "Brady said the drone followed him for about a mile and then veered away toward the bluff."

"That's dangerous," I said. "Someone could have an accident just from being distracted."

Eddie nodded. "Or the drone could hit a car." He shook his head. "I thought I'd talk to Marcus when he gets back and see if there's anything he can do."

I automatically started to smile. "He'll be back around supper time tomorrow."

"I can wait until Thursday." Eddie grinned and I felt my face get red.

I turned to Maggie. "Isn't it time for class to start?" I asked.

Maggie smiled. "Yes, it is." She stepped out into the room, clapped her hands and called, "Circle."

Eddie planted a quick kiss on the top of Roma's head.

"I'll tell Marcus you want to talk to him," I said.

"Thanks," he said and he was gone.

Roma and I took our places in the circle. Maggie had that gleam in her eye that told me she was going to work us hard. And she did. Ruby and I paired up to work on our Push Hands and Maggie spent some time watching and refining our technique. By the time we finished class with the complete form, the back of my neck was damp with sweat.

Roma and Eddie were giving Rebecca a ride home. "Eddie has some papers that Everett wants to look at," Roma said, watching him hold Rebecca's jacket for her. I noticed that Rebecca was carrying the brown paper shopping bag and Taylor was empty-handed, which told me that Rebecca had decided on both vintage evening bags. "Everett is interested in Eddie's idea for a hockey school."

I held up two crossed fingers. "I'll hold a good thought."

Roma hugged me and said good night. I sat down to change my shoes. One more day and Marcus would be home. Seeing Roma with Eddie made me realize just how much I'd missed him.

It had taken quite a while for the relationship between Marcus and me to move beyond friendship, even though at times it had felt like the entire town was playing matchmaker. It didn't help that we'd first met when I was briefly a person of interest in one of his cases. I'd stumbled on the body of conductor Gregor Easton at the Stratton Theatre. Marcus had suggested that maybe I'd been at the theater to meet the conductor—who was older than my father—for a romantic liaison. I'd taken offense at what he'd been insinuating, and *he'd* taken offense at what he saw as me nosing around in his case. I'd had no idea he'd turn into my happy ending.

It was much quieter than usual at the library the next day. As promised, Harry came in first thing and assembled the shelves and storage unit. Midafternoon I decided to start putting up the Thanksgiving decorations. I'd hung a conga line of dancing paper turkeys across the front of the circulation desk, but they were crooked, looking as though the big birds were slipping downhill. I took several steps backward to get a better perspective and bumped into a warm, solid male chest. I turned around to find Marcus smiling at me, all six feet–plus of brown-haired, blue-eyed handsome.

He looked around. "Is anyone watching?" he asked, then before I could answer he swept me into his arms.

"I don't care if they are," he said, pulling me into a long kiss.

For a moment my legs lost the ability to hold me up, so I held on to him, which wasn't exactly a hardship. This public display wasn't like Marcus. Not that I minded.

"I missed you," he said. He was wearing a gray sweater over a light blue T-shirt and smelled like coffee and the spicy aftershave he always wore.

"I missed you, too," I said, finally breaking out of his embrace. "What are you doing here now?"

"We got out early." He smiled. "Get your things."

"I can't," I said. "I'm not done until supper time."

Susan walked through the door then, grinning at me and making a shooing motion with her hands. She was wearing an origami flower fastened to what looked to be a swizzle stick in her hair.

"Go," she said, wiggling her eyebrows at me. "I'll take care of the rest of your shift. Just because I'm an old married woman doesn't mean I've forgotten about romance."

"You did this," I said to Marcus.

"Guilty," he admitted.

Susan tipped her head in the direction of the stairs. "You're burning daylight. Go!"

I hurried up to my office, grabbed my jacket and purse and left everything else. Downstairs, Marcus and Susan had their heads together. She was gesturing emphatically, the flower in her topknot bouncing as she talked.

"I'm ready," I said.

"Have fun, children," Susan said with a knowing smirk.

Marcus caught my hand and we started for the main doors. I turned back and mouthed "Thank you" to Susan. She gave a little wave.

"Where are we going?" I asked.

"Your house," he said as we started down the front steps. "I'll follow you. And don't worry about Micah. I've already been home to check on her."

I glanced in his SUV as I started for my truck. There was a cooler bag that I recognized as belonging to Susan on the backseat.

"What's that?" I asked.

"A surprise," Marcus said. He caught my arm and pulled me back to him.

It had to be something from Eric's Place, the restaurant that Susan's husband, Eric, owned. *I have great friends*, I thought, and then Marcus was kissing me again and I forgot how to think at all.

Eric had sent lasagna, salad, chocolate pudding cake for dessert and even some steamed salmon for Owen and Hercules. It was delicious. By nine thirty Marcus was yawning.

"I'm sorry," he said. "I swear it's not the company."

"I know," I said. We'd been curled up on the sofa but now I sat up and stretched. "You've had a long day."

"But a good one," he said, pulling me back down against his chest. I tipped my head back and gave him an upside-down kiss. Then I sat up again and stood up, pulling him to his feet as well.

"Are you okay to drive?" I asked.

He nodded, wrapping his arms around me. We walked out to the kitchen that way. "Don't worry," he said. "I promise I won't fall asleep driving home."

"I went to check on Micah this morning," I said. "But she must have been happy to see you and was probably a bit annoyed when you left again."

"I missed the little furball, too," Marcus said with a grin. "I've gotten used to fish breath waking me up." He pulled on his jacket and once again pulled me close for one last kiss. Or two.

I wanted to say, "Stay," but Marcus was surprisingly old-fashioned about some things.

"Breakfast at Eric's?" he asked.

"Mmm, that sounds good," I said.

He pulled away from me and was gone.

I woke up early the next morning—before Owen had a chance to breathe *his* fishy kitty breath in my face or poke me with a paw. Even though I was meeting Marcus for breakfast I made coffee. In my book there was no such thing as too much coffee.

Owen wandered down while I was getting the coffeemaker ready. There was no sign of Hercules. I gave Owen his breakfast and after he'd finished eating and washing his face he made a beeline for the back door.

"I'm leaving in an hour," I said. "Make sure you're back."

The only response was an offhanded murp.

I was washing the dessert dishes from the night before, singing along to *Ultimate Manilow* since Owen—who wasn't a fan—wasn't in the house, when I heard him meowing at the back door. He was on the top step and my heart began to pound the moment I saw him. There was a long scratch across his nose and another on his right front paw, but the most serious injury was a tear in his left ear that was matted with blood. He seemed to be more angry than anything. He looked back over his shoulder and his tail whipped across the step.

I bent down and checked him over carefully. I didn't see any other injuries but I was still worried. Owen had been in altercations before, but just minor scuffles, one with another cat and one with the Justasons' dog when he was just a kitten. That little skirmish was the reason the dog had given him a wide berth ever since.

I picked Owen up and carried him into the kitchen. I pulled my cell phone out of my bag and called Roma at home.

"It looks like he was in a fight with some other animal but I don't think it was the Justasons' dog. I didn't hear him bark and, anyway, he tends to bolt if he sees Owen," I told her.

"Yeah, he is kind of a big chicken," Roma agreed. "It sounds as though Owen's injuries aren't too serious and his shots are all up to date, although he might need stitches in that ear based on what you described."

My heart sank at the word "stitches." Owen was an uncooperative patient at the best of times. To say he was going to overreact to having to get stitches was an understatement.

"Are you sure?" I asked, looking down at the cat in my lap. He reminded me of a boxer who had just taken the match by a knockout. Although he was injured, there was something cocky in his posture.

"Not until I see him," Roma said. "And yes, I know what you're thinking, but if Owen needs stitches I can make it work. I'll see you at the clinic in a few minutes."

I ended the call and felt a wave of relief roll over me. Owen was watching me, his golden eyes narrowed.

"I know you don't exactly like Roma," I began.

He gave a sour-sounding meow of confirmation.

"But she needs to fix your ear."

Owen immediately shook his head and winced a little. I had no idea how he understood what I said but I had no doubt that he did, and given the whole invisibility thing it wasn't really that unbelievable.

"She needs to fix your ear and so you need to go to the clinic and be nice."

He didn't make a sound but the glare he gave me made his opinion very clear.

I got to my feet, nudging the chair back under the table with one foot. I wasn't sure I could trust Owen not to pull a vanishing act over this.

I bent my head close to his. "Okay, furball, here's the deal," I said. "You have to go to the clinic but you don't have to be nice and when we get home you can have an entire can of sardines. All to yourself."

Owen immediately swiveled his head to stare at

the cupboard where I kept the cats' food. I walked over to the cupboard, grabbed the oblong-shaped can and set it on the table. "Deal?" I asked, feeling a little silly over negotiating with a cat.

"Mrr," he said.

I grabbed my purse and managed to tuck my phone inside one-handed. I didn't even try to put on a jacket, trusting that my heavy sweater would be warm enough. I didn't want to set Owen down and take a chance that he'd bolt.

Roma and I both pulled into the clinic's parking lot at the same time. I'd settled Owen next to me on the passenger side of the truck, knowing if I tried to get him in the cat carrier that I would have a mutiny on my hands. I got out and lifted him from the seat.

Roma walked over and leaned in to look at Owen. She didn't make any attempt to touch him. Neither cat dealt well with being touched by anyone other than me. It was just another one of their idiosyncrasies that over time I'd gotten used to.

"Not too bad," she said. She smiled at the cat. "I have a feeling the other guy looks worse."

Owen straightened up in my arms as though this was a point of pride for him.

Roma laughed. "I swear he knows what I just said."

"I think he knows a lot more than anyone would believe," I said.

I followed Roma inside and she got us settled in one of the examining rooms. "You can set him on the table," she said to me.

I put Owen down on the stainless-steel surface. "Think sardines," I whispered. He immediately sat down and looked up at me, all the picture of innocence.

Roma ended up giving Owen a tranquilizer, which made working on him a little easier. She checked him over carefully, cleaned his scratches and managed— with me holding him—to put four stitches in his ear.

"That should do it," she said finally.

Owen sat on the exam table wearing a green fabric collar, looking slightly loopy.

Roma pulled off her gloves. "The fabric collar is adjustable and it's more comfortable. I think Owen will put up with it a bit better than with a plastic cone." She smiled down at him and he almost seemed to smile back at her, although his golden eyes didn't quite focus.

I had already called Abigail, who once she heard what had happened, had offered to open the library for me. I'd also called Marcus to tell him I wouldn't be able to make our breakfast date. Now I hugged Roma before carefully picking Owen up. "Thank you for coming in early," I said.

"For you, anytime," she said. "You should bring him back tomorrow so I can take a look at those stitches." She frowned. "Did you leave the carrier in your truck?"

"I just put him on the seat," I said. "I didn't even think about the carrier." I felt a little embarrassed. Roma had pointed out a couple of times that Owen and Hercules would be a lot safer in the truck if they traveled in the carrier. And I knew she was right. It was also impossible to do a lot of the time, since Owen would just disappear and Hercules would walk right through the side of the bag.

I had just gotten Owen settled on the passenger side of the truck when Marcus called.

"How's Owen?" he asked.

"He has stitches, but other than that, he's fine. We're just about to head home."

"I'll see you there," Marcus said. I could feel his smile through the phone.

Owen and I had just gotten out of the truck a few minutes later, when Marcus pulled into the driveway behind me. He was carrying a take-out bag from Eric's Place.

"Breakfast," he said, holding it up.

I stood on tiptoe to kiss him.

Owen meowed loudly. Translation: "Pay attention to me."

Marcus looked down at him. "Why no plastic collar?" he asked.

"Roma said this one is more comfortable and it's adjustable. She's hoping Owen might actually keep it on."

"Well, not everyone could make that collar work, but you can," he said to the cat as we started around the house. "Do you have any idea what the other guy looks like?" he asked me.

I handed him my keys so he could open the back door. "I don't even know who or what the other guy is," I said. "I'm just hoping it's not the Justasons' dog."

Marcus unlocked the door and I set Owen on the

floor just inside the kitchen. He stretched, made his way over to the table and meowed loudly. The tranquilizer Roma had given him seemed to be wearing off with no aftereffects.

"I kind of promised him a plate of sardines if he didn't bite Roma," I said to Marcus.

"You get the sardines, I'll start a fresh pot of coffee," he said.

I was just putting the plate in front of Owen when Hercules wandered in from the living room. He made a beeline for his brother. "Mrr?" he said softly.

The two cats looked at each other for a long moment and it almost seemed as though they were communicating without making a sound. Finally, Hercules looked over at me, tipping his black-and-white head quizzically to one side.

I crouched down so I was level with him and he put one white-tipped paw on my knee. "Owen's fine," I said. To my right the subject of the conversation was carefully sniffing the sardine he'd taken off the plate and set on the floor, just the way he always did with his food.

Herc made a noise that almost sounded like sympathy. I gave the top of his head a scratch and straightened up.

I could smell the coffee Marcus had started. While he got plates and mugs from the cupboard I got Hercules his breakfast. He murped a thank-you and began to eat, eyeing his brother from time to time.

"What time do you have to be at the library?" Marcus asked.

I raked a hand back through my hair. "I don't have to worry about opening—I called Abigail and she's doing that for me." I looked over at Owen again. "Do you think he can be trusted not to try to get that collar off?"

"Of course not," Marcus said, putting the sugar bowl and a small carton of cream in the middle of the table. He moved around me to get the sandwiches he'd warmed up in the microwave, dropping a kiss on the top of my head as he went past. "I don't have to go back to work until tomorrow. I'll stay here."

"What are you going to do all day?" I asked.

"We were going to paint your spare bedroom this weekend. I can at least start. I mean, if you trust me to start without you." He raised one eyebrow.

"I trust *you*," I said, taking the plate he handed me. I sent a pointed look in Owen's direction.

Marcus laughed. "I'll keep a close eye on him, I promise."

"The paint is on the workbench in the basement and you can eat whatever you find in the refrigerator for lunch. There's some pulled pork and some coleslaw."

Hercules had finished his breakfast and carefully washed his face and paws. Instead of coming and sitting next to my chair the way he usually did at breakfast time, he made his way around the table to the place Marcus had set for himself.

I laughed and shook my head as Marcus poured me a cup of coffee. "I don't think you'll have to eat by yourself," I said, gesturing at the little tuxedo cat sitting next to his chair. "'Lunch' is Hercules's favorite word, tied with 'breakfast,' 'supper' and 'snack.'"

The cat loudly meowed his agreement.

I took a drink of my coffee and watched Marcus as he tried to be discreet about sneaking a tiny bit of Canadian bacon out of his sandwich to the cats. He really was handsome, with broad shoulders, dark wavy hair and a smile that came slowly but lit up his face when it finally arrived. Both cats liked Marcus, which was a good thing because I was crazy about him. I was uncomfortably aware that I had to tell him *everything* about them soon.

3

After we finished eating Marcus stood up and made a shooing motion with one hand. "I've got this," he said. "Go get ready for work."

By the time I had done my hair and makeup and changed, Marcus had cleaned up the kitchen and started moving furniture from the spare room. Owen was supervising from the gray slipper chair that Marcus had already moved into the upstairs hallway.

I put a hand on Marcus's chest as he passed me, stopping him long enough to give him a quick kiss on the mouth. "I'll call you later," I said. I leaned over to stroke Owen's fur. "Be good," I whispered.

Owen made a face as though he were insulted by the mere idea that he'd be anything else.

When I got to the library Mary was at the circulation desk and Abigail was just coming down the stairs. "How's Owen?" she asked, walking over to me.

"He's all right," I said. "He had to have stitches and

he's wearing a collar, which he's not crazy about." I smiled at her. "Thank you for opening."

Abigail smiled. "Anytime. I'm glad Owen's all right. Let me know if you need to go home and check on him later."

I nodded. I was hoping that cat-sitting didn't turn into cat-wrangling for Marcus. Or the feline version of Jules Verne's *The Secret of Wilhelm Storitz* .

It was a busy morning. It seemed like half the population of Mayville Heights was looking for something to read. The dip in the temperatures after a day of unseasonably warm weather seemed to have nudged people into coming in for a few books so they could curl up by the fire and stay inside. I managed to find a few minutes at lunchtime to call Marcus.

"The collar is still in place, the ceiling is painted and we're having a pulled-pork sandwich for lunch," he said.

"We?" I asked. I already knew the answer to the question. The boys loved pulled pork as much as they loved sardines.

There was silence for a moment. I thought I heard a faint "mrr" in the background.

"I meant me," he said then. "*I'm* having a pulled-pork sandwich for lunch." I heard the sound again in the background. I was fairly certain it was Owen.

I laughed. "I'm sure you are."

"I talked to Mike Justason," Marcus continued. "His dog is fine but he mentioned seeing a stray in the area. I called Thorsten and he said he'll do some extra circuits of the area." Among his other jobs, Thorsten was also the town dogcatcher.

"Thanks," I said. "I'll see you tonight."

When I got home at the end of the day I found Marcus and his two furry helpers in the kitchen. "Something smells wonderful," I said.

"Chicken and rice," he said.

"I could get used to coming home to this," I said.

"I could be a kept man," Marcus teased, squaring his shoulders and jutting out his chin.

I laughed. "No, you couldn't. You'd miss being a police officer."

After supper Marcus took me upstairs to see the spare bedroom. He'd painted the ceiling and the walls. And as usual he'd done a meticulous job. "I thought we could tackle the trim on the weekend," he said.

"That works for me," I said. I turned in a slow circle. "I don't know how to thank you," I said. "It looks like a professional did the job."

He smiled and a bit of color flushed the tops of his perfect cheekbones. He gave me a long look that did crazy things to my heartbeat. "I'm sure you'll think of something," he said.

We returned downstairs and once again I was nudged out of the kitchen when I tried to do the dishes. I mock-glared at Marcus. "Okay, you win this one but don't think I don't know you're buying your allies with sardine crackers."

All that got me was three faux-innocent smiles.

"I'll drive you to class," Marcus said when I came

back carrying my towel and shoes for tai chi a few minutes later. "I have to talk to Eddie." He raked a hand back through his hair. "Did you hear about the business with the drone?"

I nodded.

"It could just be kids goofing off, or it could be someone with a weird sense of humor who gets off on scaring people, but either way it's dangerous flying those things so close to traffic."

"There've been a couple of accidents on that stretch of road as it is," I said, pulling on my gray hoodie.

Marcus shrugged. "Maybe we'll get lucky and Eddie will remember some detail about the drone that will help. There's a flying club in Red Wing that I'm going to check in with as well."

I smiled at him. Like I'd said before, I couldn't imagine him doing anything other than police work. It was in his blood.

Rebecca was waiting for me at the second-floor landing when I got to tai chi. She was holding a small brown paper bag from the Grainery that held a catnip Fred the Funky Chicken for Owen and some organic fish crackers for Hercules so he wouldn't feel left out. Roma had told her what had happened to Owen.

"Is there any point in me telling you that you're spoiling my cats?" I asked as I tucked the paper bag in my canvas tote.

"Not in the slightest, my dear," Rebecca said, reaching over to pat my cheek.

I heard Maggie call, "Circle." It was time for the

class to start, which meant I had no time to argue with Rebecca. Not that I would have won anyway.

When I turned around after finishing the form at the end of class Marcus and Eddie were standing in the doorway. Marcus smiled at me but made his way toward Maggie. I knew that Brady was still out of town. Marcus had mentioned on the drive down that he wanted to talk to Maggie.

"Call me if you want to work on Push Hands on the weekend," Ruby said on her way out the door.

I nodded, reaching for my towel. Roma came across the floor fastening the buttons of a cranberry cardigan that went well with her dark hair and eyes. "I'll see you and Owen in the morning, about nine thirty," she said.

"We'll be there," I said.

"Owen's okay?"

I blotted the back of my neck with the towel. "If he was a person I'd say he's milking this whole thing. He spent most of the day lounging on a chair watching Marcus paint the ceiling in my spare bedroom and I'm pretty sure someone"—I tipped my head in Marcus's direction—"gave him more than cat food at lunchtime. Plus Rebecca got him another chicken because he had to have stitches."

Roma smiled. "I think I'm going to be a cat in my next life."

I grinned back at her. "Me too."

The collar was still in place around Owen's neck when I got up the next morning, much to my surprise, although I noticed some threads hanging along one edge probably because he'd been chewing or clawing at it. He sat at my feet while I started the coffee.

"You're fine," I said, reaching down to stroke his fur. He sighed and went over to his dish.

My cell rang then. I reached for it, noticing it was Roma.

"Kathleen, I'm sorry but I'm going to have to cancel Owen's appointment because I have an emergency with a horse."

"It's all right," I said. "I don't see any sign of infection around the stitches and he's kept the collar on."

"That's good," Roma said, "but I'd still like to see him. I know Fridays are your late day, but is there any chance you could bring him over on your supper break?"

"I could do that."

"Okay, I'll see you around five thirty?"

I nodded even though she couldn't see me. "We'll be there."

Since I didn't have to take Owen to see Roma until later, I spent the morning cleaning and doing laundry. I took the canvas drop sheet that Marcus had used while he was painting and hung it outside on my clothesline. Not a good idea. The wind caught it before I'd even gotten it clothespinned to the line and it sailed across the backyard and over the fence into Rebecca's yard before I could manage to grab even an end of the tarp. All I could do was give chase.

I was wrestling with the drop cloth, trying to keep it from blowing away again, when Sandra Godfrey from the post office came up Rebecca's driveway.

"Hang on," she called. "Grab that end and I'll get this one." She shifted the heavy mailbag on her shoulder to one side and hurried across the grass, putting her foot on the edge of the tarp before the wind lifted it again. Together, the two of us managed to get the big piece of canvas folded into something a lot more manageable.

"Thanks," I said, hugging the bulky, folded drop cloth against my body. "If you hadn't come along I could have ended up in Red Wing."

Sandra grinned at me. "Well, for a moment I wasn't sure if maybe that's what you were trying to do." She pulled a padded envelope out of her mailbag. "Is Rebecca around? She needs to sign for this."

I shook my head. "She isn't." I looked at the package she was holding. The return address was Rebecca's son, Matthew's. "Could I sign for it?"

She shrugged. "Sure. It would save me having to take this back to the post office and it would save Rebecca a trip to pick it up." I signed where she showed me and tucked the small parcel under my arm.

"Thanks for your help, Sandra," I said.

"No problem, Kathleen," she said with a smile, shifting the heavy mailbag back onto her hip. "Try to keep your feet on the ground." With that she headed back down the driveway and I made my way back to the house.

Before I left for work at lunchtime I went looking for Owen. He wasn't hard to find. He was in the living room, sprawled on his back on the footstool, lazily staring up at the ceiling. With the collar on he looked like he was having some kind of spa treatment.

"You don't belong on that footstool," I said.

He rolled over awkwardly onto his side.

"Nice try, but I think you're fine," I said.

"Mrr," he objected.

"Well, it's a good thing we're going to see Roma at supper time."

Owen narrowed his eyes at me and his tail thumped the top of the ottoman.

"Same deal as before," I said, stroking his soft fur. "You go, you behave—more or less—and you get sardines when we get home."

He made a sound that I thought of as muttering like an old man. "For the record, behaving means no biting and no clawing. You can hiss if you want to."

He seemed to think about my words for a moment, then rolled onto his back again in the November sunshine streaming through the window. I took that as a yes.

Owen was waiting in the kitchen when I got there at supper time. He was in a bit of a cranky mood. When I tried to settle him in the carrier he yowled loudly and twisted in my arms and I could see that it wasn't going to work anyway with the collar in the way.

"Fine, you win," I told him. "*This* time!"

I grabbed Rebecca's parcel and my keys and headed out to the truck. Owen didn't even make an attempt to try not to look smug.

Roma was waiting for us at the clinic. She checked Owen's ear as well as the scratches on his nose and paw. "He's healing incredibly well," she said to me. "Keep the collar on for the weekend, but it can come off on Monday."

Owen looked up at her from the examining table, giving her his best I-am-so-pitiful look. Roma reached into her pocket and pulled out a small plastic bag about half full of star-shaped cat crackers. She set four of them in front of Owen. He meowed a thank-you before bending his head to carefully sniff the treat.

"Now who's spoiling my cats?" I teased.

"He deserves something," Roma said. "He behaved really well."

I didn't say a word. I just continued to look at her.

"He behaved well for him," she amended. "Hey, he didn't even try to bite me."

That was true, although Owen had hissed several times and his claws had come out. However, considering how much he loathed a visit to Roma's clinic, that was progress.

I gave her a hug. "Thanks for taking such good care of the little furball."

"Anytime," she said with a smile. "Owen and Hercules are kind of like family. Does that sound odd?"

"Not to me," I said, smiling back at her.

I carried Owen out to the truck and set him on the seat. He looked expectantly at me.

"You just had a treat. You don't need another," I told him.

He made a sound a lot like a sigh and turned to look out the windshield.

We were only a couple of minutes from Roma's clinic when I noticed that not only was there a lot more traffic on the road, it had slowed to almost a crawl. We inched forward a little more and then stopped. Owen craned his neck but couldn't see over the dashboard or around the collar.

"Merow?" he said inquiringly to me.

I shook my head. "I don't know." After we'd stayed put for several minutes I realized that if we didn't get moving soon I was going to be late getting back to work. I pulled my phone out of my purse and called the library. Susan answered.

"I'm stuck in traffic not far from Roma's clinic," I told her.

Owen was standing with his front legs on the passenger door, looking out the side window as though he were looking for a way to get us moving again.

"I'm not surprised," Susan said. "A tractor-trailer hauling potatoes got off the road at the wrong exit and jackknifed taking a turn too fast. Apparently there are potatoes all over the road. No one's hurt, though."

I blew out a breath, making my bangs lift in the air. "Okay, thanks," I said. "I'll be there as soon as I can."

I ended the call and discovered Owen looking at me. "Accident," I said. "Looks like we're stuck."

I had no idea who was in the small silver truck in front of me, but the driver was clearly in a hurry. I saw him look out his side window and then check the rearview mirror. He sat for a moment and then from his body language seemed to decide something. He put the truck in reverse and, using his backup camera, came back as close to my front bumper as he could. It took a little back-and-forth maneuvering, but he managed to pull into the left lane, drive ahead a couple of car lengths and turn down a side road on the left that I knew would eventually take him downtown.

"What do you think?" I said to Owen. "We could probably get down to the library."

He immediately sat up and tried to wash his face, which wasn't easy with the collar in place. Owen loved going to the library.

Because the truck ahead of me had already pulled out it was easy for me to follow. I looked both ways, headed up the wrong side of the road and turned left without meeting any traffic.

"You have to stay out of trouble at the library," I reminded him. "No going all Dr. Jack Griffin and roaming the building."

Owen shared my interest in old movies, or maybe he just liked to lie in my lap while I watched them and scratched under his chin. Either way he was familiar with the H. G. Wells character from the 1933 movie *The Invisible Man*.

"Mrr," he agreed.

I thought about how many times Owen had ended up at the building and not been on his best behavior. There was the first time, when he'd stowed away in my bag and then launched himself onto conductor

Gregor Easton's head. Of course, that had led, indirectly, to me meeting Marcus, so I couldn't really be mad about that. And I knew that I was lucky to live in a place where people wouldn't be that surprised by a cat at the library, where he really shouldn't be.

Fifteen minutes later I was pulling into the library parking lot, just five minutes late in getting back.

"You have to get in the bag if you're going inside," I told Owen, reaching for the shopping bag I kept under the seat as much for wayward cats as for groceries.

I made my way across the lot and into the building, watching out for any patrons. It was one thing for the staff to know Owen was in the building, but I didn't think it was a good idea to broadcast that information to everyone else.

There was no one near the circulation desk when I stepped inside. I waved to Mia, who was on the phone, and made it all the way to the top of the steps before I met Susan on her way down.

She grinned at me. "Hi, Kath, what's in the bag? Did you bring something to share with the class?" she teased.

I knew she had to have guessed that I had a bag of cat, but all I said was, "Stuff."

Susan slid her glasses down her nose and looked at me over the top of them. "What kind of stuff?"

I narrowed my gaze at her. "Librarian stuff."

She glanced down at the bag and started to laugh. "Sorry, Kathleen," she chortled, "but the cat's out of the bag."

It was.

Literally. Owen had managed to poke his head out, collar and all.

"Hey, Owen," Susan said.

He meowed a hello back.

Susan headed down the steps laughing. Over her shoulder she said, "Cat's out of the bag, Kathleen. I've been waiting months to use that one."

She was having so much fun I couldn't help laughing, and even Owen seemed to be amused.

Just before we closed the building I called Rebecca to ask if I could drop by with the parcel I'd signed for. I explained it was from Matthew.

"Of course you could," she said. "Thank you for collecting it from Sandra. I wonder what he sent me."

"I'll see you soon, and you can find out," I said.

"Kathleen, how's Owen?" Rebecca asked.

"Roma just checked him out a little while ago," I said. "He's healing well. In fact right now he's sitting in the middle of my desk pushing the pens on the floor." I explained about the jackknifed truck holding up traffic.

"Don't leave him in your truck. Bring him up to say hello."

I hesitated. "You know what Owen is like," I said. "He'll nose around every inch of the apartment."

"I don't mind a bit," she said. "And you know that cats are good for a person's mental health. They lower stress levels and anxiety."

Trying to win an argument with Rebecca was like

trying to win one with Owen. It wasn't going to happen. "All right," I said. "I wouldn't want you to be stressed and anxious."

"Thank you, dear," she said. "You're so thoughtful."

"And Owen does want to thank you for the chicken. This way he won't have to write a thank-you note."

Rebecca laughed. I told her we'd be there within a half hour and we said good-bye.

About fifteen minutes later I was doing my last quick survey of the main floor of the building when I noticed Mia standing by the main entrance, making a face at her phone. I walked over to her. "Is everything okay?" I asked.

"Dad's still at his office and he wants me to meet him there."

"It's raining. I'll give you a ride," I said.

She smiled. "Thank you, but I really wanted to go see Grandpa." She sighed. "Dad *says* he'll only be another twenty minutes but I know what that means. I'll be stuck there for at least an hour." She made a face. "You know how Einstein proposed in the theory of relativity that time is a relative concept?"

I nodded. I did know that—from a college physics class years ago, and I was impressed that Mia did as well.

She glanced at her phone before looking at me again. "Well, when I'm waiting for Dad I definitely experience time dilation, because it definitely slows down for me."

I smiled at her. "I'm going to take a package to Rebecca Henderson. She told me your grandfather is staying in the other apartment there. Text your dad and see if it's okay if you come with me and he can pick you up there."

A smile started to spread across the teen's face. "Are you sure?" she asked.

"Positive." There was a muffled meow from my canvas tote. "So is Owen."

She laughed and bent her head over her phone to text Simon. Then she looked at me. "Five, four, three, two, one," she counted down. Her phone rang. "Dad," she said.

Mia answered the call, listened for a moment and then said, "Okay." She held the phone out to me.

"Hi, Kathleen," he said. "Are you sure you don't mind dropping off Mia at her grandfather's?"

"I don't," I said. "I have to take a parcel to Rebecca. And she didn't ask. I offered, if that's what you're worried about."

He laughed. "You're getting to know me too well. I appreciate this, Kathleen."

"It's no problem," I said, thinking that actually most of the time I felt as though I barely knew Simon Janes at all.

I handed the cell phone back to Mia, who told her father she'd see him later.

I finished my circuit of the main floor, shut off the lights, locked the doors and set the alarm. Then the three of us made a mad dash for the truck across the puddle-splattered parking lot. Once we were inside the truck I set the canvas tote on my lap and helped Owen out. "That collar makes a pretty good umbrella," I said to him. He cocked his head as he seemed to consider the point.

I set the cat on the seat next to me and introduced him properly to Mia.

"Nice to meet you, Owen," she said, as though she were meeting another person. Then again, both Owen and Hercules considered themselves to be people, so it wasn't *that* odd, I told myself.

The rain pounded on the roof of the truck as we headed across town. Water was pooling in places on the road already.

"If Dad wasn't so paranoid about me driving in the dark and the rain . . . and, well, ever . . . I just could have taken the car and gone back to get him later," Mia said. "He's so . . . old about some things."

I laughed. "I think it's a father/daughter thing. My dad was the same way when I was your age. The first time I drove from Boston to Cape Cod by myself—which is only about an hour-and-a-half drive—I found out later that he literally sat next to the phone until I got there and called to say I was fine, and when the phone rang he made Mom answer it so I wouldn't know he'd been hovering there the whole time."

"The first time I drove by myself at night—which was just down to the community center—I found out after that Dad borrowed someone's car and followed me to make sure I made it safely."

I glanced over at her. She rolled her eyes. "It's a good thing he's not a detective, because he sucked at it. I recognized the car right away. It belonged to his assistant. There's a big Minnesota Wild bumper sticker on the front fender—'Wild' in big red letters."

"He loves you," I said.

Out of the corner of my eye I saw her smile. "Yeah, I know that," she said. "It's just, you know, sometimes it would be better if he could just do it from a distance."

A vehicle passed us then, headed in the opposite direction, driving a bit too fast for the weather. It sped through a large puddle in a low spot on the road, sending dirty water splashing on the windshield like it was thrown from a bucket. Just as the water hit, I realized it was Harry Taylor in the truck and wondered where he was going in such a rush. I didn't think the storm was going to ease up like the forecast had predicted. My left wrist, which was a pretty good weather predictor since it had been broken, still ached, which told me that there was still more wet weather ahead.

I was about to turn the corner when a woman darted out in front of me. She was wearing a dark raincoat and holding a big black umbrella, head down, walking rapidly. I hit the brakes. Luckily I wasn't going very fast thanks to the rain. The woman glanced in my direction but didn't give any sign that she recognized how close she'd come to being hit. Beside me Mia put a hand on the dashboard and put her left arm out in front of Owen. He managed to right himself and stay on the seat despite the abrupt stop. But he was annoyed and made it very clear with a loud meow.

"What's wrong with people?" Mia said. "She didn't even look. You could have run her over."

I nodded. "So remember to look both ways when you're walking, especially when it's raining." I looked at her, realizing that I sounded like a preachy adult and gave her a sheepish smile. "Sorry. I think I was channeling my mother there."

Mia smiled back at me. "It's okay," she said.

I glanced in the rearview mirror. There was something familiar about the hooded woman under the big umbrella heading down the street, something about the way she moved that I couldn't place.

Finally, I pulled in at the curb in front of Everett's house. Owen went into the bag without argument, first looking out the windshield and making a sour face at the rain.

Mia grabbed Rebecca's parcel from the floor mat on her side. "I'll bring this," she said.

We made a mad dash for the door, sprinting through the raindrops, sending water splashing onto our jackets. I caught sight of something on the sidewalk—a scarf maybe, probably Rebecca's. I grabbed the wet fabric and stuffed it in my pocket. Inside the entry Mia pushed her grandfather's bell. I could hear Owen making grumbling noises in the bag. I pulled the scarf that I'd used to keep him dry off the top. "I think you're fine," I said. The look he gave me made it clear he didn't agree.

We waited but Leo didn't come to let us in. Mia pulled out her phone and sent her grandfather a text. There was no response. "He's probably listening to music with the headphones on," she said. "I'll just go outside and knock on his window. That's what I did the last time. He gets so caught up in the music he forgets about everything else."

I put a hand on her arm. "It's raining too hard to do that. Hang on a minute." I leaned over to push Rebecca's doorbell and in a moment I could see her through the glass in the door, coming down the stairs to let us in.

She opened the door and smiled at us. "Hello, Mia," she said. "Did you come to see your grandfather?"

Mia nodded. "I think he has his headphones on. He didn't hear when I rang his bell."

Rebecca nodded. "I came up behind him yesterday when he was headed up the walkway and I almost scared him out of his shoes." She leaned down and smiled at Owen. "Hello, Owen," she said. "Thank you for coming to see me. Even injured you look as dashing as ever." She straightened and I was the focus of her smile. "Hello, Kathleen. Thank you for making the trip over here on such a wet night."

"I don't mind," I said.

We stepped inside and Mia handed Rebecca the padded envelope from Matthew.

"I wonder what he sent me this time," she said, turning the package over in her hands.

I glanced down the hall, wondering why Leo hadn't heard us by now and come out of the apartment. At that moment I felt the tote bag wriggle beside me. Before I could react Owen had jumped out and was heading down the hall to our left.

"Owen!" I called sharply.

He ignored me.

"It's all right, Kathleen," Rebecca said. "He can't get outside. He just wants to explore."

"I know. That's what I'm afraid of," I said.

We moved down the hall and found the cat sitting in front of the door to Leo Janes's apartment in his green fabric collar. He turned to look up at me and made a low murp. I knew that sound. Something was wrong. I felt my chest get heavy, like a large rock had just settled on it.

"Kathleen, can I take Owen in so Grandpa can meet him?" Mia asked.

The apartment door was pulled to, but not actually closed, I realized.

The hairs rose on the back of my neck. I tried to keep my expression neutral as I put a hand on Mia's arm. "Wait here with Rebecca for a minute," I said.

She leaned around me. "Why?"

"Stay here. Just for a minute."

I shifted my gaze to Rebecca, who put her hands on Mia's shoulders. "What's wrong?" the teen asked, fear making her voice sharp and loud. "Do you think something happened to Grandpa? Is he sick?" She tried to move forward but Rebecca slipped one arm around her shoulders and held her in place.

It seemed to me I could actually hear my own heart hammering in my chest. "Let me find out," I said.

Mia pressed her lips together and I saw the tears standing in her eyes. She nodded.

I moved over to the door. "Stay with Rebecca," I

said to Owen, who had stayed in front of the door the whole time like he was guarding it. Now he moved over to stand next to Rebecca and Mia.

I knocked on the door. "Leo," I called. "It's Kathleen Paulson."

There was no answer.

I pushed the door open and stepped inside. *Please don't let this be bad*, I prayed silently. *Please let me find Mia's grandfather listening to John Coltrane with his headphones on.*

But it was bad.

Leo was lying on the floor. I made my way carefully across the room to the man. I bent down and felt for a pulse and confirmed what I already knew.

Leo Janes was dead.

4

I took a slow, shaky breath and then another one. Leo was lying partly on his side, partly on his back, his head turned to the right. I could see some kind of injury to the back of his head. A sculpture about a foot and a half high lay on the floor nearby, two twists of angular metal curved around a central copper disk. There was blood on the curved edge of metal on one side. The sculpture had to be what had caused that injury.

My stomach clenched. I looked away and took another deep breath. "Safe journey," I whispered.

I stood up and looked around. Nothing seemed to be disturbed in the small apartment other than a photo that was lying on its side on a dark wooden table behind Leo Janes's body, knocked over maybe when he was attacked. The black-and-white, smiling image of a young woman in its inexpensive plastic department-store frame seemed a little out of place next to the other photo on the table—a candid shot of

Simon and Mia. That photo had been matted and framed in a sleek metal frame. I wondered who the woman in the old photo was, maybe someone from Leo's past he'd been hoping to reconnect with while he was in town. I felt the prickle of tears but I blinked them away. Rebecca and Mia were waiting.

I stepped back into the hallway. Rebecca still had her arm around Mia. The teen's eyes darted all around. "Where's Grandpa?" she immediately asked. She tried to pull away but Rebecca kept her arm around the teen.

"Kathleen, where's Grandpa?" Mia asked again in a shaky voice.

I took both of her hands in mine. No matter what I said, the words were going to be wrong. "I'm sorry," I began. I stopped and swallowed a couple of times.

Mia had gone rigid, so pale that I was afraid she was going to pass out.

"Sweetie, he's gone."

"No." Her voice was so quiet I almost missed the word. Mia shook her head, repeating "No" over and over as tears began to slide down her face. She tried to take a step toward the apartment, pulling against Rebecca's grasp. I folded her into my arms and she slumped against me, trembling with silent sobs. Rebecca's eyes met mine over the top of Mia's head. She shook her own head and gently rubbed Mia's back.

"My phone is in my pocket," I said, poking the right side of my jacket with my elbow. Rebecca reached over, pulled out my cell and took a few steps away from us. Owen leaned against my leg. I laid my cheek against the top of Mia's head and wished there was some way I could fix everything.

After a minute Rebecca walked back over to us. "The police are on the way," she said. "And I hope you don't mind, I called Marcus."

"I'm glad you did," I said. She slipped the phone back into my pocket.

"Take her upstairs, please," I said.

Mia lifted her face. It was wet with tears and smudged makeup. "No," she said vehemently. "I'm not going anywhere." She fixed her gaze on me. "You can't make me leave."

I looked at Rebecca, who gave her head a little shake. I turned my attention back to Mia. "The police are coming. When they get here I'm going to need to talk to them. And it's going to get really chaotic here. Please, go upstairs with Rebecca."

"I won't leave Grandpa by himself," Mia said. I recognized the stubborn set of her jaw and the flash in her eyes. In that moment she reminded me so much of Simon. There was a lump in the back of my throat that I couldn't seem to get rid of no matter how many times I tried to swallow it down. For a moment I was hit with the feeling that I couldn't do this.

I imagined my mother, what she'd do and say if she were here, and then I steadied myself. I knew she would tell me to just put one foot in front of the other. "He won't be alone. I'll stay with him," I said. I looked Mia in the eye. "I promise."

I could hear the sirens getting closer. I wiped the tears from Mia's face with my hand. "Go with Rebecca."

Mia swallowed and pressed her lips together. Then she nodded. I handed her off to Rebecca. They headed for the stairs and Owen followed, looking back over his shoulder at me before making his way up the steps.

I knew Officer Keller, the responding police officer, from Marcus's past cases. The army vet had the bearing of a former military man and an air of calm competence that was reassuring. I explained what had happened. "The door was open?" he asked.

"It had been pulled to but it wasn't closed all the way," I said.

He nodded. "Where are Mrs. Henderson and Mr. Janes's granddaughter?"

"I sent them upstairs." I hesitated. "I didn't want Mia to see . . . everything that's going to happen."

He nodded again as if that made sense to him. Then he pulled on a pair of disposable gloves. "Please stay here, Ms. Paulson," he said.

"All right," I said. I took a couple of steps back and hugged myself against the damp cold that seemed to be sinking into my bones.

Behind me I heard something and turned to see Marcus in the doorway. "Kathleen," he said, relief washing over his face. He gave me a quick hug and then pulled back to study me. "What's happened?"

I gestured at the apartment door. "Leo Janes— Simon's father—he's, uh, dead."

He frowned. "What are you doing here?"

I explained about Rebecca's parcel and how I'd offered Mia a drive to see her grandfather. "Rebecca came down and let us in. I thought Leo would have heard us talking over there by the stairs. When he didn't come out of his apartment I just had the feeling that there was something hinky going on."

Frown lines furrowed his forehead. "How did you get into the apartment? Did Mia have a key?"

"No. The door was open just a crack. I went in because I knew then that . . ." I didn't need to finish the sentence.

"Are you all right?" he said.

I pulled a hand over the back of my neck. "No, but I'll manage."

Officer Keller came to the door then. "Detective," he said.

I put a hand on Marcus's arm. He held up a finger to the officer and turned back to me. "Is it all right if I call Simon?" I asked. "Mia needs him. And if he has to hear this over the phone it should at least be from a friend."

Marcus hesitated and then nodded his agreement. "Go ahead. I can send someone to get him."

I gave his arm a squeeze and dropped my hand. The whole town knew we were a couple, but I tried not to take advantage of that when it came to his cases.

Marcus pulled on a pair of purple disposable gloves and went into the apartment. I walked back to the entryway. I wished Hope Lind, Marcus's partner, were here. I could have gone with her to tell Simon about his father in person. It really wasn't the kind of news he should get over the telephone. But Hope was in a rehab center in Minneapolis getting her mobility back after a serious injury to her leg that had required surgery to implant two plates in her ankle. She'd been hurt tracking a killer through the woods behind Wisteria Hill just before Halloween.

I wasn't sure how to tell Simon what had happened but I hoped the news would be a little better coming from me. I pressed a hand over my mouth. There was no way to make this news any better.

Suddenly I could hear my mother's voice in my head saying, "You can do this, Katydid." I pulled out my phone, found Simon's number and tapped the screen.

"Hi, Kathleen," Simon said when he answered. "Let me guess, Mia thinks I'm taking too long." There was an edge of amusement in his voice that sliced me like a knife thrust into my stomach.

"Hello, Simon," I said, working to keep the emotion out of my voice and not completely succeeding. For a moment words escaped me. Then I found them. "Mia is all right"—I knew he needed to hear that first—"but there's been an accident."

"What happened?" His voice was devoid of all emotion.

"I'm sorry," I said. "It's your father."

For a moment there was silence, then Simon said, "He's dead, isn't he?"

I nodded, then remembered that he couldn't see me. "Yes," I said. "Mia needs you."

"Where are you?"

"Your father's apartment."

"I'm on my way."

"Are you all right to drive?" I asked before he could end the call. "Marcus— The police can send someone or . . . or I can come get you." I wasn't sure if it would be all right for me to leave but I didn't want Simon to have an accident on the way across town.

"I'm all right," he said. "Stay with Mia . . . please."

"I will," I said.

He didn't say anything else and I realized he'd ended the call.

I stood there for a moment, watching the rain run down the glass panel in the heavy wooden door, then went upstairs.

Mia was curled up on Rebecca's sofa, wrapped in a knitted blanket. She was cradling a mug that I guessed held hot chocolate. Her tears were gone. She'd washed her face but she was very pale. Rebecca sat beside her and Owen was on duty at her feet with what I suspected was a saucer of chicken.

Rebecca gave Mia's arm a squeeze and got to her feet. She came over to me. "The police are here," I said, keeping my voice low.

"What do you need, my dear?" she asked. I could see the concern in her blue eyes.

I shook my head. "I'm all right," I said. But I wasn't. This was not my first dead body but I felt more off-centered than I ever had before, maybe because of Mia. It was impossible not to feel the raw ache of her pain.

Rebecca put her arms around me and gave me a quick hug. "How about a cup of coffee?" she offered.

"That would be good," I said, giving her hand an extra squeeze before I let her go.

Rebecca headed for the kitchen. I sat down on the black tweed sofa. "Your dad's on the way," I said to Mia.

Her knees were pulled up to her chest and she wrapped her free arm around them. "I bugged him until he said he'd come for Thanksgiving," she said.

I knew she meant her grandfather. "And he was happy to be here," I said. I flashed to Leo Janes at the library with his granddaughter. His happiness had been evident.

Mia held out her hand almost unthinkingly and I took it. "I don't know how to do this," she said. "I've never been in a world that Grandpa wasn't in." She chewed the corner of her lip.

I took the mug of hot chocolate and set it on the floor. Owen gave it a curious look but seemed to know this would be a bad time to investigate any further. I put my arms around Mia, who laid her head on my shoulder. "I don't think there is a right way to do this," I said. "One foot in front of the other is what my mother always says. Just keep putting one foot in front of the other and you'll end up somewhere— maybe even where you wanted to go."

"Your mother sounds pretty cool," Mia said.

"She is," I agreed.

Rebecca brought me a cup of coffee and I took exactly two sips from it before Simon appeared.

He wasn't wearing a tie and the shoulders of his leather jacket and his face were wet with rain. He swiped a hand over his face and exhaled loudly. Mia was already on her feet. She went into her father's arms and he folded her against his chest. He looked at me over the top of his daughter's head and I could see the pain in every single line on his face.

Things seemed to speed up then. Mia told Simon what happened. She seemed steadier with him there. Marcus came in just as she was finishing. He told Simon and Mia how sorry he was about Leo and I noticed that his response was more personal than the usual, "I'm sorry for your loss."

"I'm sorry to interrupt," he continued, "but I need to ask you a few more questions, Kathleen."

"I have questions, Detective," Simon said.

"I understand," Marcus said. "Just let me get a few more details from Kathleen and I'll do my best to answer them."

"You can use the kitchen," Rebecca said.

"Thank you," he said. He gestured for me to go ahead of him and I touched Mia's shoulder as I passed her.

Marcus and I sat at the small round wooden table in the kitchen. "I just want you to walk me through what happened one more time, from the moment you realized the apartment door was ajar."

"Okay," I said. I explained how I had knocked and called out Leo's name. "I know I should have just stopped and called nine-one-one right there. I just thought . . ."

My hands were flat on the table and Marcus covered one of them with one of his own. "It's okay," he said. "You said you gave Mia a ride because she was coming to see her grandfather. Why didn't she just ring his doorbell when you first came in?"

"She did," I said. "Leo didn't answer when she rang the bell. Mia thought he was listening to music but something felt off to me." I told him briefly again how I had stepped inside the apartment, seen the body and realized that Leo was dead. "I tried to tread carefully and I only touched his neck. I, uh, I didn't want to mess up any potential evidence."

He nodded. "I wish you didn't know that."

I knew he was referring to the fact that this wasn't the first case of his I'd been mixed up in.

"Yeah, me too," I said.

He leaned back in his chair. "I just have a few questions for Rebecca and then I'll talk to Simon."

I got to my feet. "I'll get her for you."

He raked a hand back through his hair. "Do you think Rebecca would mind if I had a cup of that coffee?" he asked, gesturing at the pot.

"Of course not." I managed a small smile. "You know Rebecca." There were several stoneware mugs on the counter next to the coffeepot. I gestured at them. "Pour yourself a cup and I'll go get her for you."

He got to his feet, stretching his neck to one side.

I paused by the doorway. "Are you going to tell Simon how his father died?" I asked.

For a moment he didn't move. Then he turned to look at me, his movements slow and deliberate. "What do you mean?"

"I saw his head," I said. "I saw that metal sculpture or whatever it was on the floor." I swallowed. "And the place where his skull was crushed. I know he was murdered."

5

Over the next few days Marcus was surprisingly closemouthed, even for him, about the murder. He canceled our plans twice and I tried hard not to ask any questions although I had plenty of them. Tuesday morning brought a third cancellation.

"I'm sorry," he said when he called about nine thirty. "I know I said I'd take you to lunch today to make up for bailing on our dinner plans last night, but I have a meeting with someone from the medical examiner's office."

"It's all right," I said. "I want you to find out who killed Leo Janes. If anything changes or if your meeting finishes early, call me."

By twelve thirty he hadn't called and I was getting hungry, so I decided to walk over to Eric's for some chicken-noodle soup and maybe a big gooey brownie. I'd gotten out of the habit of walking around town and I really did miss it. I almost always met someone I knew and it was fun to see what was on display in the bookstore's front window or what the latest fashions were at Abel's Boutique.

Downtown Mayville Heights is laid out more or less like a grid. The streets that run from one end of town to the other all follow the sweep of the shoreline of Lake Pepin, which meant Eric's was just down the street from the library. The cross streets mostly cut straight up the hill, all the way up to Wild Rose Bluff, where a lot of the stone that was used on many of the older buildings had come from.

When I'd first arrived in town it had taken a while for me to learn my way around, mostly because of the way streets and buildings were named—and sometimes renamed. For instance, Old Main Street followed the shoreline from the Stratton Theatre, past the library and the St. James Hotel all the way to the marina. *Main* Street continued from the marina to the edge of town, where it joined the highway.

Old Main Street was originally Olde Street, with an E at the end. It had been the main route from the lumber camps to where the marina is now. Over time Olde Street had morphed into Old Main Street. Still, having two Main streets made giving directions to people from out of town very confusing, compounded by the fact that the St. James Hotel had reverted to its original name, the St. James Hotel, after a decade of being just the James Hotel.

Ruby Blackthorne was standing at the counter at Eric's when I stepped inside, waiting for a take-out order I guessed. There was a heavyset man with her wearing a woolen tweed coat with a striped black-

and-maroon scarf knotted loosely at his neck. From the back he looked vaguely familiar.

Like Maggie, Ruby was an artist, albeit a lot more flamboyant. She'd added a streak the color of lime Jell-O to her hair since our last tai chi class and another piercing in her right ear. Ruby was also the current president of the artists' co-operative, and the two of us had been working together a lot recently, looking for ways the artists' co-op and the library could offer programs that would bring in visitors to both places.

Ruby turned as I came up beside her. "Hi, Kathleen," she said.

I smiled. "Hi."

"Claire just went to get our order," she said. "She'll be right back." She gestured to the man beside her. "This is my friend Elias Braeden. Elias, this is Kathleen Paulson. She's our head librarian."

Elias Braeden offered his hand and as I took it I realized I'd seen him before. He was the man who had come into the library just last week, the man who Leo Janes had thought for a moment looked familiar. "It's a pleasure to meet you, Kathleen," he said.

Elias was a bit above average height with broad shoulders and a muscular build evident even under his heavy coat. His hair was a mix of gray and brown, as was his close-cropped mustache. He had piercing dark eyes and a lined, lived-in face.

"Do you remember me telling you that I worked as a singer and dancer at a resort for three summers when I was in art school?" Ruby said.

I nodded. "I remember." Ruby had shown me photos

of herself dead center in a kick line wearing high heels, sequins, a feathered headdress and very little else.

"Elias owned the resort. I've known him since I was a little girl. He was a friend of my grandfather."

"Ruby's very talented," he said.

"Yes, she is," I agreed. "She did some wonderful paintings of my cats."

"So you own Owen and Hercules? Ruby showed me the photos she took of them."

I nodded. "Actually it's more like they own me," I said with a smile.

Claire came out of the kitchen then, carrying a large paper take-out bag.

Before Ruby could move Elias put a hand in front of her. "I suggested lunch," he said. "This is on me. No arguments."

"Like arguing with you would be anything other than a waste of time," Ruby said with an indulgent smile. It was clear she was very fond of the man.

Elias moved to the counter and pulled out his wallet. He had massive hands, like a wide receiver, I noticed.

Ruby turned to me. "Elias is here because he's thinking of buying the Silver Casino." The casino was about halfway between Minneapolis and Mayville Heights. "He used to work for my grandfather when I was a little girl. That's how they got to be friends."

I nodded. Ruby's grandfather, Idris Blackthorne, had been the area bootlegger, among other things, and had run an ongoing high-stakes poker game out of a small cabin in the woods close to Wisteria Hill.

Given Elias's size and huge hands, it wasn't hard to imagine the kind of things he'd probably done for Idris. His presence alone had probably been very intimidating.

Elias rejoined us then, holding the take-out bag.

"Kathleen, Elias is a fan of old buildings," Ruby said. "Any chance you could give him a tour of the library while he's here?"

"I'd be happy to." I smiled at the older man. "But I think you've already visited the building. Didn't I see you come in one day last week?"

"You did," he said. He had a charming smile, warm and genuine. "I had a bit of time to kill before a meeting but I'd love a tour if you happen to have the time someday."

"I'd be happy to show you around," I said. "Please stop in when you have time."

"I may take you up on that."

We shook hands. His grip was firm but not overpowering. "It was good to meet you," I said.

Ruby waved good-bye to Claire. "I'll see you at class, Kathleen," she said.

They headed for the door and I moved over to the counter. I could smell Eric's chicken soup and my stomach rumbled in anticipation.

Mia walked in for her shift just before four thirty that afternoon. Mary and I were looking at the book drop, which was sticking again, mostly because someone—some delinquent hooligan, as Mary had put it—had jammed about two packages of chewing gum—

strawberry flavored based on what we could smell—into the channels for the pull-out door. I was wondering if I should try to dig the gum out myself or just give in to the inevitable and call Harry, when Mary elbowed me.

"Kathleen," she said, sotto voce.

I turned to see what she was looking at. "Give me a minute," I said. I brushed off my hands and walked over to the teen. "Mia, you didn't have to come in to-day."

"I wanted to. That's okay, right?" She looked a little uncertain. One hand played with the zipper pull of her jacket.

"Of course it is," I said.

Mary joined us. She smiled at Mia. "I have something for you upstairs in the staff room. I found a couple of photos of your grandfather when he was about your age. I thought maybe you'd like to have them."

Mia nodded and managed a smile. "I would like to have them. Thank you."

"I'm going to try not to worry and hover," I said. Beside me Mary made a strangled sound in her throat. I looked at her, narrowing my eyes.

She put one hand on her chest. "It's dry in here," she said. "Got a little frog in my throat."

I turned back to Mia, who was still smiling. "If you need anything I'm going to trust you to ask."

The phone rang then at the circulation desk. "I'll get that," Mary said, bustling across the tile floor.

"There is one thing," Mia said, ducking her head. "You can say no if you want to."

"What is it?" I asked.

"Would it be too weird? Would you sit with Dad and me at the service on Friday?"

Simon had told me that since Mayville Heights was where Leo had grown up, he and Mia had decided here was where his father should be buried.

"Of course," I said. I'd been planning on going to the service for Leo and if I could be there for Mia— and Simon—I was happy to. I'd felt helpless from the moment I'd found Leo Janes's body and I was glad to finally be able to do something that might make a difference to Mia.

I stopped at the library after tai chi class to check on Mia. According to Abigail, she was handling being at the library just fine. While I was there I noticed more than one person share their sympathies with her and it seemed to do her good to hear how many people had known and liked her grandfather. The next evening went just as well.

Thursday night after tai chi I drove out to Marcus's house.

He had called just as I was leaving for class. "I haven't seen you in days," he'd said. "I have pumpkin chocolate-chip cookies."

"Well, for cookies I guess I could drive out," I'd teased.

Marcus was just ending a conversation on his cell when I stepped into the kitchen. He looked tired, I thought. There were shadows under his eyes and I could see that he'd run his hands through his hair multiple times.

"Hope says hello," he said, setting his cell on the table. He leaned forward to kiss me.

"How's she's doing?" I asked.

"Good." His mouth twisted to one side. "I think. She said physio is going well, but you know what Hope's like. She keeps things pretty much to herself."

I nodded. He was right about his partner. She did keep things to herself, which was why he had no idea she'd been in love with him for years. "You called her to talk about the case," I said, hanging my purse on the back of the closest chair.

"I did want to see how she was, but yeah, I wanted to run the case by her as well."

"Do you have any suspects?" I asked.

Marcus hesitated. I waited for him to say he couldn't talk about the case the way he had so many times in the past. But instead he said, "You're not going to like it."

I pulled off my jacket and put it on the back of the chair as well, to buy a little time. I realized he had to be referring to Simon.

"Simon didn't kill his father," I said. "If that's what you're thinking you need to look somewhere else."

Marcus just looked at me without speaking.

"C'mon, Marcus, you have to know there's no way he would do that. First of all, he's not that kind of person, and second, Mia is the most important person in the world to him. He would never hurt her."

He raked a hand through his hair, something he did a lot when he was stressed. Then he suddenly shook his head and said, "Do you want a cup of hot chocolate?"

"Please," I said. I'd warmed up at class but suddenly I was cold again.

When he didn't say anything else I sat down, curling one leg up underneath me. "Why?" I said. I didn't need to say another word. Marcus knew what I meant.

He exhaled loudly and opened the refrigerator to get the milk. "Simon and Leo Janes had a volatile relationship and spent periods of time when they didn't talk," Marcus said.

"Lots of fathers and sons have difficult relationships," I said. "And as for not speaking, for a while that was you and *your* father."

"Which, believe me, I've reminded myself of more than once," he said. "I'm guessing you know about the affair Leo Janes's brother, Victor, had with Simon's mother. There was bad blood between them for more than twenty years."

I nodded. "By that logic Victor Janes should be a suspect."

"He had nothing to gain," Marcus said. "Simon, on the other hand, does. He was Leo's beneficiary and by Simon's own admission Leo wanted his son to give Victor a second chance because he's sick, but Simon found it hard to forgive the man who he felt was responsible for his mother's death and the breakup of his family." He looked back over his shoulder at me. "They had recently had a very heated conversation in

the hotel bar that was seen and heard by several people."

"That doesn't prove anything," I said. "You and
your father have had some pretty heated discussions.
So have we."

He put two mugs in the microwave and turned
around, leaning back against the counter. "This is not
the same thing."

Even if I hadn't known him so well I would have
known he was holding something back. His blue eyes
didn't quite meet mine. So I didn't say anything. I just
waited.

"This stays between us," he finally said.

I nodded.

It had taken a long time for Marcus and me to work
out our differences, and now I couldn't imagine my life
without him in it. My parents had been married
twice—to each other both times. As crazy as they made
each other—and the rest of us sometimes—they were
miserable without each other. Just the way I was miserable without Marcus.

"Simon doesn't have an alibi, at least not one we
can verify, for the window of time around his father's
death."

"Yes, he does," I said. "He was in his office, working. Mia talked to him before we left the library. *I*
talked to him."

Marcus took the mugs out of the microwave and
added the Jam Lady's cocoa mix and a couple of her
homemade marshmallows to each one. He handed me
my cup, set a plate of the promised cookies at my

elbow and came to sit across from me at the table. "Simon did talk to you, but he'd had the calls to his office phone forwarded to his cell phone and the cell tower logs show he wasn't at his office. The call pinged off a tower near Everett's building—near his father's apartment, Kathleen. He says he was just driving around, trying to clear his head after a frustrating day, but he can't prove it."

"That doesn't prove he was in his father's apartment or even close to the building." I turned the mug of hot chocolate in circles on the tabletop. "You're the one who explained the problems with cell phone evidence to me when that woman was on trial for killing her husband in Red Wing back in the spring. Simon could have been in his office and if the tower near him was experiencing a heavy call volume his calls could have been picked up by another tower closer to the apartment."

Micah wandered in from somewhere, probably drawn by the sound of our voices. She jumped onto Marcus's lap, cocked her head at me and meowed softly. I leaned over and scratched behind one ear. She immediately began to purr.

I looked over at Marcus. "I know you don't know Simon very well," I said, "but I do know him well enough to know that his life revolves around Mia and he wouldn't have killed his father even by accident. He would *not* do that to her. Please, trust me on this."

"I do trust you," he said. "That's the reason I'm telling you."

* * *

I stayed out at Marcus's for another hour, only reluc-tantly pulling myself away because I needed to check on Owen and Hercules. I'd only been home for a few minutes when Simon called.

"Hey, Kathleen, Mia told me that she asked you to sit with us at my father's service. I wanted to tell you that you don't have to do that."

I was upstairs and I dropped down onto the edge of the bed. The closet door moved and Hercules stuck his head around the side of it. When he saw it was me he came over and jumped onto my lap. I started strok-ing his fur. "I'm happy to be there for Mia, but I'm not family and I don't mind sitting elsewhere if it makes you uncomfortable."

"It doesn't," he said. "I didn't want you to be un-comfortable. Thank you for caring so much about my kid."

"She's easy to care about."

"Yeah, that she is." I could hear the love in his voice. "I should have said this before: Thanks for talking to her about things that she doesn't always feel she can say to me. Sometimes I wish—," He stopped and cleared his throat. "Sometimes I wish her mother were alive. I can't always give her what she needs."

"Mia adores you," I said. "I know you would do anything for her."

I paused and after a moment Simon said, "I get the feeling there's something you want to say to me?"

I shifted sideways a little, moving Hercules, who made a disgruntled face at me. My mother would have said, "In for a penny, in for a pound," an expression she'd picked up from the English wardrobe mistress while doing a production of *My Fair Lady*.

"Yes," I said. "Why did you lie to me—and to Mia—about being in your office the night your father died?"

"I didn't kill my father."

"I know that," I said.

"Then why does it matter where I was?" His blunt manner teetered on the edge of rudeness on occasion, which meant if he liked you, you knew it, and if he didn't, he didn't care.

I gritted my teeth and squeezed my eyes shut for a moment. When I opened them again Hercules was sitting up, watching me curiously. "All I ask is that people be straight with me, Simon. If there's something you don't want to tell me, ever, that's okay, but don't lie to me."

"You said you know I didn't kill my father."

"That's because I know you would never do anything to hurt Mia. And I know how much her grandfather's death has hurt her."

Simon was silent for so long I thought he'd hung up. Finally he spoke. "You know about my father's brother being in town."

"Yes." Hercules nudged my hand with his head. Translation: "Scratch behind my ear."

"I'm sure Detective Gordon has told you that my father and I disagreed about that."

"I knew that you and your father had words."

Simon laughed but the sound had no humor. "That's one way to put it." Then his voice softened. "My father left me a voice mail message saying he wanted to talk to me about Victor. I didn't want to have the same stupid argument because, you're right, it wasn't good for Mia. That's why I left the office, in case my father decided to show up. I just drove around because I needed to figure out what to do. Sitting and thinking doesn't work for me. I need to move, so I just drove around for a while. I can't prove it. I did see a deer by the side of the road and a drone flying over a field. I lied to you and to Mia on the phone because I was trying to keep her out of this thing with my father as much as I could." He sighed. "I didn't do a very good job of it. And I'm sorry I didn't tell you the truth." I could hear traffic noise and I wondered where he was.

"I understand what you were going through," I said. "I'll meet you at Gunnerson's about nine thirty." Gunnerson's Funeral Home was where Leo Janes's funeral was taking place.

"That's fine," he said. "And, Kathleen, I appreciate everything you've done, for Mia and for me."

He ended the call before I could reply.

I set my phone down on the bed. Hercules was watching me and as odd as it would probably sound to most people if I'd tried to explain it, I knew he'd been listening to my side of the conversation. He glanced over at the phone and meowed, inquiringly, it seemed to me.

Being able to walk through walls or disappear

weren't the only skills my cats had. They seemed to have an uncanny ability to, well, solve crime. They were like two small, furry Sherlock Holmeses. Sometimes I thought explaining *that* to Marcus was going to be harder than explaining the whole walk-through-walls/vanishing-act thing.

I started to stroke Herc's fur again. "No," I said. "I don't think he told me everything, either."

Simon and Mia were just getting out of Simon's car when I arrived at the funeral home the next morning. Mia was pale but composed in a dark blue dress, her hair pulled back in a simple ponytail. She came around the car and hugged me.

Simon was wearing a dark suit with a crisp white shirt and conservative striped tie. He was close to six feet tall, long and lean with a direct gaze. Simon generally kept his sandy hair buzzed close to his head but recently he'd let it grow out a little. The first time we'd met I thought that he didn't look anywhere near old enough to be the father of a seventeen-now-eighteen-year-old, and I still felt the same way.

"Good morning," he said. I hesitated and then hugged him as well.

A dark green SUV pulled up then. I recognized Denise, Simon's assistant, as the driver. Victor Janes was in the passenger seat. Denise smiled at me as she got out of the vehicle and came to give Mia a hug.

Simon offered his hand to Victor. They shook hands and then Victor touched Mia's shoulder for a brief moment.

"Victor, this is our friend Kathleen Paulson," Simon said.

The older man nodded at me. "We met at the library. Thank you for coming, Kathleen."

"I'm sorry about your brother," I said.

There was an awkward silence before Denise touched Simon's arm. "We should probably go inside," she said. "People will be arriving soon."

We headed across the parking lot. Simon was ahead of me, his back ramrod straight in his dark suit, and I had a sense of just what this civility with his uncle was costing him.

Daniel Gunnerson Senior was waiting for us inside. Gunnerson Senior was a short, squat man with thick, white hair combed back from his face and sparkling blue eyes. He reminded me of the actor Malcolm McDowell, with whom my mother had once done a production of *The Taming of the Shrew*. Both men had the same impish grin, although there was no sign of it today on Daniel Gunnerson's face. This morning his blue eyes were serious. He was wearing a conservative charcoal suit and a gray striped tie. He shook Simon's hand. "Would you like to see the chapel?" he asked in a low voice.

"I would, thank you," Simon said. He glanced at me and I gave a slight nod to let him know I'd take care of Mia.

Denise and Simon followed Daniel. Simon took a few steps and then stopped and turned to his uncle. "Victor, would you like to come with us?" he asked.

I saw the older man swallow hard. "Thank you. I

would," he said. He gave Mia a smile that was just really a slight movement of his lips and went with Simon and his assistant.

Mia watched them go. "Did you know that funerals predate modern man? The Neanderthals probably followed some sort of ritual for their dead thousands of years ago." She shrugged. "I couldn't sleep last night and I ended up Googling funerals."

"I did know that," I said.

Mia smiled. "I forgot that you know pretty much everything."

I smiled back at her. "Not everything."

Mia looked in the direction of the chapel again and suddenly she looked profoundly sad. "I want to tell you something but you're going to think I'm a bad person."

I put my arm around her shoulders. "There's nothing you could tell me that would make me think you're a bad person. You could tell me that you glued the covers of every book in the library together and I still wouldn't think you're a bad person."

"There's no way you wouldn't be mad," Mia said.

I smiled. "I didn't say I wouldn't be mad, I said I wouldn't think you're a bad person."

She laid her head on my shoulder. "I wish it was him," she said in a small voice.

I realized she meant she wished Victor were dead instead of her grandfather. "That just makes you human."

"Mary's right," Mia said. "You don't know how to be mean."

I grinned and shook my head. "I promise you that I do."

She raised her head so she could look at me. "What was the last mean thing you did?"

"Yesterday I threw a can of creamed corn at a squirrel that was chewing on one of my Adirondack chairs in the backyard."

"No." Her eyes widened.

"Yes."

I'd also yelled and stomped my feet on the back steps, but the squirrel had simply looked at me like I was a toddler having a tantrum and then gone back to chewing on the arm of the chair.

"Did you hit the squirrel?" Mia asked.

I shook my head. "Not even close." I leaned my head against hers. "It's okay to feel mean and petty, just try not to act that way."

I looked out the window by the front door. Two cars pulled into the parking lot, one behind the other. "Are you okay? Are you ready?" I asked.

Mia nodded. "I can do this," she said. The look in her eyes reminded me of Simon and I had no doubt she could handle the day. I just wished that she didn't have to.

I was surprised at how many people showed up for the funeral, although I shouldn't have been. Mayville Heights was a small town and people knew one another going back generations. More than once I'd found out that someone I knew was third cousin twice removed of someone else I knew. It could be a little claustrophobic at times but from the perspective of someone who had moved around a lot as a child I found it warm and welcoming.

Mary and her husband arrived with Mary looking uncharacteristically sedate in a dark blue dress. Rebecca and Everett came in behind them. While Everett was talking to Simon, Rebecca walked over to me. "How is she doing?" she asked, tipping her head toward Mia, who was talking to Mary.

"Better than I would have done at the same age," I said.

"She has the same vein of inner resilience that both her grandfather and father have," Rebecca said. "Leo was a good man. You would have liked him if you'd been able to get to know him."

I thought about the one time I'd met Leo Janes at the library and the love and pride I'd seen on his face when he looked at his granddaughter. I had liked him.

Rebecca was wearing a tie-dyed, pale blue silk scarf at the neck of her navy blue suit jacket. It reminded me of the scarf I'd found on the sidewalk the night of Leo's death. "I forgot to tell you," I said. "I found your scarf."

"What scarf would that be, dear?" she asked.

"It's just like this one," I said, reaching out to finger the ends of the silky fabric around her neck. "Only in shades of yellow instead of blue. I found it on the sidewalk the night . . . the night Leo . . ." I couldn't finish the sentence.

Rebecca touched my arm. "I didn't lose a scarf," she said. "I don't own any yellow scarves at all. Someone walking by must have dropped it."

Across the room Everett caught her eye and raised

an eyebrow. She gave my arm a squeeze. "I'll talk to you after the service," she said.

I nodded.

Harrison Taylor came in with Harry Junior and Larry—Harrison's younger son—all three men dressed in dark suits and ties. Harrison shook hands with both Simon and Victor. He took Mia's hands between his own large ones and said something to her that made her smile.

I watched Harry Junior speaking with Simon and I couldn't help wondering again why he and Leo had argued in the gazebo.

Marcus walked in then dressed in his dark blue suit with the blue tie my mother had sent him from Los Angeles the last time she'd been there. Simon caught sight of him at the same time and, as I watched, he excused himself from Harry and turned to Marcus. Marcus offered his hand and Simon took it, leaning in as he spoke. I saw Marcus nod at whatever the other man was saying.

The conversation was brief. Marcus made his way over to me. I reached for his hand and gave it a squeeze.

"How's Mia?" he asked, looking over at the teen standing tall and poised next to her father and uncle.

"All right," I said. "I wish she didn't have to go through this."

"I wish no child did," he said.

"Are you here to watch Simon or to look for other suspects?" I asked.

"I'm here because it's my job," he said. "Simon

wants to talk to me this afternoon. Do you know why?"

Before I could answer Daniel Gunnerson came out to collect the family for a private moment before the service. Simon turned to look for me.

"I have to go," I said. "I'm sorry."

Marcus's hand brushed mine. "Go," he said. "I'll bring you dinner later."

The service was simple but very moving. Mia held on to her father's hand with one hand and mine with the other.

Mary spoke from the heart about her friendship with Leo when they were young. More than once people laughed at the memories. She told the story about Leo kidnapping the mascot of the high school in Red Wing and how the first Christmas she and her husband were married, Leo came and helped put up the Christmas tree after Mary had kicked her husband and burst into tears when he said she had a crooked eye because it turned out the tree had a decided list to the left after she'd fastened it in its stand. She finished by laying her hand on the urn at the front of the room, saying, "Rest well, my friend."

Simon reached for Mary's hand as she passed on the way back to her seat and she blew Mia a kiss.

Simon spoke briefly about his father, about how Leo had encouraged him to go after his dreams. He smiled a tight smile. "He made me the man I am today, for better or worse."

To my surprise Victor Janes went to the podium.

Mia tightened her grip on my hand so much that my fingers began to go numb. I suspected Victor speaking hadn't been planned. I felt a pang of sympathy for the man. He was the one with a serious illness, trying to atone for his past mistakes, and now his brother was dead. He'd run out of time but not in the way he'd likely expected.

Victor cleared his throat and looked out over the rows of people, all friends of Leo or of Simon and Mia. "Leo was the older by seven minutes and he always felt that gave him the right to act like a big brother," he said.

From the corner of my eye I saw Simon's shoulders tense.

Victor stared down at the podium. "He was a great brother and I wish I'd said that more often." He looked at the copper urn for a long moment and then took his seat again.

Mia spoke last. She talked about what a great grandfather Leo was, how he'd played tea party with her and dressed up at Halloween but how he'd also read poetry to her and corrected her when she said "like" too much. Her voice was strong and her hands on the edge of the podium were steady, although unshed tears shone in her eyes.

"The world was better with my grandfather in it and it's a little less with him gone," she said.

Then she turned and looked at the polished urn. "Walt Whitman was one of Grandpa's favorite poets." She took a breath but she couldn't hold the tears back any longer. They slid down her face but her voice was strong. "'O Captain! my Captain! our fearful trip is done; The ship has weather'd every rack, the prize we sought is won.'" She blew a kiss to the urn and I felt a tear slip down my own face.

There was a reception in the big front room of the funeral home after the service. I carried a cup of coffee around but didn't actually drink from it. There was no way I could swallow anything past the lump that seemed to be permanently stuck in my throat.

Harrison Taylor came up behind me. "That coffee has to be colder than a witch's—"

I flashed a warning look at him.

"Kiss," the old man finished, a devilish gleam in his eye. "No appetite?" he asked, tipping his head toward my cup.

I set it down on the table to my right. "Not really."

"I'm the same way," the old man said. "I get that this is part of how people grieve and, hell, I think it's good for the family to hear stories and memories about their loved one, but I'll be damned if I can understand how anyone can go from sitting in Daniel Gunnerson's back room to stuffing their face with potato salad." He patted my arm. "The boys would say I'm raving. How are you?"

I smiled at him. "I'm fine, Harrison. How are you?"

"I'm fine, girl," he said. "Damned sorry to hear about Leo Janes."

I nodded. "I only met the man once but I liked him."

"He was that kind of person," Harrison said. "And he'd be proud of that granddaughter of his today."

"Mia's mother died when she was a baby, didn't she?" I asked. Neither Mia nor Simon ever spoke about Mia's mom.

"In childbirth."

I glanced over at Simon, talking to Brady Chapman. "I had no idea."

The old man nodded. "She and Simon were just teenagers. There were some kind of complications with the delivery." He leaned on his cane and looked across the room at Simon. "Her parents tried to take the baby. Simon dug his heels in. He wanted to raise her himself. Lord knows what Leo must have thought, and he's the only one who ever did because he backed that boy one hundred percent. The whole thing ended up in court." He gestured with one deeply veined hand. "You know the rest."

"I had no idea," I said.

"Most folks don't." He rubbed his chin with one hand. "That man of yours know who did this?"

"He's working on it," I said.

"No offense intended, but it probably wouldn't hurt if he had some help."

I stood on tiptoe, put one hand on the shoulder of his black suit and kissed his cheek. "You're not subtle," I said.

He gave a snort. "I'm too old to be subtle," he said.

I looked at my watch. It was getting late and I needed to get to the library. I promised Harrison I would be out soon for supper and headed over to say good-bye to Mia.

"Call me or text me anytime," I said. "I mean it."

"I will," she said. She hugged me tightly.

Simon put a hand on her shoulder. "I'm just going to walk Kathleen out. I'll be right back," he said.

"I'm okay," Mia said. Simon caught Denise's eye and she nodded. I knew she'd keep a close eye on Mia. Like me, she'd been doing that all morning.

I didn't realize how warm it was inside the funeral home until we stepped outside.

"I didn't know he knew so many people," Simon said as we crossed the pavement toward my truck.

I thought he looked tired, the lines around his eyes pulling tighter than they had when we'd first arrived for the service.

"It's not just your father all these people care about," I said. "They care about you and Mia as well."

We reached the truck and Simon pulled at his tie, loosening it a little. "My father loved this place," he said. "After my mother died we moved to Green Bay and then Milwaukee. Dad went back to school and got his PhD in math. He taught for twenty years at Marquette University." He swiped a hand over the top of his head. "He loved math the way some people love the New York Yankees or Star Wars movies."

I smiled.

"And he loved to play blackjack and poker. Would you believe Dad was banned from a couple of casinos?" He kicked a rock, sending it skittering over the pavement.

I thought about the smiling man I'd met who doted on his granddaughter. It was hard to imagine Leo as a card shark. "What did he do?" I asked.

Simon gave me a wry smile. "Your guess is as good as mine. He always claimed he didn't cheat. He said the odds were stacked overwhelmingly in favor of the house and he was just evening things up a little."

"I wish I'd gotten to know him better," I said.

"You would have liked him."

I nodded. "I already did."

"Thank you for everything you did for Mia today," Simon said.

"She's special," I said, turning to look back at the funeral home for a moment.

"She's not the only one." He leaned over and his lips brushed my forehead, then he turned and headed back across the lot.

Abigail was working the front desk when I got to the library. "How was the funeral?" she said.

"Sad," I said.

"And Mia?"

I sighed and ran a hand through my hair. "She got up and spoke and she was so grown-up, but underneath all that she's still a little girl who misses her grandfather."

Later that afternoon I was pushing an empty book cart back to the front desk when Harry Junior came in. He lifted a hand and I joined him.

"I just took a look at the loading bay door and it definitely needs a new seal. That's where the rain's getting in."

"That's better than a whole new door," I said. "How do we get a new seal?"

"That's what I wanted to tell you," he said. "Thorsten thinks there's one at the town depot. I can go over and check if you want me to." He pulled off his Twins cap and smoothed a hand over his mostly bald scalp. "Do you need me to write you up a requisition for Lita?"

"I will," I said, "but I have enough in the repairs budget, so if they've got it, get it and go ahead and install it. There's rain in the long range for the first of next week."

"I'll get right on it."

"I talked to your father at the service. He's looking hale and hearty."

Harry smiled. "As much as I hate to admit it, this new romance of his seems to be agreeing with him." He pointed a finger at me. "And if you tell him I said that, those blackberries you like so much from my backyard might mysteriously disappear."

I held up both hands. "I didn't hear anything."

He smiled.

"It was good of you and Larry to come to the funeral as well," I said.

He suddenly looked uncomfortable, shifting his weight from one side to the other. "Leo Janes and the old man were friends a long time ago. It was the right thing to do." He shrugged. "I better get over and get that seal. I'll let you know when the door's fixed."

I watched him go, and Harrison's nudge that I should get involved in the investigation into Leo Janes's death came into my mind. I flashed to Simon in the funeral home parking lot and to Harry Taylor just now. I had no idea who had killed Leo Janes, but I did know that at least two people were probably hiding things.

6

Saturday morning I had a meeting with Ruby and Taylor King at the library. We'd gotten a small grant from the state to offer a summer reading club for elementary school kids. Ruby was going to run the program with help from Taylor. Ruby had lots of experience with that kind of thing—she'd been doing various art programs in the local schools for several years. Taylor had helped with the Reading Buddies Halloween party and I'd seen firsthand how good the teen was with little kids.

We went over what I was hoping to accomplish with the program. Both Ruby and Taylor had some good suggestions to improve my ideas and when we wrapped up just before ten thirty I felt satisfied that when the time came, the summer reading club was going to be a big success.

I was just coming back downstairs from grabbing a quick cup of coffee around eleven thirty when Elias

Braeden walked in the front door. I raised a hand in hello and he smiled and walked over to me.

"Good morning, Kathleen," he said. "I was hoping I could take you up on your offer of a tour of the library. Is this a good time?" He was wearing a black quilted jacket with a standup collar over a gray sweater.

"All I was going to do was shelve some books," I said. "So yes, it's a good time." We headed over to the front desk, where I introduced Elias to Abigail. "I'm going to give Elias a tour of the building," I said.

"I like old things," he said with a self-deprecating shrug.

"Me too," Abigail said, smiling up at him. "They always have a story." She gestured toward the entrance. "Make sure Kathleen tells you the story behind our sun."

"Why don't we start there?" I said. We moved a few steps closer to the entryway. A carved and pieced wooden sun, more than three feet across, hung above the door frame. Above it were stenciled the words "Let there be light." A carving of the sun and those same words were over the entrance to the very first Carnegie library in Scotland.

Elias looked at me, a frown creasing his forehead. "Wait a minute, this is a Carnegie library?" he asked.

I nodded.

He tipped his head back to study the sun. "That's beautiful work."

"Oren Kenyon's," I said. "He lives here in Mayville Heights and he's as much an artist as he is a carpenter."

I took Elias outside onto the steps to show him the wrought-iron railing Oren had also fabricated. The center wrought-iron spindle on each side of the landing divided into a perfect oval about the size of my two hands and then reformed into a twist again. The letters M, H, F, P and L for "Mayville Heights Free Public Library" were intertwined, seemingly suspended in the middle of the circles.

Elias ran his hand over the metal. "Mr. Kenyon is an incredible craftsman," he said.

We went back inside and I showed off the restored mosaic tile floor, the wide ornate woodwork and the stained glass window that made rainbow patterns of light on the floor when the sun streamed through it.

"I'm impressed," Elias said. "It's been a long time since I was in this building. You've restored it to its glory days."

"Thank you," I said. Renovating the library had been a massive project filled with massive headaches. There were times I doubted it would ever be completed, let alone completed in time for the centennial celebration, but we managed to make it happen. I loved showing off the finished product. "You've known Ruby her entire life," I said. The words weren't really a question.

He nodded. "Since she was five days old. She probably told you that I worked for her grandfather."

I nodded. "Is that how you knew Leo Janes? When you were in here before I thought you seemed to recognize him."

"Yes, I recognized him," Elias said, glancing at his

watch, a Citizen Eco-Drive, powered by light. It seemed to represent the man, understated and practical. "But not from when I worked for Idris. About six months ago I threw Mr. Janes out of my casino."

I remembered what Simon had told me about his father being banned from several casinos. "What exactly did he do?" I asked.

If Elias thought I was nosy it didn't show on his face. "He was cheating," he said flatly.

"You don't mean he was hiding cards up his sleeve, do you?" I said.

Elias shook his head. "No. At least I don't think he was. I don't actually know what he was doing. That was the problem." He shifted his weight from one foot to the other. "I think he was counting cards and had people helping him, but I could never prove it." He narrowed his eyes. "You know he was a math professor?"

I nodded.

"I did a background check on Mr. Janes. I found photos online of him with several of his students. Some of those same students turned up on the surveillance footage when Mr. Janes was in my casino." He paused. "At my blackjack tables."

I didn't know what to say, and that *did* seem to show on my face. "Kathleen, Leo Janes cost me more than a million dollars, money that I don't believe he won fair and square."

I realized then that Elias had been talking about Leo in the past tense. "You know that Leo is dead," I said.

"Yes." The smile disappeared from his face. "Kathleen, I know that he was murdered. I think you're far too polite to ask the next obvious question but I'm not nearly that well-mannered. For the record, I didn't kill Leo Janes."

I thought it was a little strange for him to say that.

"I did come to this area on business. Ruby may have told you I'm thinking about buying the Silver Casino."

"She did."

"I did want to talk to Leo once I learned the man was in Mayville Heights, too, but I give you my word that I didn't kill him. I didn't even see Leo the day he died." He gestured with one hand. He seemed relaxed, confident. "And for the record, I was on the road between Minneapolis and Mayville Heights on Friday night."

"I've offended you," I said. "I'm sorry."

Elias shook his head. "No offense taken, Kathleen. I know the rumors and the stories about businessmen like me, but I don't beat people up in back alleys when they cheat me. That's what lawyers are for." He glanced at his watch again. "I have to get going," he said. "Thank you for the tour."

I watched him make his way to the main doors, raising a hand in acknowledgment to Abigail at the front desk. Elias Braeden was an intriguing mix of bluntness and charm, but he had worked for Idris Blackthorne, so no matter what he said about leaving his problems to be handled by his lawyers I couldn't shake the feeling that he could be "hands-on" if he felt the situation warranted it. Could he have gotten hands-on with Leo Janes?

Roma and Maggie showed up at five to one. "Hi. What are you two doing here?" I asked.

"We came to steal you for lunch," Maggie said, grinning and holding up a take-out bag from Eric's.

"Do you have time?" Roma asked.

"She does," Susan said, moving behind me with an empty book cart. She smiled at me and pushed her cat's-eye glasses up her nose. "Abigail and I can close. There isn't that much to do. It's been dead quiet all morning." She made a shooing motion with one hand. "Go!"

"I have time," I said.

Maggie smiled at Susan. "Thanks," she said. She turned to me. "It's beautiful outside. How about a picnic in your gazebo?"

"I'd like that," I said.

I'd met Maggie when Rebecca convinced me to try her tai chi class. Mags was the instructor, tall and slim and unbelievably flexible, with cropped blond curls and green eyes that reminded me of Hercules. Our friendship had begun the night I arrived early for class and found her online at the website for the popular celebrity dance show *Gotta Dance*, voting for the *Today* show's Matt Lauer. I was a fan of the show as well, although cutie Kevin Sorbo had been getting my votes.

Tai chi was also where I'd met Roma. When the class had formed a circle to begin our warm-ups

Roma had been beside me. She was new to the group as well and we'd bonded over our mutual inability to master White Crane Spreads Wings. I sometimes wondered if Mayville Heights would have started to feel like home so quickly if I had turned Rebecca's invitation down.

We walked around the building to the tall wooden gazebo in the back overlooking the water. Maggie had brought turkey-and-bacon sandwiches on thick slices of honey-granola bread. Roma handed me her insulated travel mug. "Coffee," she said with a smile.

"Because how could we forget that?" Maggie said drily. She and Roma were drinking lemonade.

I ate about half of my sandwich and then eyed the two of them. "So what's up?" I asked.

Roma set down her lemonade. "There's something I'd like to ask you."

"If you'd like me to feed the cats for you next week the answer is yes."

She smiled and shook her head. "No. Kathleen, I know you already said you'd be a bridesmaid, but I'd like you to be my maid of honor."

I stared at her. I hadn't expected the question. "But what about Maggie?" I said. "She's the reason you and Eddie met. She should be your maid of honor."

Roma and Eddie had gotten together after Maggie had made a full-sized, very lifelike Eddie Sweeney mannequin for a display about the history of sports in this part of the state for Winterfest a couple of years ago. The only way she'd been able to get Faux Eddie from her studio to the community center was in the front seat of Roma's SUV. That had started a rumor that Roma and the Minnesota Wild star were seeing each other, and pretty soon it wasn't just a rumor.

"I may have indirectly gotten things started, but there wouldn't be a wedding if you hadn't urged Roma to throw caution to the wind and listen to her heart." Maggie paused, a dill pickle halfway to her mouth. "And that was a lot of clichés in one sentence."

"I wouldn't be marrying Eddie if it weren't for both of you," Roma said. "Which is why I want you both to be my maids of honor." She looked from Maggie to me. "Please say yes."

"Yes!" Maggie and I said in unison.

Roma threw an arm around each of us and hugged us. Then she straightened up and gave me a sly smile. "And when you and Marcus get married Maggie and I will be your maids of honor."

I felt my face flood with color. Roma and Maggie exchanged a look. They were getting a kick out of my flustered reaction. I held up both hands. "Okay. I might, *might* have been thinking about spending the rest of my life with Marcus."

"So ask him," Maggie said, popping the pickle in her mouth.

Roma tucked a stray strand of hair behind one ear. "I highly recommend it," she said with a smile.

I took a sip of my coffee and eyed Maggie. "What about you and Brady? And don't give us that 'we're just friends' speech."

Maggie shrugged. "I don't know if I want to get married at all, let alone if Brady would be the guy."

She took a bite of her sandwich, chewed and then realized we were waiting for something more from her. "What if you get married and then you wake up some morning and realize you don't love that person anymore?" She gestured with her sandwich and little bits of shredded lettuce fell onto her lap.

"What if you get married and then you wake up every morning for the rest of your life thinking how lucky you are to be able to spend one more day with that other person?" Roma asked. "Except for the mornings that you want to smack them with a burned bagel because they're all cheery and full of sunshine and don't need coffee to turn into a human being."

I laughed. "I hope Eddie knows how lucky he is," I said.

"Because most days I resist the urge to hurl burned breakfast food at him?" Roma said with a laugh.

"No, because he gets to spend all the rest of his days with you." I held up a hand. "And yes, I know I sound like the heroine of some romantic novel. It's still true."

"I'm the lucky one," she said, looking down at the ring on her left hand.

"What kind of wedding dress are you going to wear?" Maggie asked.

Roma made a face. "Do I really need one?"

"You don't need one, but you'd look beautiful in one," I said.

I caught Maggie's eye. "Shopping trip!" we both said.

"Maybe," Roma said, "but nothing lacy or poufy or

big. And I don't know about white. I'd just like something very plain and simple."

Maggie made a sound in her throat that made me think of Owen when he was annoyed.

"Roma, you do know you've pretty much just described those big recycled paper bags Harry uses out here when he collects the dead leaves and plants, don't you?"

She laughed. "I just want to marry Eddie. I don't have a clue what to choose for a dress."

"We'll find you the perfect dress," Maggie said, licking mustard off her little finger. "I promise, no pouf, no white." She frowned. "There are lots of possibilities. There's ivory, vanilla, linen." She studied Roma. "Cornsilk would look good with your hair. Or maybe ecru."

I reached for my coffee. "I have no idea what ecru is but I'm sure you'd look good in it. And maybe those big sleeves. I don't know the name of them."

"Mutton," Maggie said. She looked at Roma, all seriousness, although I saw the glint in her green eyes. "How do you feel about hoopskirts?"

Roma folded her arms over her chest and smiled at us. "You do realize that as the bride it's my prerogative to choose the maid-of-honor dresses? How do you two feel about chartreuse?"

"When I was in art school I dated a guy with a chartreuse Volkswagen Microbus," Maggie offered, seemingly unconcerned about wearing a yellow-green maid-of-honor dress for Roma's wedding.

I picked up the dill pickle spear that was lying on

the wax paper that had been around my sandwich and set it next to the bit of crust left from Maggie's sandwich. She smiled a thank-you at me.

"The color chartreuse gets its name from a type of liqueur made by a group of French monks starting back in the eighteenth century," I said.

"It's a tertiary color," Mags added.

"That means you mix a primary and a secondary color together?" I asked.

She smiled at me. "Exactly."

Roma rubbed the space between her eyebrows with two fingers. "Okay, you can stop with the history of chartreuse. We'll go wedding dress shopping next week. But no hoopskirts and no sleeves named after meat."

"Deal," I said, grinning at Maggie over the top of Roma's head.

Roma took a drink of her lemonade and gestured at me with the bottle. "Have you spoken to Thorsten?" she asked.

"No," I said. "Why?"

"Because I think he found the dog that tangled with Owen. Yesterday afternoon he brought in a stray he found running loose a little farther up Mountain Road from your house."

I reached for my coffee. "What makes you think it's the dog Owen encountered?"

"It had several infected scratches on its muzzle and one shoulder. They look like something a cat's claws did."

"Is the dog going to be all right?"

Roma nodded. "Yes, but if you hear of anyone who wants a dog, please let me know. He's thin and he's obviously been on his own for a while, but he's a good-natured dog." She gave me a sheepish grin. "Don't tell Owen I said that."

We sat there for another five minutes talking and then Roma stood up. "This was fun," she said. "And I hate to go, but I do need to go check on a horse." She hugged Maggie and me, promising she'd call to work out a time for our shopping trip.

"Do you think I could take another quick look at the photos?" Maggie asked as we walked around the side of the building.

"Sure," I said. "And you don't have to hurry. There are some things on my desk I need to take care of."

"Did Keith get a price for you on the glass to cover the photos if you decide to put them out on a table for people to look at?" Maggie asked as I unlocked the building and we stepped inside.

I nodded. "It's a lot more expensive than I expected. I don't have much money left in my discretionary budget." I put my keys in my pocket. "And I still think we need some kind of hook, some kind of enticement to people who aren't regular library users to come in and see the photos."

"Maybe Bridget would do a story about them for the paper."

"Mary said Bridget's already working on an article for the paper about the letters." Mary's daughter owned the local newspaper.

"Do you know anyone who got one of them?"

We started up to the second floor. "No," I said. "And no one who has been in has talked about getting one." I nudged Maggie with my elbow. "Do you think there were any misplaced love letters hidden behind that wall?"

"Probably not," she said. "I know whatever was walled up in that little anteroom has been there for more than twenty years, but I think handwritten love letters went out of style long before that." She smiled. "I think you just have romance on your mind because we were talking about Roma's wedding dress."

I unlocked the door to the workroom and Maggie walked over to the table, where I spread out the photos. Her green eyes lit up. "Oh, Kath, these are incredible. I didn't really get a good look at them at the meeting."

"I know," I said. "Just based on the clothing some of them are from the early 1960s."

"You don't have any idea how they got walled up in that room?"

"Not a clue."

"So all these photographs belong to the library now?"

"Uh-huh. Unless we can figure out whom they're of and return them—which would be the best outcome. I don't want all of these photos to just end up in a box on a shelf. I'd like to know who all those people are."

Maggie picked up a five-by-seven image of a group of kids standing arm in arm at the water's edge. "We could see if Lita recognizes anyone. And maybe Harrison Taylor."

I leaned against the long worktable. "If we show the pictures to enough people we probably could figure out who they're all of, but as I said at the meeting, I don't think they'd stand up to being handled so much."

Maggie was staring off into space. I knew there was an idea rolling over in her mind. That's why I'd asked her to get involved in the first place. I knew she'd probably be able to come up with some way to display the photographs and entice people to come in to see them. "I have an idea, Kath," she said, "but I need to check on a couple of things first."

"I knew you'd be able to figure something out." I looked in the direction of my office. "I have about an hour or so's worth of paperwork to do if you want to hang around for a while and look through those."

She nodded, blond head already bent over the pile of pictures in front of her on the table.

I'd been working for about half an hour when Marcus called. "Would you mind if I bailed on our plans and went to Minneapolis with Eddie?" he asked.

"Yes," I said. "I'd probably spend the evening sobbing into my pillow."

"Even if I promised to make it up to you by cooking dinner tomorrow night at your house *and* making pudding cake *and* doing all the dishes?"

"Hmmm," I said, leaning back in my chair. "That does sound delicious. Okay, you have a deal. Why are you and Eddie headed to Minneapolis?"

"Guy he played with retired a couple of years ago from the LA Kings. He's been doing hockey-skills workshops all over the country. He's in Minneapolis for some kind of meeting. Eddie's going to take him to dinner and pick his brain about running a hockey school. I'm going along to drive and think of things that Eddie forgets."

Eddie had plans to start a hockey school in Mayville Heights now that he was retired and he and Roma were getting married.

"Have fun," I said. "I'll be sad and lonely while you're gone but I'm pretty sure that pudding cake you mentioned will cure that. You will be making a double batch, right?"

Marcus laughed. "For you, absolutely."

"I could go out and check on Micah," I said. "It'll be late when you get back."

"Umm, yeah, if it's not too much trouble. I was gone all morning and she gave me the silent treatment when I came back. I gave her some of your sardine crackers. I'm not sure I'm back on her good side, though."

"I think she's like Owen. He'll milk being miffed as long as he can to get as many treats as possible," I said, swinging slowly from side to side in the chair. I was almost positive it wasn't the only thing the two cats had in common.

Marcus said he'd call me in the morning and I said good-bye. It took me another twenty minutes or so to finish up my paperwork. I drove Maggie over to her studio and went in to take a look at her latest collage.

On my way out I met Ruby coming up the stairs. "Hi, Kathleen," she said. "How's your day going?"

She was wearing her *Ginger Did It Backward in High Heels* T-shirt.

"Good," I said. "Elias came in this morning. I gave him a tour."

She smiled. "Thank you. He has this thing for old buildings. He grew up in some pretty bare-bones places. I think that's why."

"You've known Elias a long time."

"All my life." She frowned. "Is there some kind of problem?"

I shifted uncomfortably from one foot to the other. "When he was in the library before—the first time—Leo Janes was there and I had the feeling they knew each other."

Ruby shrugged. "So? Elias lived here years ago. It's a small town. A lot of different people know each other."

"I know, but he told me one of the reasons he came to town was to talk to Leo."

"Maybe they knew each other when they were kids."

I shook my head. "He thought Leo had cheated him out of a lot of money—more than a million dollars."

She laughed. "Good dog, this isn't some mobster movie, Kathleen. Elias didn't have Leo Janes whacked. He's a reputable businessman. He belongs to the Chamber of Commerce. He sponsors a kids' hockey team."

"Hey, I like Elias," I said, holding up a hand. "And I'm not saying he had Leo killed, but is it possible that someone who worked for him went to see Leo and things got out of hand?"

She shook her head. "No." She took a breath and let it out slowly. "Look, I'm not saying that Elias doesn't have a bit of a reputation for being hardheaded, and yeah, some of that probably does come from working for my grandfather, but there's a line he wouldn't cross and hurting someone is it. Trust me."

I didn't see any point in continuing the conversation. "Thanks," I said.

Ruby smiled. "Hey, no problem," she said. She moved past me and I continued down the stairs.

"Trust me," she'd said. I wanted to. I did. I wanted to trust Elias Braeden, too. I just wasn't sure if I should.

I left Riverarts and headed out to Marcus's house. There was no sign of Micah in the backyard. I let myself into the kitchen and called for the little ginger tabby. Nothing. In the middle of the table there was a loaf of bread and a Mason jar filled with the Jam Lady's marshmallows and a note from Marcus. *I love you,* the note said, and it was signed with several large X's for kisses.

"I love you, too," I whispered.

At that moment Micah appeared on the empty chair beside me. Not launched herself from the floor or jumped from another chair. Appeared, as in the opposite of disappeared.

For a moment the air almost seemed electric, the way it did before a thunderstorm. Micah cocked her head to one side and meowed at me.

"Does Marcus know you can do this?" I asked the cat and immediately felt foolish. Did I really think she was going to answer me?

The cat wrinkled her whiskers and meowed again almost as though she were saying, "Maybe." And given what I'd just seen her do, who was I to say that she wasn't?

I thought about all the times lately that Marcus had told me the little cat had "snuck" unseen into his SUV. "I'm going to have to tell him," I said. "As soon as this case is over I'm going to have to tell him."

I left Micah with some sardine crackers and a promise to bring an actual tin of sardines next time I came out. She licked her whiskers and I had the feeling that the ability to disappear wasn't the only skill she shared with Owen.

When I got home there was no sign of Owen, but one of my hats was in the middle of the kitchen floor. I bent down to pick it up and discovered that there was a funky chicken head inside. I sat back on my heels. "Do you have any idea what this is all about?" I said to Hercules, who had just come in from the living room.

"Mrr," he said, blinking his green eyes at me. In other words, he didn't know, either.

Hercules had gotten his name from Roman mythology. At least that was what I told people. For the most part it was the truth. He had been named after Hercules, the son of Zeus. As portrayed by the very yummy Kevin Sorbo. Or as Maggie liked to teasingly describe him, Mr. Six-Pack-in-a-Loincloth.

Owen, on the other hand, was named because of the book *A Prayer for Owen Meany*—John Irving— which I'd been reading when I brought the boys home.

Whenever I put the book down Owen sat on it. His name was either going to be Owen or Irving and to me he didn't look like an Irving.

I dumped the soggy chicken head in the trash and shook my hat over the can to get the bits of catnip out. I went upstairs to change, trailed by Hercules. I told him about my day and he murped at intervals as though he was actually listening.

About twenty minutes later, I was peering in the refrigerator to see if I had any Parmesan cheese to top a plate of spaghetti when Owen came up from the basement. He walked past me, stopped in the middle of the floor and looked all around the kitchen. Roma had been keeping an eye on his ear ever since the collar had come off. It seemed to be healing well.

Owen looked at me. It was hard to miss the accusatory glare in his golden eyes. "Merow!" he said loudly.

"It wasn't your hat, it was my hat," I said, setting a Mason jar of spaghetti sauce on the counter. "And hats don't belong in the middle of the kitchen floor."

He looked around the room again and then seemed to zero in on the trash can. He stalked over to it and meowed again, turning back to look at me over his shoulder.

"Yes, I threw out your chicken head," I said. "It was wet, it was disgusting and it was inside *my* hat."

I saw his muscles tense and I knew he was about to launch himself at the can.

"Knock that can over and I will vacuum up every chicken part in this house." It was an empty threat.

My best guess was that I knew where maybe half of his stash was, but Owen didn't know that. He glared at me. I folded my arms over my chest and glared back at him. Hercules suddenly became engrossed in checking out something on the floor under the chair next to where he'd been sitting. Who knows how long the standoff would have gone on except Hercules sneezed . . . which scared him the way it always did. Startled, he jumped, the way he always did. Except he was under the chair. His head banged the underside of the seat. He yowled in indignation and flattened himself against the floor, turning from side to side as though he thought someone had hit him over the head.

Owen sat up and took a few steps toward his brother. I immediately moved the chair and bent down to Hercules. "Let me see," I said. He was still looking around suspiciously.

"You banged your head on the chair," I said. "Let me take a look."

He made grumbling noises in the back of his throat but he let me feel the top of his head. He didn't pull away from my carefully probing fingers and didn't even wince as I examined the top of his head. "I think you're going to be okay," I said. Could cats get concussions? I wondered. Hercules seemed all right; annoyed and a little embarrassed but otherwise fine.

I got him a couple of bites of cooked chicken from the fridge and gave one piece to Owen as well. I noticed Hercules gave the offending chair a wide berth as he made his way over to his water dish, shooting it a green-eyed glare as he passed.

Owen disappeared after supper, probably checking his various stashes of funky chicken parts to make sure they were still hidden. Hercules was still a bit out of sorts. He followed me around the kitchen as I cleaned up and did the dishes and twice I almost tripped over him. Once the dishes were put away I set my laptop on the table. "Want to help me look up a couple of things?" I asked the cat.

"Mrr," he said after a moment's thought. It sounded like a yes to me. I picked him up and settled him on my lap. He put one paw on the edge of the table as I pulled the computer closer and turned it on.

"I'm kind of curious about Simon and his family," I told Hercules. "Let's see what we can find." Simon Janes had no Facebook or Twitter accounts but there was still a fair amount of information about him online. He'd started his development company in college when he rented a room in a run-down house about fifteen minutes from campus. On the weekends he went home to see baby Mia, who stayed with Leo. Simon persuaded the landlord to let him fix up the old house instead of paying rent. He did the same thing in another place the next year. In his third year he used the money he hadn't spent on rent as a down payment on a tiny two-bedroom house, renovated it and then rented out rooms to his friends. By then Mia was living with him full-time.

I tried to imagine what Simon's days had been like, going to class, going home to see Mia every weekend and then having her with him all the time, trying to make time to study and working on whichever old house he was living in. It had been all I could do to manage my classes and a very early breakfast shift at an off-campus diner that catered to early risers, hunters and people just getting off the night shift. "Simon wasn't afraid of hard work, as my mother would say," I said to Hercules.

The cat seemed less impressed. He pawed at the keyboard and somehow I found myself looking at a newspaper article about the death of Meredith Janes outside Chicago. Hercules leaned in toward the screen as if he was reading the copy. He paused for a moment, looked back at me and meowed. Clearly he thought this was important somehow. So was it?

"Fine, I'll read it, too," I said.

The piece was the second of a three-part series on accidents along a stretch of twisty road. The police had spent a lot of time investigating Meredith Janes's accident. There was some question at the time that another car had been involved, possibly forcing her off the road, but in the end police found no evidence at the scene or on the car and the investigation was closed, the accident blamed on road conditions and excess speed.

But what caught my attention as much as the article was the photo of Meredith Janes. It was the photo I'd seen lying on the side table when I'd found Leo Janes's body. Something had been bothering me about that picture, or more specifically, the frame. There had been one other photo on the table—of Simon and Mia. It had been professionally matted and framed in an expensive metal frame. The old photograph in the inexpensive plastic department-store frame had seemed oddly out of place next to the professionally presented image of Simon and Mia. I remembered Rebecca saying that Leo never forgave his brother or his wife. I wondered why he had a photo of her in a place he was only staying at for a few weeks if he felt that way. Did it have anything to do with Leo's decision to give his brother a second chance?

I remembered what Marcus had said when I'd suggested the animosity between the two brothers gave Victor a motive to kill his brother: *"He had nothing to gain."* Was that actually true?

Hercules seemed to finish reading before I did. He sat patiently on my lap and I could see him watching me out of the corner of my eye. When I finished I reached over and scratched the place above his nose where his black fur turned to white.

"Fine, you win, smarty pants," I said.

He licked my chin, cat for "I told you so."

I looked at the computer screen again. Marcus had said once that I had the mind-set of a detective. I wanted to know the what and the why about everything. I found myself wondering those things about the photo of Meredith Janes in her ex-husband's apartment. What was it doing there and why did he have it? And was Victor Janes connected in any way?

Maybe I needed to find out.

7

Marcus called Sunday morning to tell me the trip to Minneapolis had been a success. Eddie had learned a lot about setting up a hockey school from his former teammate and they'd split a huge platter of wings. I was curled up in the overstuffed chair next to my bed with a book and a certain gray tabby cat sprawled half on my lap, half on my chest.

I thanked him for the bread and the marshmallows. I'd toasted some of the bread at breakfast and there were four marshmallows in the cup of hot chocolate at my left elbow.

"You're welcome," he said. "Do you want to check out the flea market down at the community center this afternoon? I'm looking for a bench to set by the back door. And no, I didn't forget that I'm cooking dinner for you."

Somehow Owen heard the word "dinner," probably because he had exceptional hearing—when it suited him. He lifted his head and meowed loudly.

"Is that Owen?" Marcus asked.

"Uh-huh," I said. "He seems to think you should make him supper, too."

Marcus laughed. "He can have cat food, cat food or cat food. Roma threatened to ban me from ever getting another slice of her apple pie if I don't watch how much people food he and Hercules are getting. So no more pizza for Owen—at least until pie season is over."

Owen and Hercules clearly weren't "ordinary cats" and I suspected they didn't have ordinary digestive systems, either, but that didn't mean they should eat like a pair of frat boys on spring break.

"I agree with her, at least on the pizza," I said. "How would you like to be woken up by a cat with morning pizza breath licking your chin?"

"I'd much rather be woken up by you licking my chin," he said, and it seemed that I could feel his breath warm against my ear even though that was impossible.

He picked me up at twelve thirty and we headed downtown to the flea market, which was being held in the community center parking lot. There were a lot more people there than I'd expected. We'd been walking around less than five minutes when I caught sight of Maggie and Brady. I waved but she didn't see us, so we made our way over to them through the crowd.

"Isn't this fantastic?" Maggie asked. She was carrying a string bag over one shoulder and I could see a stack of postcards and a child's Spirograph inside.

"Everything *and* the kitchen sink," Brady said, gesturing at a huge stainless-steel sink at a nearby stall. "There's a guy here from upstate with a PAC-MAN arcade machine."

"Tabletop or upright?" Marcus asked.

"Upright. I'm thinking about maybe buying it."

Marcus raised an eyebrow and grinned. "I may have to hit the bank for some rolls of quarters."

"I haven't played PAC-MAN in years," I said.

"I didn't know you liked arcade games," Maggie said.

"One year my parents were doing summer stock and there was an arcade next to the theater." I smiled. "I got pretty good at a couple of games. I have excellent hand-eye coordination."

Marcus looked at me. "You may have beaten me the first time we played road hockey but there is no way you're better at PAC-MAN than I am."

I'd beaten him at our most recent game of road hockey, too, but I didn't point that out. I shrugged. "Well, if Brady buys the game maybe we'll find out."

"Want to go take a look?" Brady asked. Both he and Maggie seemed to be getting a kick out of the conversation.

"Absolutely," Marcus said, his blue eyes never leaving my face. He had a competitive streak I'd learned about when I'd played road hockey against him at my first Winterfest. And won. When it came to road hockey games with Marcus, I was undefeated.

"I'll come find you in a little while," I said, smiling sweetly at him.

Marcus and Brady headed toward the back corner

of the lot. "It's going to be Winterfest all over again, isn't it?" Maggie asked.

"Yes," I said.

"You're really good at that game, aren't you?"

I nodded. "Yes."

Maggie slipped the strap of her bag up onto her shoulder. "I take it your mother never told you to let the boys win so they'd like you."

That made me laugh. "Mags, you've met my mother," I said. "Do you really think she'd ever give advice like that?"

She shook her head. "Not really."

We started walking. "She told me to do my best, play fair and never throw a game for a guy. She said, 'The only person you might annoy is your first ex-husband.'"

Maggie laughed. "That sounds like your mom."

She led me to a stall along the street side of the parking lot. "Take a look at these," she said, indicating several large cardboard cartons sitting on the ground in front of the booth.

I took a few steps closer. "Picture frames?" I asked.

She nodded. "I can get one of those boxes for twenty dollars—maybe less. I was thinking I could get everyone at the co-op to take two or three and paint them or whatever and we could use them to frame those photos. What do you think?"

"I think it's a great idea," I said. I pulled out my wallet and handed her two twenties. Maggie crouched down and began looking through the boxes, deciding which ones she wanted to buy.

I looked around. I knew it would take a while for Maggie to make up her mind. I couldn't see Marcus and Brady anywhere but as I turned in a slow circle I did see someone I recognized: the woman I had seen walking in the rain the night Leo Janes was killed, the same woman I'd seen coming out of the building the time I'd gone to pick up Rebecca for tai chi. The scarf I'd found the night of Leo's murder hadn't belonged to Rebecca. Maybe it belonged to this woman.

"Mags, I'll be right back," I said.

"Okay," she said, fluttering one hand over her shoulder at me. I knew she'd be busy for a while.

I made my way over to the woman, who was looking at a collection of vintage cookie jars. I tapped her on the shoulder. "Excuse me," I said. "Did you by any chance lose a yellow tie-dyed silk scarf on Hawthorne Street? The night we had all the rain?"

She turned. "I did," she said. "Don't tell me you found it?"

"I did," I said. "It was lying on the ground and I picked it up." I realized then that I hadn't introduced myself. "I'm Kathleen Paulson."

"Celia Hunter." She was maybe five feet tall without the chunky-heeled, low, brown boots she was wearing. She was a little older than I had guessed when I'd seen her walking. There were fine lines around her eyes and her hair, cut in a sleek, asymmetrical bob, was completely gray.

"I'm the head librarian at the library here in town," I said. "I could leave your scarf at the front desk for you."

She smiled. "Thank you. It's not expensive but it was a gift, so it has a lot of sentimental value for me." Her hazel eyes narrowed. "You were at Leo Janes's funeral," she said.

I nodded. "Yes, I was."

"Leo's wife, Meredith, was my best friend."

Meredith Janes. Her name seemed to keep coming up.

"So you grew up in Mayville Heights?" I took a step to the right to get out of the way of a woman pushing a chubby-cheeked baby in an umbrella stroller.

Celia's smile returned. "Yes. I haven't been back in years. So much has changed and yet so much is the same. I heard that the library has been restored."

"For the building's centennial, yes," I said. "You can see it when you come to get your scarf."

"I'll try to get there tomorrow," she said. "I'm staying at the St. James so I'm close by. I plan on being here another week." She hesitated, brushing a bit of lint off the sleeve of her caramel-colored jacket. "I actually came to see Leo. Did you hear about the mail that was found behind the wall at the post office?"

I nodded.

"One of those pieces of mail was addressed to me. It was sent by Meredith the day she died. I came here to show it to Leo."

I looked around, hoping I could spot Marcus. This had to mean something.

Something flashed across her face for a moment, like a cloud passing over the sun. "Kathleen, excuse me if I'm being, well, too presumptuous, but you're friends with Leo's son, Simon, aren't you? I mean, I saw you sitting with him and his daughter at the service."

I was picking at the cuff of my sweater, I realized. I put my hand in my pocket. "Yes, I am."

"Then maybe you can give me some guidance." She pressed her lips together for a moment. "Once I got here I had second thoughts about showing Leo the letter Meredith had sent me all those years ago. I, uh, I was afraid it might be painful for Leo so the first time I visited him I didn't mention it. I just said I was here and wanted to say hello."

I wasn't sure what to say, so I just nodded. "The second time I went to see him I had the letter with me but Leo obviously had something on his mind. He was distracted. He looked at his watch a couple of times and then he apologized. He said he was waiting for a phone call. I told him we could get together another time. I was at the door when his cell phone rang. He asked the person on the other end to hold on and then he said he'd call me in a day or two and we could have lunch. I left. That was the day he died."

She sighed. "This is my long-winded way of saying that I never did show Leo the letter. I'd be happy to let Simon read what his mother wrote but I don't want to cause him any more grief than he already has to deal with."

"What are you asking?" I said.

"I know this is a lot to ask when you don't know me, but would you be willing to read the letter and tell me if I should show it to Simon?"

I smoothed a hand back over my hair. "I don't think I'm qualified to make that decision for Simon," I said.

"I understand," she said.

"I think you should get in touch with him. You could tell him what it says in general terms, then he could decide if he wanted to read it himself."

She nodded. "That's a good idea." She glanced at her watch. "I should be able to make it to the library tomorrow or Tuesday."

I glanced around again and still couldn't see Marcus. "Celia, do you mind if I ask if you've spoken to the police?"

Her eyes narrowed and she looked puzzled. "No. Why would I talk to the police?"

"Because you're one of the last people Leo saw the night he died."

For a moment she didn't say anything and she seemed focused on something beyond me. Then her attention came back to me. "I assumed Leo had a heart attack, but that's not what happened, is it? Somebody . . . Leo didn't die of natural causes, did he?"

The fact that Leo Janes had been murdered wasn't a secret, but it wasn't common knowledge yet, either. Surprising, because that sort of news usually made it around town pretty quickly.

"The police are still looking into that," I said. "You might know something that can help them and not realize it."

Celia nodded. "Of course. I'll go to the police station first thing in the morning."

"I think that's a good idea."

"I'm glad you came to speak to me," she said. "I'll see you soon."

She turned and headed toward the street. I walked back to Maggie, who had two boxes of frames at her feet and was just getting some money from the stall owner. She turned to me, smiled and handed me a ten-dollar bill. "Two boxes for thirty dollars," she said, "and I think I could have gotten him down a little more. No one is lining up to buy these."

She bent down and picked up one of the boxes and I got the other. "Guy who owns the stall doesn't have to drag these two boxes home and I saved a little money—everyone is a little happy and a little had."

I smiled at the expression. I'd heard Burtis use it before. Brady's father had several small businesses, most of which were legal. No matter what Maggie said about her relationship with Brady Chapman, I knew they were becoming important parts of each other's lives.

"Did you find anything interesting?" she asked.

"In a way, yes," I said, thinking about my conversation with Celia Hunter.

She glanced over at me. "You didn't buy anything?"

"It wasn't that kind of interesting."

Maggie shrugged. She was probably the only person I knew who would accept that kind of an answer.

"If we can find Brady I can get his keys and put these in his truck," she said.

"Do you know where that arcade game was?" I asked. The box of frames was heavier than it looked.

Maggie stopped, took a couple of steps to the side

to get out of people's way and looked around. Her green eyes narrowed and her mouth moved as she muttered to herself. "Over there," she said, "just to the left of the place with the copper birdbaths."

We headed across the parking lot and suddenly I caught sight of Brady. He was shaking hands with someone I didn't recognize. "Mags, I see Brady," I said. "I think he bought the PAC-MAN game."

"I knew he would," she said. "You should have seen his face when he first saw it." She smiled. "He has the money, and how often can you buy happiness?"

I pretended to think about the question. "That depends on how often Eric has chocolate pudding cake on the menu."

She laughed. "Okay, so some of us can buy it more easily than others."

Brady had bought the arcade PAC-MAN machine. He and Marcus had grabbed Larry Taylor, who happened to be walking by, and the three of them got the game loaded onto Brady's truck, strapped in with some bungee cords of Larry's.

"We'll take these boxes," Marcus said, taking the carton from Maggie's arms. "Where do you want them? Home or at Riverarts?"

"Thank you," Mags said. "Studio, please."

We followed Brady's truck over to the former school and put the two boxes of frames up in her studio.

"Do you need some help to get that thing off the truck?" Marcus asked Brady when we were back on the street again.

Brady shook his head. "There will be lots of bodies at the house—that's where I'm taking it."

Maggie told me she'd call me in the morning to set up a time to start measuring some of the photos.

"Thanks for taking this project on," I said, giving her a hug.

"I'm excited about it," she said. "See you tomorrow."

Marcus headed up the hill. I replayed the conversation with Celia Hunter in my head. I was so focused on my thoughts I didn't realize he'd spoken to me.

"Sorry," I said, shaking my head.

"Where were you?" he asked.

"Do you have Leo Janes's cell phone?"

"Yes," Marcus said, his eyes darting sideways at me briefly.

I remembered what Celia had said about Leo getting a call on his cell just as she was leaving the apartment. "Did he get a phone call a short time before he died?"

"I can't tell you that, Kathleen," he said, his expression and voice shifting into what I called "cop mode."

"Did the person Leo spoke to tell you that someone was leaving his apartment at the time of the call?"

Marcus put on his blinker and pulled over to the curb. He put the SUV in park and turned to me. "You know something. What is it?"

"When Mia and I got to the building that night I saw a silk scarf on the walkway. I picked it up and put it in my pocket. I thought it was Rebecca's. It wasn't, she just has one that's very similar."

He nodded.

"Later, I realized the first time I'd gone over to Rebecca's I'd passed a woman coming out of the building and she was wearing the scarf." I held up a hand. "I know this doesn't make much sense."

He folded his arms over his chest and shifted a little in his seat. "Keep going," he said.

"I saw her, while Maggie was looking at those picture frames. I went and spoke to her. Her name is Celia Hunter. She was a friend of Leo's wife. She was with Leo not long before he died."

He pulled one hand over his mouth. "Why didn't she get in touch with us when she heard he was dead?"

I reached over and brushed a bit of dried leaf from his sleeve.

"She said she didn't think it was important. Remember, not everyone knows Leo was murdered. And by the way, how did you get Bridget to sit on that?"

"It wasn't me," Marcus said. "I think the prosecuting attorney made some kind of deal with her."

"I told Celia she needed to talk to you and she said she'd come to the station in the morning."

"She's from out of town," he said.

I nodded.

I could see his mind working. "Describe her to me."

"She's around sixty, gray hair about this long." I tapped my jawline with my index fingers. "She's maybe five feet tall but no more."

He didn't write anything down but that didn't mean he wouldn't remember.

I blew out a breath, lifting my bangs in the air. "I'm

sorry I didn't tell you about the scarf. It didn't occur to me that it might have belonged to anyone other than Rebecca."

He smiled. "It's all right. You said this woman admitted it was hers?"

"Uh-huh."

Marcus started the SUV again. "It's not evidence. It could have been on the ground for days. Don't worry about it."

"Are you sure?" I said as he pulled away from the curb.

"It wasn't her, if that's what you're thinking."

I snugged up my seat belt. "How do you know?"

He glanced at me again. "This stays between us."

"Absolutely."

"I have the medical examiner's report, and the person who hit Leo with that heavy piece of sculpture was strong and tall. I don't think Leo obligingly bent down for his killer."

"And there was nothing there he could have been sitting on," I finished, remembering what the room had looked like when I'd found Leo's body.

Marcus put on his blinker and turned onto Mountain Road. I realized that the medical examiner's report may have eliminated Celia, but it didn't do anything for Simon.

8

Marcus made chicken with apples and leeks for supper and my favorite, Eric's chocolate pudding cake, for dessert. "You're a really good cook," I told him, licking the back of my spoon after having a second helping.

He smiled. "You might be a little biased."

"I don't think so," I said solemnly. I leaned across the edge of the table to kiss him.

His phone rang.

I made a face. "No," I groaned.

Marcus's lips brushed mine. "Remember where we were." He picked up the phone and immediately his expression changed. "What happened?" he said.

It was police business, I realized. I got up and started clearing the table. Owen was sitting to the right of Marcus's chair, fastidiously washing his face. Hercules had gone into the living room once he figured out he wasn't getting any pudding cake.

Marcus said, "Okay," several times. His mouth

pulled to one side. "No, no, I'm on my way," he finally said. He ended the call and turned to look at me. "I'm sorry, Kathleen. This has to do with a case."

Leo Janes's case? I wondered. Marcus stood up and pulled me into his arms. "Rain check?" he asked.

"Absolutely," I said.

He gestured at the sink. "I'm sorry to leave you with the dishes."

"That's okay," I said. "Owen doesn't mind lending a paw." The cat held up one front foot and gave me a puzzled look.

Marcus laughed. Then he grabbed his coat. I kissed him and he was gone.

Owen didn't actually help with the dishes, but he did sit at my feet and keep me company while I did them.

Once everything was dried and put away I set my laptop on the kitchen table. "Want to help me look up a couple of things?" I asked. He tipped his head to one side, seeming to consider the idea, then he yawned, stretched and disappeared. As in I couldn't see him anymore. "You could have just said no," I said.

Hercules poked his head around the living room doorway then. "Mrr?" he said inquiringly.

"I was talking to your brother," I said, hooking a chair with one foot.

"Mrr," he said again.

"Do you want to help me look up a couple of things?" I asked.

He almost seemed to shrug, then he made his way over to me. I picked him up, sat down and let the cat get settled on my lap. "Claws," I reminded him when his poking got a bit too pointed.

Once Hercules was settled, I turned on the computer. He looked over at the chair where Marcus had been sitting. Then he looked over his shoulder at me. "Work," I said. The answer seemed to satisfy him. He put one paw on the edge of the table and turned all his attention to the laptop screen.

I'd read a bit about Meredith Janes's accident but I wanted to know more. The accident had been big news in the Chicago area and there were a number of articles besides the original one I'd read.

I didn't learn anything new. I read three different newspaper articles but in the end there wasn't anything suspicious about Meredith Janes's death. It was nothing more than a very sad accident. One article had several photos of the stretch of road where her car had gone over the embankment, including one of a clearly distraught Victor Janes, his face drawn and gaunt.

"Okay, this is a dead end," I said to the cat. I stretched one arm up in the air and rolled my head from side to side to work out the kinks in my neck. Just then my cell phone rang. It was lying on the table and I reached for it. At the same time Hercules craned his neck as if he was trying to see the screen and find out who was calling. It was Simon. "Hi, Simon," I said.

"Hi, Kathleen," he said. "I'm sorry to bother you, but I need a favor."

Simon was the kind of person who didn't ask for favors. "Sure. What is it?"

"Mia is working on some project for one of her

classes. She's out at the Taylors'. I'm supposed to pick her up in about half an hour but—" I heard him exhale. "I'm at my office. Someone tried to break in. Harry was having a beer when I dropped her off so he can't drive her."

"Are you all right? What about Denise?" I leaned forward in my chair, which got me a glare from the black-and-white eavesdropper on my lap.

"Denise is fine. So am I. No one was here. The office has a good alarm system. Whoever it was didn't manage to get in. All they did was damage my door and make a mess in the entrance." He muttered a swear word under his breath.

I could hear voices in the background and it occurred to me that the break-in was probably the call Marcus had gotten.

"I really need to stay here, Kathleen. Is there any chance you could pick Mia up and bring her here?"

"Of course I can. Text her and let her know I'm coming."

"Thank you," he said. "Normally I'd ask Denise but she's in Minneapolis. She's having dental surgery first thing tomorrow."

"It's not a problem, Simon," I said. "We'll see you soon."

I ended the call. Hercules jumped down from my lap as I closed my web browser. He headed across the floor to the kitchen door. "You're not coming," I called after him.

"Merow," he said right before the door seemed to shimmer and he walked right through it.

I shut off the computer, grabbed my purse and my gray hoodie. Hercules was standing in front of the outside door. He looked up at me as I pulled on my sneakers.

"What part of 'you're not coming' are you having trouble with?" I asked.

He made a face as if he were seriously considering the question, then he walked through the porch door. I hated when he did that. It was impossible to get the last word.

Hercules was waiting at the bottom of the steps at the edge of the pool of light cast by the outside fixture. He walked around the side of the house with me.

"You're only doing this because you know I don't have time to argue with you," I said. When I looked down at him his green eyes were firmly fixed on what was ahead of him. I was on ignore.

I unlocked the truck and Hercules jumped onto the seat, walking his way over to the passenger side. He sat down, curling his tail around his feet, and looked out the windshield, satisfied that he'd won the battle.

I backed out of the driveway, and headed for Harry Taylor's house. Hercules didn't make a sound the entire way there. He was content to sit next to me and look out the window. When I pulled the truck in at the side of the big farmhouse he moved to the middle of the seat. I turned to look at him. "I have no idea where Boris is. Unless you want to end up nose to nose with him, stay in the truck."

Hercules immediately lay down on the seat. He'd gotten the message.

Boris was Harry's German shepherd, although he spent most of his time with Harrison. The big dog was gentle and friendly with a keen intelligence that showed in his brown velvet eyes. I'd called him a pussycat once. Both Owen and Hercules had seemed deeply offended.

The outside light was on at the side door to the house and I could also see a light on in the kitchen. I knocked and after a moment Harry came to the door. He was wearing a red plaid flannel shirt and gray-framed reading glasses.

"Hello, Kathleen," he said. "What are you doing out here?"

I was colder than I'd expected and I tugged at the drawstring around the neck of the hooded sweatshirt. "Simon asked me to pick up Mia," I said.

He frowned. "Everything okay?"

"Pretty much," I said. "Someone tried to break into Simon's office—they didn't succeed—but he's with the police so I came to get Mia."

"I'm sorry to hear that. He's been through enough. He doesn't need that."

I nodded.

"The girls are over with the old man," Harry said, gesturing at his father's small house at the far left of the cleared area near the trees. "They're doing some project about the history of the town and he knows more than damn near anyone except for maybe Mary Lowe or Rebecca."

"Thanks," I said.

Harry held up a hand. "Hang on. I'll walk over

with you." He reached behind him for his jacket, pulled it on and stepped out into the landing, tucking the reading glasses into his pocket.

"Your father was friends with Leo Janes," I said as we walked across the gravel parking area.

Harry nodded. "They played poker together and some hockey back in the day." He'd pulled up his collar against the sharp bite of the night air and his hands were jammed in his pockets.

"What about Victor?" I asked.

"Not so much, at least as far as I know. From what the old man said those two may have been twins but they were very different people. You know the old saying, looks can be deceiving."

"It seems to me people don't really like Victor Janes," I said.

"Can't say you're wrong." Harry stopped walking and looked at me. "I'm sorry to hear he's so sick and all, but at the end of the day Victor ran off with his brother's wife. People in this town have long memories for something like that." He shrugged. "On the other hand, it's easy to turn Leo Janes into a saint now that he's dead."

It wasn't like Harry to speak ill of someone who wasn't around to defend himself. Again I wondered what Harry and Leo had been arguing about the day I'd seen them by the gazebo. I was about to ask him but he'd started walking again.

I hurried to catch up with him. Harry knocked on the side door of his father's house and didn't wait to be invited in. "Dad, it's me," he said, opening the door and stepping inside.

"You checking up on me?" Harrison Senior called.

Harry looked at me and shook his head. I leaned around the kitchen doorway. "Yes," I said. "I am."

The old man was sitting in his favorite chair next to the woodstove. His granddaughter Mariah was at his feet on a tufted black leather footstool and Mia was sitting cross-legged in the chair opposite, a notebook open on her lap, her cell phone resting on one knee. Boris was at her feet.

"Kathleen, girl, what are you doing out here?" Harrison smiled at me and made a move to get to his feet.

"Stay where you are," I said. I crossed the room, leaned over and gave him a hug. "I came out here to see if you're behaving yourself."

"Well, as a matter of fact, I am," he said. He gave me a conspiratorial wink. "I'm trying to be a good role model for the girls."

"Of course," his son added drily behind me.

Mia smiled at me. "Dad texted and said there was some kind of problem at his office so you were coming to get me."

Boris had gotten up and padded over to me. I dug my fingers into the thick fur of his neck and gave him a scratch and he sighed happily. "How are you, boy?" I said. He leaned his warm weight against my leg. "So have you filled the girls in on all the history of the town?" I asked.

"How old exactly do you think I am?" Harrison asked, and I could see the mischievous twinkle in his eyes.

"They say age brings wisdom," I said. "I think you

are a very wise man. I also think there's still more for you to learn."

He threw back his head and laughed. "You have the soul of a diplomat," he said.

I smiled then I looked at Mia. "Are you ready?" I asked.

She nodded, closing her notebook and reaching for a black backpack I hadn't noticed at her feet. Mariah got up and moved the footstool back against the wall.

Mia got to her feet as well. "Thank you for your help, Mr. Taylor," she said.

He reached up and caught one of her hands, giving it a squeeze. "Anytime, child," he said. "Come back and see us anytime."

She smiled. "I will."

Harrison started to get to his feet.

"You don't have to get up, Dad," Harry said behind me.

"You think I was born in a barn?" the old man countered. "I have better manners than to expect a lady to see herself to the door."

Harry held up one hand. "I'm here," he said.

"And I can certainly hear you and see you," his father said.

Mariah had stashed all of her things in a camouflage messenger bag. Now she threw her arms around her grandfather. "Thanks, Pops," she said.

He kissed the top of her head. "You're welcome, my girl."

I took his arm and we headed for the door. The

girls were already outside looking for the Big Dipper in the clear night sky.

"Take good care of that child, Kathleen," Harrison said quietly to me. "She's been through more than a child her age should have to face."

"I will. I promise," I said.

"And come out and see me when you can sit for a bit."

"I promise I'll do that as well," I said. I stood on tiptoe and kissed his cheek.

"Lock up after us," Harry said to his father. "And remember you have that appointment at the dentist tomorrow."

"Not likely you'd let me forget," the old man grumbled.

I raised a hand in good-bye and he closed the door. Harry listened for the snap of the dead bolt before he moved.

I touched his arm. "Have a good night," I said.

He nodded. "You too, Kathleen. And Dad's right. Come out when you can stay awhile."

"I will," I said.

Mariah had started for the house and Mia was standing waiting for me on the gravel.

We headed for the truck. Hercules was looking out the driver's-side window.

"That's not Owen," Mia said. "Is it Hercules?"

"Yes, it is," I said. "He called shotgun." I unlocked the passenger door for her and walked around the truck to the driver's side.

"Hey, Hercules," Mia said. "Thank you for coming to get me."

Always modest, the cat ducked his head and meowed softly.

"He's so handsome. He looks like he's wearing a tuxedo."

Herc murped at her and moved a bit closer. He liked to be complimented on how he looked.

I fastened my seat belt, started the truck and headed down the long driveway as Mia kept talking to Hercules. Once we were on the road I saw her look in my direction.

"So what happened at my father's office?" she said. "What did he tell you?"

"He just said something happened. Did someone break in?"

"They tried. They didn't succeed."

She sighed. "I bet Dad's piss— Mad," she said.

I flipped my turn signal on. "I don't blame him," I said. "When someone spray painted graffiti on the loading-bay door at the library back in the spring all I could think of was finding whoever had done it and standing over them while they scrubbed off every speck of paint. I know it wasn't personal but it felt that way. Your father probably feels the same."

"Do you think it was someone looking for something to steal who killed my grandfather?" Mia asked.

I didn't, but I also didn't want to say that to her. "Maybe," I said. "The police look at every possibility."

"They're looking at my father."

"Yes," I said. "It would be irresponsible not to. If

they don't and someone else is arrested the first thing that person's lawyer will do is point out that your father wasn't investigated."

"Mrr," Hercules said.

"See? He agrees with me." Out of the corner of my eye I saw her smile.

"I know," she said. "When people are killed more than half the time it's by someone they know and about a quarter of the time it's someone in their family."

I shot her a quick glance. How on earth did she know that?

"I was on the FBI website," she said by way of explanation.

"There's something wrong with Snapchat?" I said.

Mia laughed. "No, I just like knowing things."

"I get that," I said. "I like knowing things, too."

"But I should have fun while I'm young," she finished.

I looked sideways again and smiled. "You're stealing my best speeches," I said.

We drove in silence for a minute or so. Then Mia said, "Do you miss your family?"

I nodded. "Very much. But my mother has been going back and forth to Los Angeles and my brother is on the road with his band, so even if I were in Boston it doesn't mean I'd see them that much."

Mia reached into her pocket and then extended her hand. I shot a quick look in her direction. A small, brown acorn sat in the middle of her palm. "My grandfather said acorns were good luck," she said. "I've been carrying it around since the funeral. How crazy is that?"

"I grew up around theater people," I said. "I know all about charms for good luck." I remembered sitting in the middle of my parents' bed in their place in Boston as my mother went through her closet in what I knew would be a futile effort to cull some things from the space. My father's clothes lived in the closet in their office.

"What about this?" Dad had asked, holding up a black woolen winter coat with a gray faux-fur collar and wide bands of faux-fur trim on the sleeves. My mother had taken the coat from his hands. "Not that. That style is coming back. I might wear it this winter."

I'd pressed my lips together to keep a smile from getting loose as my dad gave a sigh of exasperation. "Okay, then what about this?" He held up a long, silky dress. It was a pale sage green with an empire waist and a pleated cape collar.

Mom shook her head and reached for a pair of black leather pants. "I can't get rid of that. That's my lucky dress."

Dad swiped a hand over his mouth. "There's no such thing as a lucky dress," he said.

She raised an eyebrow and gave him what I thought of as her Mona Lisa smile. "You got lucky the first time I wore that dress," she said.

He pulled her to him with one arm, tipped her back into a sweeping dip and kissed her. I fell over sideways on the bed and pulled a pillow over my head in embarrassment. I could still hear them laughing.

I smiled at the memory and glanced in Mia's direction again. "When I left Boston my mom gave me a sixpence for good luck. It's English money."

Mia nodded.

"I still carry it in my wallet. Mayville Heights may be home now, but that doesn't mean I don't miss my family back in Boston."

"Sometimes I think I miss my mother," Mia said, her voice thoughtful. "I didn't get to know her so I think what I really miss is the idea of her."

"I get that," I said. "I've felt the same way about grandparents. Mine died before I was born, so I wasn't missing them, I was missing the idea of grandparents. Sometimes I still feel that way."

"My dad and my mother were just teenagers when they had me," Mia continued. She was twisting one end of her long scarf in her hands. "She died right after I was born and her mom and dad—my other grandparents—tried to take me away from my dad. They said he wouldn't be able to take care of me. It all went to court and the judge let me stay with Dad. He told me that my grandfather never tried to talk him out of raising me. Grandpa and my dad fight about stuff because they're both stubborn people."

I noticed she referred to Leo in the present tense.

"But he would never have hurt Grandpa, because he loves me."

I exhaled slowly. "I know that," I said. "Give the police a little time and they'll figure it out, too."

I hoped I was right.

9

Simon was waiting for us in the entrance of the brick building that housed his office and several others. He was wearing a brown leather jacket over jeans and a rust-colored sweater. He smiled when he caught sight of Mia. She went right over to him and gave him a hug. "Kathleen said someone tried to rob you but they didn't get into the office."

He nodded. "They tried my office and two other ones on this floor." He smiled at me over his daughter's head. "Thanks for picking her up."

"Anytime," I said. "I got to see Harrison, so it was good for me, too."

"Police are almost done and then we can head home," Simon said to Mia. He pointed at a wooden bench near the doors. "Go sit and we'll be leaving in about fifteen minutes."

She cocked her head to one side and studied her father. "You just want to talk to Kathleen without me listening."

Simon swiped a hand over the stubble on his chin. "Yes, I do, so please go sit over there so I can do that and she can go home."

Mia grinned at her dad. "Okay." She went over to the bench and opened her backpack.

"I don't know what I would have done without your help," Simon said.

"I'm happy to do anything for Mia," I said. And I was, although I suspected picking up Mia was a bit of a contrivance on Simon's part. I could see that he was interested in me and this was a way for the two of us to spend time together, even if just for a few minutes. Simon knew Marcus and I were together but he wasn't the type of man to just walk away without at least trying to get what he wanted.

Down the hallway behind us Marcus came out of Simon's office. He stopped when he noticed me standing with Simon. I raised a hand in hello and for a moment I thought he was going to join us, but he just nodded and moved to speak to another police officer in the hall.

"Kathleen, can I ask you something?" Simon said.

"Sure," I said, pulling my attention back from Marcus.

"The police still consider me a suspect, don't they?"

I looked away from him for a moment, studying the exposed brick wall to my right. "At this point everyone is a suspect."

"So yes."

"They're still gathering evidence," I said, finally shifting my gaze back to him.

"There's something I need to—want to—tell you," he said. His expression was serious and one hand was playing with the band of his watch. "My father and I had an argument a couple of days before he was killed. We had more than one, actually."

"Okay," I said. I wasn't sure why Simon was telling me this. I already knew he and Leo had had a relationship that was contentious at times and Marcus had told me about their disagreement at the hotel bar.

"This was a very public argument in the parking lot over at Fern's." He shifted restlessly from one foot to the other.

Fern's was Fern's Diner, home of Meatloaf Tuesday and also where Harrison Taylor's lady friend, Peggy Sue, worked.

"Families have arguments," I said. "Even the police know that."

The lines in his face seemed to deepen. "One of the last things my father said to me was, 'You're killing me.'"

It took me a moment to find the right words to say what I wanted to say. "Simon, I only met your father once, but he didn't seem like the kind of person who would want you to get stuck on something he said when he was angry."

He studied me for a long moment, as though he thought he could find some answers on my face, and then his expression softened. "Mia's right," he said.

I was lost. "About what?"

"About you being nice."

I shook my head. "I'm starting to dislike the word," I said, giving him a wry smile.

Simon shook his head. "You shouldn't. We act like being nice is somehow a bad thing. It's not. The world needs more nice people."

"Well, this so-called nice person thinks that the police aren't going to arrest you because you had an argument with your father in the parking lot of Fern's."

I glanced over at Mia. She was bent over her notebook, holding her cell phone with one hand.

"It isn't any of my business, but what were you arguing about?" I asked. "I know it's been difficult having your uncle here."

Simon nodded. "Dad and I did have words over that more than once, but it's not what the fight at Fern's was about."

I waited. Simon's mouth moved but it took longer for words to come. Finally he said, "You have to have heard about my mother. Mayville Heights is a small town, after all."

"I've heard," I said.

"We never talked about my mother—my choice, not his." His fingers played with his watchband again. "I knew that Dad was angry and hurt for a long time, but I really thought he'd put that part of his life to rest a long time ago." He looked past me for a moment and then shook his head. "He hadn't." He focused on me once more. "A few weeks ago I found out that he had hired a private investigator to look into the car accident that killed my mother."

Meredith Janes's death. Was it possible it was connected to what happened to Leo?

"Did you ask him why?" I said.

"I asked him why, all right. Why he was doing it, why he hadn't told me, why he thought there was any point to digging up such a painful part of both our pasts after all this time. Just before he hired that investigator Mia was doing a school project, a family tree. I know they talked about . . . my mother. Dad started reading some of the old news coverage. He said he'd never been satisfied with the investigation."

He sighed. "Kathleen, a few years ago I went to Chicago, to the police station. I talked to the detective who investigated my mother's car accident. I looked at the reports. There was no big conspiracy. The road was wet, she was speeding—which according to everyone she knew was something she'd done since she got her driver's license. She went off the road and over an embankment. She died. End of story." He shook his head. "You're the only other person aside from Dad I've told this to, and I waited a long time before I told him. I hate that my mother still has so much power in my life."

Mia looked up and smiled over at us then dropped her head over her phone again.

"He wanted me to be part of this ridiculous investigation. This fool's errand. I said no. He tried to change my mind. That's what we were fighting about." He shrugged.

"Simon, you don't actually think your mother's accident and what happened to your father are connected, do you?" I said. I didn't say that I did.

"I don't want to, but . . ."

"But what?"

The lines around his mouth tightened again. "He told me he'd hired an investigator. The day before the funeral I went all through his apartment. Victor had asked Everett if he could stay there for a few days. He said it made him feel closer to Dad." He sighed softly. "I didn't want Victor to know what Dad had been doing. I found the contact information for that investigator and I called him. He said my father told him that he'd found something out about my mother, something that was key."

"But he didn't say what that was."

Simon shook his head. "I hired him, Kathleen, the detective. He says there may have been a witness, a woman who was walking her dog the night my mother's car went off the road. If there's any chance what happened to my father is connected to my mother's death, I have to know."

"Have you considered talking to your uncle?"

He shook his head. "Not a chance in hell. My father may have been giving Victor a second chance but that didn't mean he would have ever confided in him."

I put a hand on his arm. "Simon, tell the police," I said.

A smile pulled at his mouth but there was no warmth in it. "I already did. I don't think they're taking me very seriously."

I raked a hand back through my hair. I cared about Mia and I cared about Simon. "How can I help?"

Simon glanced down the hallway. There was no

sign of Marcus. "I don't want to interfere in your life," he said.

"How can I help?" I repeated.

He looked over at his daughter again and his face softened. "I know that Dad and Mary Lowe go way back. Someone saw them together at a place out near the highway. They looked like they were having a pretty serious conversation."

"The Brick," I said, nodding my head.

Simon frowned. "How did you know?"

Mary may have looked like the stereotypical sweet, cookie-baking grandmother, which in fact she was, but there were a lot more layers to her, including her love of dancing, corsets and feathers. "That's a story for another time," I said.

"Would you talk to Mary?" he asked. "See if she knows anything? I think she'd be more likely to tell you before me."

"I can do that," I said. "She's working tomorrow. I'll see what I can find out."

Simon smiled then. "How many times are you going to come to my rescue?" he said.

I smiled back at him. "How many times do you need?"

Mia had gotten to her feet and now she walked over to us. "Excuse me," she said. "Are you done? Because I'm hungry."

"Yes, we're done," I said.

"Thank you for coming to get me," she said, wrapping her arms around me in a hug.

"Anytime," I said.

"Thank you," Simon said. "For everything."

I smiled. "Like I said, anytime."

Hercules was waiting for me in the truck. "Thank you for being so patient," I said, sliding behind the wheel. He yawned and I realized he'd probably been napping the whole time I was gone.

We headed up the hill and I filled Hercules in on what Simon had told me about his father hiring an investigator to look into Meredith Janes's death.

"This means something," I said.

"Merow," the cat said.

I glanced over at him. "Okay, so now all we have to do is convince Marcus."

We'd only been home about twenty minutes when my phone rang. Hercules was just eating the last of the four crackers I'd given him. He meowed at me but didn't even lift his head.

"Yes, I heard that," I said.

It was Marcus.

"Hi," I said. "Where are you?"

"At the station," he said, "wrestling with paperwork."

He sounded tired. I tucked one leg underneath me. "You want to know what I was doing at Simon's office."

"I do, but I don't want to sound like a suspicious boyfriend or an equally suspicious cop by asking. You can see I'm on the horns of a dilemma."

I laughed. "So you were going to do what, just dance around the subject?"

"Pretty much," he said. "I'm tired; all my creativity has checked out for the night."

"It's not that complicated," I said. "Simon was supposed to pick up Mia out at Harry's. I went to get her."

"That was nice of you," he said.

I wondered if he was at his desk or leaning against the wall in the hallway for a bit more privacy.

"Marcus, have you looked into the possibility of a connection between Leo Janes's death and the accident that killed his wife?"

"Simon mentioned that."

I pulled up my other leg and propped my chin on my bent knee. "You didn't answer my question," I said.

"No, I didn't."

"What if there's a connection?"

"A connection how?" he asked.

I blew out a breath. "I don't know how. Simon told me his father had hired someone to look into his ex-wife's accident. Don't you think it's an awfully big coincidence that Leo Janes started asking questions about what happened all those years ago and suddenly he's dead?"

"Coincidences do happen, Kathleen." I recognized that reasonable tone. When we'd first met it had frustrated me.

"I don't think it's a coincidence," I said.

"So you think what?" Marcus asked. "That Meredith Janes's death wasn't an accident and now after twenty years the killer decided to get rid of her husband?"

The idea sounded better in my head than when he said it out loud.

"How do you know Victor Janes didn't do something to his brother?" I said.

The idea had been in the back of my mind like a wisp of a song.

"He has an alibi. He was in a cancer survivors' chat room when Leo was murdered."

"Which he could have accessed from his smartphone," I countered.

"Victor had one of those phones with the battery problems. His actually overheated and stopped working *that* day. The company had to overnight a replacement. He was close to twenty-four hours without a phone."

"Oh," I said, feeling a little deflated.

"I know you care about Mia, Kathleen, and I know you like Simon."

I got the sense that he was choosing his words carefully, which told me I probably wasn't going to like what he said next.

"Simon didn't kill his father," I said, speaking each word slowly and carefully.

Marcus cleared his throat. "Look, Kathleen, I trust your instincts. You have to know that by now. But I can't just ignore the evidence because of those instincts."

"And I can't ignore what my instincts tell me just because you believe your evidence says something else."

There was silence for a moment, then he said, "I'm sorry I called your cell phone."

I hadn't expected him to say that. "Umm, why?" I asked.

"Because you could have hung up on me. Regular phones can be very satisfying to hang up . . . so I've heard."

I laughed. "I wouldn't hang up on you," I said. "Pour coffee on your shoe? Maybe."

He laughed as well. He'd gotten my reference to a time in our past when I'd come very close to doing just that.

"I love you," he said. I could feel the warmth of his smile as though he was in the room with me.

"I love you, too," I said.

"I'll talk to you tomorrow," he said. "Sleep well."

I set the phone on the table and sighed. Hercules was watching me, pensively it seemed, his head cocked to one side. "How am I going to convince Marcus that there are other people who could have wanted Leo Janes hurt if not dead?"

"Mrr," the cat said, his green eyes narrowing a little.

"Yes," I said. "I'm thinking about Elias Braeden."

"Merow?" Hercules said. It almost seemed like there was a question in the sound.

"I know what Ruby said and I'm not saying Elias wanted Leo dead. Maybe . . . maybe things just got out of hand. He was killed with that piece of sculpture. It wasn't premeditated." I picked up my mug. It was empty. I set it back on the table again. "What I'd like to do is talk to someone other than Ruby about Elias."

Hercules yawned and stretched, seemingly bored with the conversation. He made his way over to the refrigerator and used one paw to push his food dish toward me.

"You just had a snack," I said. "That's it until breakfast."

He stared at me without blinking, his green eyes locked on my face for a good thirty seconds.

I got to my feet, picked up the empty bowl and set it back beside the refrigerator. "Like I said, that's it until breakfast."

As I turned around my gaze passed over the front of the refrigerator. I had a coupon for half a dozen cupcakes from Sweet Thing stuck there along with a notice about a Christmas arts and crafts market in Red Wing and a flyer about the holiday cookie-decorating contest being sponsored by Fern's Diner.

Fern's Diner, where I'd had breakfast with Burtis Chapman more than once. Burtis, who had also worked for Idris Blackthorne as a young man and likely knew Elias Braeden.

I scooped up Hercules. "You are a furry genius," I said.

He nuzzled my cheek and tried to look modest but didn't quite get there.

By five forty-five the next morning I was on my way over to Fern's Diner. Burtis's shiny black truck was in the parking lot behind the squat, brown-shingled building. I found Burtis inside perched on a stool with his elbows on the counter and his hands wrapped around a heavy china coffee mug. He was wearing a blue plaid shirt with the sleeves rolled back over a long-sleeved gray T-shirt and his Twins ball cap was sitting on the counter at his elbow.

Burtis Chapman was a massive man, with wide shoulders and a barrel chest, intimidating if you didn't know him. His face was lined and weathered and the little bit of hair he had left was snow white. He was good friends with Marcus's father, Elliot Gordon. In fact, the two of them had gotten more than a little intoxicated just a few weeks ago when Elliot had been in town. They'd hijacked the jazz trio playing in the bar at the St. James Hotel and sung Bob Seger's "Old Time Rock and Roll." The other bar patrons seemed to enjoy the impromptu concert; hotel management, not so much, and I'd had to go rescue them before the police were called.

Burtis looked up and smiled when I stepped into the diner. "Well, aren't you a sight for sore eyes," he said. He slid off his stool and gave me a hug.

"Feel like some company for breakfast?" I asked, shrugging out of my jacket.

"You, girl? Always."

He patted the empty stool beside his, then took my jacket and hung it on a nearby hook.

Peggy Sue came out of the kitchen and slid an oversized oval plate in front of Burtis. "Hey, Kathleen," she said with a smile. "What can I get you besides a cup of coffee?" She was wearing her regular uniform of red pedal pushers and a short-sleeved white shirt with *Peggy Sue* stitched over the left breast pocket. Her red-framed glasses had been replaced with a black cat's-eye style a lot like Susan's pair. Her hair was in a bouffant updo with sideswept bangs, lacquered in place I was guessing with half a can of hair spray.

I pointed at Burtis's plate. "That looks good to me."

"It'll be ready in a jiff," she said. She relayed my order to the kitchen and poured me a cup of coffee. Peggy and Harrison Taylor (Senior, not Junior) had been, as he liked to call it, "keeping company." The age difference between the two had made his family a little nervous, especially Harrison's daughter Elizabeth, who was fiercely protective of her biological father. But they—and the rest of us—quickly came to see how good Peggy was for the old man. She made him laugh, and she got him to have his blood pressure checked more frequently. She hadn't been able to get him to cut down on his coffee consumption, but that was an impossible task no matter who was trying.

Burtis had already started in on his breakfast. I added cream and sugar to my coffee and took a long sip. It was hot and strong, just the way I liked it.

"What are you doin' here so early?" he asked. "And don't tell me it's for the pleasure of my company, because I may have been born at night but it wasn't last night."

"I do like your company," I said, "but there is something I wanted to talk to you about. Actually, someone."

"Leo Janes." He nudged a bite of scrambled egg onto his fork with the half slice of toast he was holding in his massive left hand.

"Sort of," I said.

That got me a smile. "Now, how exactly are we 'sort of' going to talk about Leo Janes?"

"By talking about Elias Braeden."

"I heard he was in town on some kind of business," Burtis said, spearing a chunk of fried potato. It disappeared into his mouth.

"Did you know him when you worked for Idris?" I asked.

Peggy came back with my plate then. It held bacon and sausage, fluffy scrambled eggs, Yukon gold potatoes fried with onions and whole wheat toast. She topped up our coffee and then headed toward the booths with the pot.

"I knew Elias back in the day," Burtis said. "We don't run in the same circles now." He grinned at me.

"Do you think he could have had anything to do with Leo Janes's death?" I asked. I picked up my fork and started eating. The eggs were fluffy and the potatoes tasted of onion and dill.

"Not likely," Burtis said. "From what I know of Elias now, he's more likely to bury you with lawyers and paperwork than he is to just have you buried somewhere." He reached for his coffee cup. "I take it Leo was still playin' cards."

"Enough to get banned from more than one casino in the state."

"And one of them belonged to Elias."

I nodded. "Leo had some kind of system worked out. And it looks like there were other people involved."

"He was smart as a whip, you know. He'd figure

the odds of a certain card turning up in his head and then bet according to that. It gave him an edge, not to mention he had a hell of a poker face. How much did he take Elias for?"

"Around a million dollars."

Burtis shook his head. "I don't care for cheaters myself and I can imagine how Elias felt. It's a wonder he left Leo with a pot to"—he gave me a sideways glance—"bake beans in," he finished. "So you think what, Kathleen? That Elias had Leo killed over what he won?"

I reached for my coffee again. "I don't know. Elias told me what he wanted to know was how Leo was cheating. He'd figured out that Leo had some of his students involved but beyond that . . ." I shrugged. "Do you think it's possible they had an argument and things just got out of hand?" The image of the back of Leo Janes's head flashed in my mind. "Tell me I'm crazy," I said.

"You're not," he said. "Elias has come a long way from the days when he used to move beer through the back wood for old Blackie. I told you before, it wasn't what the old man did, it was what people thought he did that kept 'em in line. Elias learned that lesson. He's a respectable businessman now—more or less— but just because you take the boy outta those woods doesn't mean you take the lessons he learned outta him."

"I'll keep that in mind," I said. "Thank you."

We ate in silence for a couple of minutes. Then I felt Burtis's eyes on me. "I hear you've been bragging about hanging around a few arcades in your younger days."

I knew he was referring to my telling Marcus I could beat him at PAC-MAN. I gave an offhand shrug. "My mother always said it's not bragging if you can do it."

Burtis gave a snort of laughter. "That it isn't," he said.

We finished our breakfast and I told him about the box of photos from the old post office that the library had "inherited." I lost the argument about paying for my own breakfast and I promised Burtis I would come out to the house to play a game of PAC-MAN with him, although I may have said I'd come out to beat him at a game of PAC-MAN. He left with a promise that he'd stop by the library once the photos were on display to see if he recognized anyone.

I took Celia Hunter's scarf with me to the library and Marcus called midmorning to tell me she'd arrived at the station first thing, just the way she'd said she would. "It wasn't her," he said. "She's too tiny to have hit Leo Janes."

I made a face, glad that he couldn't see me. Everything seemed to point back at Simon.

Mia came in right after school. Mary had brought in an album with the photos of Meredith Janes that she'd promised to show Mia.

"Is that your mother?" I asked Mary, pointing to a young woman leaning on a hoe and squinting into the sun in one photograph. It wasn't so much that they looked alike, it was something about the way the young woman in the photo was standing, her unself-conscious stance, that made me think of Mary.

"Yes, it is," she said. "She lived to be ninety years old, you know, and she was sharp as a tack until the day she died. In fact, if she'd stayed off the roof of the barn when it was raining she'd probably have made it to one hundred."

Mia and I exchanged looks.

"But that's a story for another day," Mary said, making a dismissive gesture with one hand. She flipped several pages in the album. "That's your grandmother, Mia."

Mia and I both leaned in for a closer look. Meredith Janes looked to be about sixteen in the photograph. She reminded me of Simon. She had the same challenge in her dark eyes.

"She was so beautiful," Mia said softly.

"Inside and out," Mary agreed.

We spent the next few minutes looking at the rest of the photos. There were several more of Meredith and one of Mary in a bathing suit with one hand on her hip and the other behind her head in a bathing beauty pose.

"Wow! Look at those legs," I said admiringly. Harrison would have said Mary had legs up to her neck. In fact I recalled him using those exact words about her once.

"I've always been told they're my best feature,"

Mary said with a sly smile. She pulled an envelope out of her sweater pocket and handed it to Mia. "I made copies of the pictures of your grandmother. I thought you'd like to have them."

"Thank you," Mia said, her voice suddenly husky with emotion. She turned to me, both hands holding the envelope. "I'm just going to put these upstairs and then I'll get started on the shelving."

I nodded. "That's fine." I watched Mia head up the stairs. Then I turned to Mary. "That was really nice of you," I said.

"I'm sorry she never got to know Merry. She really was special."

"She must have been," I agreed, "if she was friends with you."

"You're really shoveling it today," Mary said, waving away my words with one hand, even as she was smiling at me.

About quarter to five, Victor Janes came into the building. I was dealing with a balky keyboard in our computer area. He stopped at the circulation desk to speak to Mia and I could see from her body language that she was uncomfortable. I got up and joined them.

"Hello, Victor," I said.

He turned to me with a smile that seemed a little forced. "Good afternoon, Kathleen," he said. "How are you?"

"I'm well, thank you. Could I help you find something specific?" I asked in my best friendly, helpful-librarian tone.

"I was hoping that Mia could help me," he said.

I felt a surge of annoyance followed by a twinge of guilt. I didn't like the man. Maggie would have said his energy was off and I felt the same way. On the other hand, I felt guilty for feeling that way about someone who had been fighting a serious illness.

Mia was so tense her shoulders were hunched up to her chin and Mary was openly looking daggers at Victor from across the room.

"I need Mia here," I said. "But I can help you with whatever you're looking for."

Victor hesitated, then he nodded. "Thank you, Kathleen. I was wondering what you could recommend for some escapist reading. I like mysteries with some kind of historical connection."

"I can think of several series you might like," I said.

He glanced at Mia again. "I hope we can spend some time together before I leave."

"School takes up a lot of my time, Uncle Victor," Mia said in a tight voice.

I led Victor over to the shelves and showed him two different authors' books. He chose one but since he didn't even look at the back cover or flip through the pages I doubted that he'd really come for reading material. He seemed desperate to connect with what family he had left, which was understandable given that he'd just lost his only brother.

I wanted to tell him not to try so hard, but it wasn't any of my business.

It wasn't any of Mary's business, either, but that

didn't stop her. Mia was gone when we got back to the checkout desk. Mary took the book and Victor's temporary card and checked the book out for him.

"Victor, let the child be," she said when she handed them back to him.

I shot her a warning look, which she ignored.

"She's my niece, Mary," he said.

"That you've seen how many times in the last seventeen and a half years?"

"And you know who prevented that."

She nodded. "I know whose actions did."

His jaw muscles tightened. He took a deep breath and let it out and then swallowed down whatever had been his first impulse to say. "I can't argue with that, Mary," he said. "But I don't exactly have a lot of time to right all the wrongs."

Mary's expression softened. "Don't push, Victor," she said. "It's not going to get you anywhere." She looked at me then. "I'm just going to straighten up the magazines." She came around the desk and headed across the room.

Victor looked at me. "I'm sorry, Kathleen," he said. "My family is . . . messy."

"All families are messy," I said.

"You've probably heard that I have some time constraints as far as fixing my relationships."

I nodded. "I'm sorry."

"I didn't have enough time to fix things with my brother," he continued. "I knew that could happen but I never thought Leo would be the one who would end up dead." He gave his head a shake and held up the book. "Thank you for your help," he said, and with that he made his way to the front doors.

Mary must have been watching for Victor to leave. She came back to the desk. "I owe you an apology, Kathleen," she said.

"If you're trying to apologize for looking out for Mia you're wasting your time," I said, "because there's nothing to apologize for."

She smiled and patted my arm. "I like you," she said. She looked over at the front doors. "I don't like Victor. I'm sorry he's sick and I'm sorry he lost his brother but I can't pretend I like him."

"Were you ever friends?" I asked. "I mean when you were kids?"

She gave a snort of disgust. "No. To use an expression of my mother's since we were talking about her, he's always been as useless as a bag of smoke."

"But you and Leo were friends."

Mary nodded and brushed a bit of lint off the front of her sweater.

"You know, we actually went out for a bit. Nothing came of it and I'm glad we were able to stay friends because we were much better friends than anything romantic."

I knew I could beat around the bush to try to find out what I wanted to know or I could just ask. It seemed easier to do the latter.

"Did Leo tell you that he was looking into his wife's death?" I asked.

Mary wasn't one for prevaricating, either. "Yes," she said. She narrowed her eyes. "How did you find out? Did Simon tell you?"

I nodded. "Do you know what happened that made Leo think there was something to find?"

She shook her head. "I don't know. He said time has a way of catching up with you sometimes. I asked him what the heck did that mean? He laughed and said, 'You might say I came upon a key fact that changed everything.' That's all he'd say."

The phone rang then and she leaned over the counter to answer it.

Based on what he'd told Mary, Leo had found some new piece of information, something that had changed his opinion about the accident that killed his estranged wife. But how had he found that piece of information? And more important, what was it?

10

I headed home after work to change and have a quick bite of supper. I was meeting Maggie and Roma at Abel's to look for a wedding dress.

Maggie was standing on the sidewalk outside the small boutique when I got out of my truck. She was wearing a red duffel coat and a red-and-white-striped scarf. "Roma is on her way," she said.

"What are the chances we're going to be able to find her a dress?" I asked.

Maggie held out one hand and waggled her fingers from side to side. "Fifty–fifty," she said.

"This is where Rebecca's wedding dress came from and it was beautiful," I said, pulling up the collar of my black peacoat. "I'm going to think positively."

Roma arrived then, parking at the curb behind my truck. She hugged us both and then studied the display of holiday dresses in the front window of the shop. "Are you sure I'm not too—"

Maggie held up a hand. "If the next word out of

your mouth was going to be 'old' you might want to rethink what you were going to say."

Roma closed her mouth, pressing her lips together, but there was an amused sparkle in her dark brown eyes.

We headed inside. Avis, who owned the store, was behind the cash register, her silver-framed glasses slipping down her nose as she waited on a customer. She smiled at us. "Go ahead and look around," she said. "I'll be with you in just a minute."

Maggie led us to the back of the store, where the more formal dresses were displayed. Roma fingered the chiffon overskirt of a petal pink, knee-length gown. "This is pretty," she said.

Maggie shook her head. She reached for the fabric and draped it over the back of her hand. "Uh-uh," she said. "That color is too pale for you." Something on the back wall caught her attention and she moved ahead of us.

"Kathleen, what if I really can't find a dress I like?" Roma said.

I put my arm around her shoulders. "Then I'll loan you my big fuzzy bathrobe."

"Be serious," she said.

"Who's saying I'm not?" I retorted. "Look, we want your special day to be, well, special, but if you want to get married in your jeans or my fuzzy bathrobe or a garbage bag held up by duct tape that's fine with us. We love you no matter what."

Roma swallowed hard. Then she shook her finger at me. "You better not make me cry. I promised Olivia

I'd send her pictures of the dresses and I don't want my nose to be all red."

Olivia was Roma's daughter and I knew Roma wished she could have been with us.

I held up both hands. "I promise not to be nice for the rest of the night."

Avis joined us then and after a bit of consultation Roma decided she would like to try on a couple of more traditional gowns. The first was a strapless sheath.

Roma disappeared into the dressing room and Avis grabbed her tablet to see if she could order the chiffon wrap that went with the dress. She didn't have it in stock. She tapped the screen a couple of times and exhaled loudly. "I cannot get used to this new tablet," she said, her voice edged with frustration. "I just got it yesterday and I'm still figuring out the new software." She rolled her eyes. "I left my old one too close to the radiator. It turns out heat isn't good for rechargeable batteries."

"Neither is vinegar and water," Maggie offered, slipping off her jacket. "Or so I've heard," she added, cheeks turning pink.

Avis smiled and gestured toward the far wall. "I'm just going to see if I have something else that Roma might like."

"I'm going to need a roll of double-sided tape to make this dress work," Roma said when she came out of the dressing room. She put one forearm under the boned and underwired corset bodice of the dress and made a show of hiking up her chest, complete with a grunt for the effort.

I made the mistake of looking at Maggie. We both dissolved in laughter.

The second dress was a strapless mermaid-style gown. Roma looked beautiful but once again Mags and I couldn't contain our laughter when Roma tried to sit down and discovered she couldn't, no matter how she contorted her body.

The next dress was a fairy-tale tulle-and-lace creation. When Roma sat down on the bench beside us the skirt puffed out and up with an audible push of air so that Roma was surrounded by a cloud of tulle.

I pressed my hand against my mouth so I wouldn't laugh.

Maggie frowned and tipped her head to one side. "It's not that bad," she said. "The skirt may be a little too poufy."

Roma looked at Avis. "How do I pee?" she asked.

Avis made a dismissive gesture with one hand. "Oh, that's no problem," she said, as a customer carrying two sweaters and a black pencil skirt approached us. "You get one friend to hold up the skirt and the other gets your underwear down." She headed toward the woman with the sweaters. "I'll be right back," she added over her shoulder.

"I call dibs on holding up the skirt," Maggie said.

She and Roma both looked at me. "If I have to help you get your underwear down so you can pee on your wedding day I am not wearing chartreuse," I said firmly.

Maggie was struggling not to laugh.

Roma looked down at the froth of fabric, lace and

sequins around her. "How do you feel about helping me pee right now?"

In the end none of the dresses Roma tried on worked and after an hour we adjourned to Eric's Place to figure out what to do next.

"I can just wear a regular dress," Roma said, dropping two marshmallows into her cup of hot chocolate.

"It was just one store," Maggie said. "And a special day deserves a special dress."

I nodded and since no one was looking at me dropped three marshmallows into my cup. "Maggie's right. As my mother says, how many times do you get married in life? Two, three times, tops."

Roma smiled.

Ella King was standing over by the counter, probably waiting for a take-out order. Maggie suddenly said, "Ella."

"I see her," I said.

Maggie shook her head. "No, I mean Roma needs Ella."

"What do you mean I need Ella?" Roma asked.

"She could design a dress for you."

"Really?" Roma looked uncertain.

Maggie nodded and got to her feet. "I'm going to see if she has a minute." She walked over to Ella and they spoke for a minute, Maggie's hands gesturing as she talked, then Ella came back to the table with her.

She smiled hello at us. I stood up and got a chair from a nearby table for her.

"Maggie says you're having trouble finding a wedding dress," she said to Roma as she sat down.

Roma nodded. "Yes. I need one I can walk in, pee in and that doesn't require the use of double-sided tape anywhere on my body."

Maggie smiled at me across the table.

Ella nodded as though she'd heard that before. "Do you have a particular style that you like?"

Roma picked up a spoon and stirred the marshmallows in her cup. "I'd like something simple and sleek with no lace or tulle—or boning." She made a face.

Ella pulled a fine-point Pitt pen out of her purse. She grabbed a napkin and quickly sketched something, then she pushed the napkin across the table.

Roma looked at the drawing and a smile stretched across her face. "Yes," she said. "That's what I want."

"I could make it for you," Ella said, "if you'd like."

Maggie and I leaned over to look at the sketch. The dress Ella had drawn had a sleek, fitted silhouette with sheer, long sleeves, a draped neckline and a flowing overskirt. The dress was Roma.

Roma looked at us.

"Yes," Maggie said.

"Yes," I echoed.

Ella smiled, and a flush of color touched her cheeks. "Call me tomorrow," she said to Roma. "I'll do a better sketch and we can get together to talk about fabric." She got to her feet.

"I will," Roma said. "Thank you so much."

Ella said good-bye and walked back over to the counter, where Nic was waiting with a large take-out bag.

Roma looked at us, her expression a mix of excitement and a bit of shock. "I'm actually getting married," she said.

I laughed. "What did you think all that lace was about?"

"What color are you thinking about?" Maggie asked, leaning forward for another look at Ella's sketch.

I caught Nic's eye as Maggie and Roma talked about blush versus ecru. I pointed at the carafe of hot chocolate and he nodded. I glanced at the napkin Ella had left on the table. Roma's dress was going to be beautiful. She was going to be beautiful. I wished every problem could be solved so easily.

Hercules moved back and forth between the bedroom and the bathroom as I was getting ready the next morning, which I didn't seem to be doing fast enough for him. Spending some time with Mia on Sunday night seemed to have motivated him to help figure out who had killed Leo Janes and he clearly wanted to keep going. He sat in front of the closet making grumbling sounds in the back of his throat and when I pulled my head out he was gone. I guessed that he'd given up and gone to wait for me in the kitchen.

When I got downstairs I found him sitting on top of my messenger bag, which I'd left on one of the kitchen chairs. Since Hercules knew my laptop was inside, I wondered if he was suggesting we needed to do some more research.

I had called Simon after I'd gotten home from dress shopping to share what Mary had told me. "I'm sorry," I'd said. "It doesn't really help, does it?"

"It was a long shot," Simon said. "Thanks for trying. Maybe the PI will be able to track down the
so-called witness or maybe he'll come up with something else."

It occurred to me that I hadn't told Simon about my
conversation with Celia Hunter. "Simon, did your father ever mention a woman named Celia Hunter to
you?" I asked.

"The name doesn't ring a bell," he said. "Why? Who
is she?"

"She was a friend of your mother. She's here in Mayville Heights." I hesitated. "She came to talk to your
father."

"Does she know he's dead?" he said, his voice tightening.

I was in the big wing chair in the living room. I
stretched my legs out on the footstool, which Owen
took as an invitation to jump up and sprawl over
them. "Yes," I said. "She talked to him a couple of
times before he died."

"Do you think she has anything to do with this
kick Dad was on to find out more about my mother's
accident?"

I rubbed my shoulder with my free hand, wishing
I could see his face. It was hard to read him when I
couldn't see his expression. "Not directly. I don't see
how she could have been the source of whatever information he came across. But she did have a letter from
your mother." I let out a breath. "You know that they
found some mail along with that cache of old photos
when they took down that wall at the post office?"

"Kathleen, are you saying there was a letter from my mother in that mail?" He sounded skeptical and I didn't blame him.

"According to Celia Hunter, and it wouldn't be that difficult to check." Owen had rolled onto his back and his back paws were moving through the air like some sort of low-impact aerobic workout. "She's going to be here for a few more days," I said. "If you want to read the letter she offered to show it to you."

I heard him exhale. "Yes," he said. "Do you have a phone number for her?"

"She's staying at the St. James."

"I'll call her," Simon said. "Thank you. I seem to be saying that a lot to you."

"My mother would say it's a sign you have good manners," I'd said, lightly. I'd hesitated for a moment. "If you want company call me. Either way, please let me know what happens."

"I will," he'd said. "Good night."

Now, Hercules meowed loudly from his perch on top of my bag. Owen had other priorities. He was sitting next to his food dish and he meowed just as loudly as his brother had in case I'd somehow forgotten it was breakfast time. Hercules, however, could be determinedly single-minded when it suited him. He jumped down from the chair and sat directly in front of me, staring up at me with serious green eyes. But Owen was not going to let anything get between him and his first meal of the day. He meowed a second time, a bit louder than he had the first time. Hercules turned to glare at his brother, his tail flicking restlessly across the floor. There almost seemed to be a challenge in his gaze. It was like waving a red flag in front of a bull. Owen immediately dropped his head and began nudging his dish across the floor toward me. As far as he was concerned everything else could wait until he'd eaten. Hercules stayed where he was. If Owen wanted to get to me and his breakfast, he was going to have to go through his black-and-white sibling. I could see where this was heading.

"That's enough," I said.

They didn't even look at me. Owen was glaring at Hercules through slitted golden eyes. Hercules was unmoving, except for his lashing tail, like an ebony-and-alabaster statue.

I brought my hand, palm flat down, on the table. Hercules jumped at the sound. Owen's head came up, catching the edge of his dish. Unfortunately he'd been pushing his water bowl across the floor, not his food dish. There wasn't very much water in the bowl, but what there was splashed in his face. He yowled in outrage and began to vigorously shake his head.

I grabbed a dishtowel and hurried around the table. "Let me see," I said getting down beside him on the floor. I'd heard Mary use the expression "Mad as a wet hen," but it seemed to me that "Mad as a wet cat" was a better description of someone truly outraged. I put a hand on Owen's back as he continued to shake his head. "Let me see," I repeated. I wiped his face with the towel. His wet fur was sticking up and there was a sullen expression on his face.

"Are you all right?" I asked, using a dry edge of the

towel to smooth down his fur, being extra careful around his ear. His pride was clearly wounded but other than that he seemed fine. The contents of the dish had hit him but the bowl itself hadn't.

I wiped up the water, got breakfast for both cats and a bowl of granola with almond milk and fruit for myself. Owen muttered to himself the entire time he was eating. Hercules glanced in his brother's direction a couple of times but wisely kept his distance.

When I finished my own breakfast I cut the last sardine in the fridge in half and gave a piece to each cat. "I'm sorry," I said to Owen. "That little incident with the water was partly my fault. I did hit the table a little harder than I meant to."

Suddenly I thought of Harry Taylor smacking the top of the rain barrel after Leo Janes had walked away from him that day out by the gazebo. Could Harry be connected in some way to that piece of information Leo had discovered? I had no reason to think he was, but Harry wasn't acting like himself, and it wasn't as though I had anywhere else to start.

I checked my watch. Talking to Harry would have to wait. I was meeting Marcus out at Wisteria Hill to feed the feral cat colony that called the old carriage house on the property home. Roma was assisting on an early surgery in Red Wing and I'd volunteered Marcus and me to take care of the cats' breakfast.

Marcus was waiting for me, leaning against his SUV, as I crested the top of Roma's driveway. He gave me a quick kiss. "Good morning," he said with a warm smile.

"Umm, good morning to you, too," I said. I gestured at the house. "Roma left everything we need in the porch. I have her key."

We walked across the gravel parking area, collected the cats' dishes along with food and water and then headed for the carriage house.

"How did the shopping go last night?" Marcus asked.

"Good," I said. "And that's all I'm telling you because Eddie isn't allowed to know what the dress is like. Apparently it's bad luck."

Marcus laughed. "I didn't think Roma cared about those old superstitions."

I grinned back at him. "It's not Roma. It's Maggie."

We made our way around the side of the weathered old building. Marcus pushed the heavy wooden door open and we stepped inside. I waited a moment for my eyes to adjust to the dim light.

It was because of Marcus that Roma had discovered that there was a feral cat colony out at the old estate. He'd found an injured Desmond and taken the big black tom to her clinic. Desmond was the clinic's cat although he spent more time at Roma's house than at the clinic these days. He had one eye and was missing part of an ear. Even though he wasn't that big, his appearance and his attitude made him seem larger and very imposing. He'd backed more than one unruly dog under a clinic chair.

After Marcus had shown up with Desmond, Roma had gone out to Wisteria Hill to see if there were any more cats. She'd discovered nine in total. Now there

were just seven. It had taken multiple attempts to cap-
ture them all. Roma had taken the cats back to the
clinic, where they had been neutered. Then they had
been returned to Wisteria Hill with Everett Henderson's tacit, if not expressed, approval.

There was no sign of any of the cats now, which
was typical. I looked around for any indication that
anything was amiss but saw nothing. I remembered
how surprised I'd been to learn Roma hadn't tried to
find homes for the cats.

"They're not used to people," she'd explained. *"And
they wouldn't adapt well to living with them."*

Marcus and I set out the food and water and then
retreated back by the door to wait. I leaned against his
chest and he wrapped his arms around me, the warmth
of his body keeping me warm.

After several minutes I heard a sound down near
the feeding station. "Lucy," I whispered.

The little calico cat may not have been the largest
in the small colony, but she was its leader. She moved
into view, sniffing the air, then she turned in our direction.

"Good morning, Lucy," I said in a low voice.

Lucy and I had a connection I couldn't explain.
She'd come closer to me than she would to anyone else
and sometimes it even seemed like she understood
what I was saying to her. Roma believed it was because Lucy trusted me for some unknown reason, the
same way Owen and Hercules had put their trust in
me the day I'd come across them up here as tiny kit-
tens. I sometimes wondered if Lucy, like the boys, had

some kind of special ability and that was why we had connected.

The little cat moved closer to us, stopped and meowed softly. Then she made her way to the feeding station.

"You're welcome, Lucy," I whispered.

The rest of the colony made its way out to eat then. We both looked each cat over carefully for any sign that it was unhealthy or injured in any way.

"They all look good," Marcus said softly against my ear.

After the cats had eaten they made their way back to their shelters. Lucy stopped to look in our direction before she disappeared again. Once the cats were gone, Marcus and I cleaned up the feeding station and set out more fresh water. Then we collected the empty food dishes and everything else and made our way back outside again.

"So how did breakfast with Burtis go?" Marcus asked as we started around the side of the carriage house.

"Delicious," I said. "I have to ask Peggy what's in the fried potatoes besides onion and dill."

"Bacon fat," he said. "Lots of bacon fat."

I bumped him with my hip. "How did you know I had breakfast with Burtis?"

He squared his shoulders. "Have you forgotten you're dating an ace detective?"

I put a hand on his shoulder and came up on tiptoes to kiss his cheek. "No, I have not," I said.

Marcus laughed. "You're not the only one who talks to Burtis, you know."

"What did he tell you?" I asked.

Marcus shifted the empty water jugs to his other hand as we started for Roma's side porch. "Probably no more than he told you: It's not what a person has done that makes them intimidating, it's what our mind thinks they've done."

I nodded. "I realize it's what Hitchcock said: 'There is no terror in the bang, only in the anticipation of it.'"

He nodded.

"So is Elias Braeden a suspect?" I asked as I fished Roma's key out of my pocket.

Marcus raked his free hand back through his hair. "As far as I'm concerned just about everyone is a suspect right now."

We put everything back in the porch and I followed Marcus down the driveway and back into town. He waved as he drove past Mountain Road and I turned down the hill.

Harry was at the library when I pulled into the parking lot, shoveling leaf mulch into a wheelbarrow from a large bin on the back of his truck. I'd known there was a good chance he would be. He had told me he was bringing some mulch for the bed at the back of the library where the rain chain had been vandalized and water had washed away much of the soil and mulch already there.

"Hi, Kathleen," he said. "I thought I'd get an early start at this."

"That's fine with me," I said. "I'm going to put the coffee on. Why don't you come in later and have a cup?"

He rubbed his gloved hands together. "Thanks. That sounds good."

"It was good of your father to help Mia with her project," I said. "With Leo dead she didn't really have many people to ask."

"The old man likes kids," Harry said. "And Lord knows he's got enough stories about this town." As I'd noticed before, once I mentioned Leo's name Harry seemed to tense; the muscles in his neck looked like thick ropes.

"I better get back at it," he said. "And I will take you up on that coffee later."

I nodded and headed for the front steps. Harry wasn't quite avoiding me, but it was close.

Midmorning I was talking to the leader of the senior quilters about a Christmas exhibit of their quilts when Patricia suddenly stopped midsentence and touched my arm. "Kathleen, either Abigail has taken up semaphore or she's trying to get your attention."

I looked over at the front desk. Abigail held up a hand and then pointed at the phone. "Excuse me for a minute," I said to Patricia. I walked over to the desk.

"It's Harrison Taylor for you on line one," Abigail said. "And I thought maybe you needed a break. Patricia can talk your ear off."

"Thanks," I said. "She's not really that bad. She just likes to get every detail nailed down."

"Nailed down, stapled, glued and cemented," Abigail said with a grin.

I reached for the phone. "Good morning, Harrison," I said.

"Good morning, Kathleen," he replied. "How are things at the library?"

"They're going well," I said. "Your son came and repaired that washed-out flower bed at the back of the building and someone brought in four books that were due eight years ago."

"Did you make him or her pay a fine?" Harrison asked.

"I thought about it," I said, turning so I could lean back against the desk. "Then I realized one of the books may be a first edition of Clement Moore's *The Night Before Christmas* with illustrations by William Wallace Denslow."

"I take it that's a good thing."

"The book could be worth several thousand dollars to the right collector."

"Then you have something to celebrate," he said. "So how about coming for supper tomorrow night?"

I liked spending time with Harrison and maybe I'd get the chance to talk to Harry. "That sounds wonderful," I said. We settled the details and I hung up.

The rest of the morning passed quickly. Abigail and I went over the plans for our Christmas programming and then I spent some time looking through the book suggestions people had left on our "What Would you Like to Read?" bulletin board display. Maggie came in after lunch to sort through the photos and decide which ones she was going to frame first.

"Are you going to have enough frames?" I asked.

She nodded. "In fact it looks like I may be able to get some of the mail and display that as well. Did you hear that Thorsten Hall got a Christmas card from an old girlfriend?"

"Very romantic," I said.

Maggie laughed. "Not exactly. It was a religious card with a picture of a snow-covered church on the front. Inside it said, *God Loves You* and underneath she'd written, *I still think you're a jerk!*"

"You're making that up!"

She put one hand on her chest. "I swear I'm not."

I thought about Meredith Janes's letter to her former best friend. I wondered what it said.

Marcus had hockey practice while I was at tai chi but we met afterward for hot chocolate at Eric's.

"Want to split a cinnamon roll?" he asked.

"They haven't been out of the oven very long," Claire said. "They're still warm." That was all I needed to persuade me.

"Okay," I said.

Marcus smiled at Claire. "One cinnamon roll, two plates," he said.

"I'll be right back," she said.

Eric's cinnamon rolls were as good as Mary's. That's because he used her recipe. And so far I hadn't been able to wheedle, whine or bribe it out of either of them.

Marcus must have guessed what I was thinking.

"Do you think you'll ever convince Mary to tell you what her secret ingredient is?" he asked.

"No," I said. "And I've tried everything I can think of to make mine come out the same."

"But yours are good," he said. He'd tried just about every batch I'd made.

"I've gotten close." I held up my thumb and index finger about a half an inch apart. "But there's a little something missing." I lined up the sugar bowl and cream pitcher on the table. "Mary says she'll leave me the secret in her will."

Marcus nodded solemnly. "Other words, she's never going to tell you."

I laughed. "Pretty much." I leaned my elbows on the table and smiled at him. "What are you trying to sweeten me up for?" I asked. To his credit he didn't try to pretend.

"We're bringing Simon Janes in for questioning to-morrow. I didn't want you to find out from . . . from anyone else."

"He didn't kill his father," I said. I was beginning to sound like a broken record.

"I'm not saying he did." He picked up a spoon from the table and flipped it end over end in his fingers. "Do you remember Schrödinger's cat?" he asked.

I frowned, unsure of how we'd gotten from talking about whether or not Simon had killed his father to quantum mechanics. "I remember," I said slowly. "It's a thought experiment that Erwin Schrödinger came up with that's really a criticism of the Copenhagen interpretation of quantum superpositions."

Marcus laughed. "Well, here's what I remember: a steel box, a cat, a vial of poison. The cat could be dead or it could be alive. Until you open the box you don't know which."

"Yes."

"Until someone is charged with Leo Janes's murder Simon could be guilty and he could be innocent and this idea of Schrödinger's murder investigation made a lot more sense in my head."

I reached across the table and gave his hand a squeeze. "I get it," I said. "You're just doing your job. I can live with that."

I thought about what Marcus had said as I drove out to the Taylors' after work Wednesday night. Harry might know something that could help solve Leo Janes's murder or he might not. Until I opened the box, until I came right out and asked him, there was no way to know. I wondered how the Austrian physicist would have felt about his thought experiment becoming part of pop culture.

Harry opened the door when I knocked and the rich smell of onions, garlic and tomatoes welcomed me as I stepped inside. "It smells wonderful in here," I said as he took my coat.

"Italian beef stew. I hope you like it."

I smiled at him. "I already do. Anything that smells that good has to taste at least as wonderful."

Boris padded over to meet me. "Hi, boy," I said. I handed the paper bag I was carrying to Harry. "Half a dozen of those organic dog biscuits Roma's friend makes and Maggie sent you a bottle of blueberry syrup."

"That's a bribe," Harrison said. I went over to give him a hug, trailed by the dog.

"Why is Maggie bribing you?" I asked.

"You know that mail they found stuffed behind that wall at the post office?"

I nodded.

"There was a Christmas card addressed to me. She wants me to let her use it for some exhibit she's putting together for you."

"And you don't want to?" I asked, taking the chair opposite him. Boris leaned against my knee and I scratched the thick fur on the top of his head. He gave a contented sigh.

"I don't mind one bit, but if she wants to send me a bottle of her blueberry syrup to soften me up, who am I to say no?"

We talked about the mail and the photos that had been hidden behind that wall at the post office for the past twenty years. "Do you think someone put them there on purpose?" I asked Harrison. "Or do you think they ended up there somehow by accident?"

"Neither and both," he said.

"You do know that doesn't make sense?" Harry said.

"Sure it does," Harrison said. "Do you remember Campbell Larsen?"

Harry nodded. "He was the postmaster."

"Named after his mother, not the soup," the old man said. "Father's side was Danish. That's where the Larsen came from. Mother's side was Scottish."

"What does Campbell Larsen have to do with that stuff they found at the post office?" Harry asked. He was still standing in the kitchen doorway.

"He had some kind of dementia. He ended up in a nursing home."

His son was nodding. "I remember that."

"Well, he did some danged odd things before anyone figured out what was wrong with him. I think he put that stuff back there and in his mind he probably had a good reason for it."

"That's as good an explanation as any," Harry said. He glanced over his shoulder. "We should be ready to eat in about ten minutes."

Harrison got to his feet. He pointed a gnarled finger at me. "Before you ask, no, there isn't a thing you can do. Sit there and talk to Boris."

I smiled. "Yes, sir." I turned all my attention to the dog, who seemed happy to get it.

"You're driving?" Harrison said.

I nodded. "I am."

"Well, I'm not," the old man said, heading for the fridge and, I was guessing, a bottle of Thorsten Hall's wine.

Harry served his Italian beef stew with slices of crusty multi-grain bread. I took one bite of the thick, spicy creation and closed my eyes with happiness. "Any chance I could get the recipe?"

"Sure," Harry said. "There's not that much to it.

Onions, garlic, tomatoes, carrots, potatoes, celery, beef and my secret ingredient, half a bottle of Thorsten's red wine."

"He made the bread, too," Harrison said, using a chunk to soak up some of the spicy liquid in his bowl.

"Bread machine made the bread," Harry said.

"It's good," I said. I could taste molasses and I thought seven-grain cereal.

"He's a good cook," the old man offered. "Baffles me why he can't get a woman."

"Don't start," Harry warned.

His father paused his spoon in midair. "When did I stop? I've been telling you for years that you need a woman."

Harry glanced at me and I saw a smile pulling at his mouth. They'd had this conversation dozens of times before. "Doesn't seem to be working for you," he said.

"That's because you're bull-moose stubborn."

"Dad, did you ever hear the expression 'People who live in glass houses shouldn't throw stones'?" Harry asked.

"Is that your way of saying you think I'm stubborn?"

"Yes," Harry said.

The old man shook his head. "Every bit of your stubbornness comes from your mother, may she rest in peace."

I was losing the struggle not to laugh. A bit of carrot went down the wrong way and I started to cough. I reached for my water glass.

"You all right?" Harry asked.

I nodded.

"Okay, no more talking about who has all the stubborn genes in this family," he said. "I don't want Kathleen to choke to death."

"Fine with me," Harrison said. He turned to me. "Anyone figure out who killed Leo yet?"

"Marcus is working on it," I said.

"I hope he's getting some help," he said.

I shot him a look but didn't say anything.

"How many enemies could Leo have had in town? He hasn't lived here in close to twenty years."

"It doesn't mean someone couldn't still have a problem with him," I said.

I watched Harry out of the corner of my eye. His head was bent over his food but he was clenching his jaw. Maybe it was none of my business, but I needed to know what Harry's beef had been with Leo Janes. I leaned forward and looked directly at him. "Like you, for instance."

His head came up and his eyes met mine and I saw a flash of anger in his gaze.

Harrison was shaking his head. He swore and then immediately looked at me and apologized. "I told you to let that go," he said.

"Let what go?" I asked.

Harry pushed his bowl away. "Kathleen, no offense, but it's not really any of your business."

I set my spoon down. "You had an argument with Leo at my library, so you pretty much made it my business." I took a deep breath and exhaled slowly.

"Harry, I don't for a moment think you had anything at all to do with Leo's death, but that doesn't mean that whatever had the two of you so angry didn't."

His shoulders were rigid and I found myself hoping I hadn't permanently ruined our relationship. "It doesn't," he said.

"Then why keep it a secret?"

"You know damn well I'm going to tell her if you don't," Harrison snapped.

Harry held out both hands. "Be my guest."

The old man looked across the table at me. "You know Ruby's grandfather, Idris Blackthorne, used to run a poker game out in that shack he had in the woods by Wisteria Hill?"

I nodded.

"I played a few times, probably a few times more than I should have," Harrison said. "I got in over my head one night." He made a face. "I thought I had a good hand, a sure thing, and those kind of things rarely are. I lost my watch. To Leo." He shook his head at the memory. "Few years later when I had a bit of money I tried to buy it back from him."

"He wouldn't sell it to you."

"No, he wouldn't, and if I'm being fair I was a bit of an asshole so I can't really blame him."

His son gave a snort of derision. His father let it pass without comment.

"So you were arguing over that watch?" I said to Harry. I was confused. So much anger over an old watch that had belonged to his father didn't make sense to me.

He pulled a hand across his mouth. "He told me he wasn't even sure he still had the watch but he'd take a look when he had the chance. He said he didn't see what the big deal was."

"That makes two of us," Harrison commented.

I saw a flash of anger again in Harry's eyes but his voice was quiet and steady when he spoke. "Do you remember where you got that watch?" he asked his father.

"Your mother got it for my birthday," Harrison said. And then recognition spread across his face. He swore again. "It was the last gift she bought me before she had that stroke."

Now I got why the watch was so important.

Harry let out a breath. "Dad, I've tried to be supportive of your relationship with Peggy Sue. Hell, she got you to go for a checkup, which is more than Larry and I have ever been able to do, so in my book she gets points for that. I want you to be happy." He swallowed. "And I'm damn glad we have Elizabeth, no matter how she came into our life."

The old man nodded but he also hung his head. Harry's younger sister, Elizabeth, was the result of a relationship Harrison had had when his wife, Harry's mother, was in a nursing home after a debilitating stroke that eventually ended her life.

"But I don't want my mother to be forgotten. I thought if you had the watch, maybe you'd remember her once in a while. When I heard Leo was in town it seemed like a good chance to try to get it back."

Harrison's expression changed. "Remember her

once in a while? There's not a day that goes by that I don't think of your mother. I loved her with everything I had. And yes, I'm grateful to have Elizabeth and to be part of her life—which by the way is thanks to Kathleen—but I'm ashamed of how I betrayed your mother."

I wrapped one arm around my midsection and pressed the back of my hand to my mouth. I'd handled this badly. I'd upset two people I cared about for nothing. Harry's argument with Leo Janes had nothing to do with his murder. "Harry, I'm sorry," I said. "You're right. This is none of my business."

"No," he said. "*You're* right. There's more and I shouldn't have been keeping it to myself. At my age I should know better."

"I don't understand," I said.

"Day before he was killed Leo called me at the house. He said he'd found the watch and he asked if I could do something for him. He said he'd give me Dad's watch whether I helped him or not."

"So what did he want?" I asked.

"Well, it didn't make sense, but Leo wanted me to put him in touch with Lisa."

"What for?" Harrison said, frowning. Lisa was Harry's ex-wife.

Harry tented his fingers over the top of his water glass. "I don't know. I figured it had to have something to do with insurance." He looked at me. "Lisa's a claims adjuster for Activa Life," he said.

"Did you talk to her?" I asked.

"I did. I explained that he was giving me Dad's

watch. She knows about it. I asked if she'd talk to Leo."
He looked from his dad to me. "I told her she didn't
have to help him but I'd appreciate it if she'd talk to
him. She said she would. That was it. Pretty much."

"Did you talk to Leo again?" I asked.

"I called him with her number. He told me to come
over and pick up the watch." He rubbed a hand over
his bald head.

"You were there, the night he was killed. I passed
you on the way over there. It was raining."

Harry nodded. "I rang the bell but he didn't answer
the door and yes, I was mad when I left." He looked
at his father then. "I didn't kill Leo."

"Good Lord, we know that!" Harrison exclaimed.

I nodded. The idea that Harry could have killed
Leo Janes or anyone else was unthinkable.

Harry went on to explain he'd talked to Marcus.
Footage from a security camera on a nearby house
confirmed how quickly Harry had been in and out.
He wasn't a suspect.

And I was glad of that, but that meant Simon still
was.

11

Harrison got to his feet.

"What are you doing?" his son asked.

"What do you think I'm doing? I'm calling Lisa to find out what Leo wanted to talk to her about." A cordless phone handset was sitting on the nearby buffet. He picked it up and brought it back to the table.

Harry stared at his father. "How do you know her phone number?"

"What? I'm not allowed to check on my daughter-in-law?"

"We're not married anymore, Dad."

The old man nodded his head. "I know that. You two aren't married. That has nothing to do with me." By then he had punched in a phone number and lifted the handset to his ear. A warm smile spread across his face when Harry's ex-wife answered. "Hello, my girl, how are you?" Whatever her response was made him laugh. "Well, I think I'm in damn fine shape for the shape I'm in," he said. He listened for a moment.

"You're right," he said. "I didn't just call to check in. My son says he asked if he could give your number to Leo Janes."

I watched as the smile slipped off his face, replaced by a frown that pulled his bushy eyebrows together. "Well, that's a surprise."

There was a pause.

"I appreciate that," Harrison said then. "It was good of you to say you'd talk to him. You have a good night. I'll be talking to you soon." He ended the call and set the phone on the table.

"Leo didn't call before he died, did he?" I said. That seemed obvious from Harrison's side of the conversation and the way his expression had changed.

He shook his head. "I can't believe you went to so damn much trouble just to try to get that watch back," he said to his son. "The fact that you did means a hell of a lot to me and I'm sorry I let you think I forgot your mother."

"I'm sorry I didn't get the watch before I gave him Lisa's phone number," Harry said.

Harrison shrugged. "Water under the bridge, son." He looked across the table at me. "Eat up, Kathleen. I made gingerbread."

"More like Peggy made gingerbread and you watched her," his son commented. The glint of a smile was back in his eyes.

"Never you mind," Harrison countered. "I can cook. I have all sorts of talents." He grinned and wiggled his eyebrows at me.

I laughed and dropped my head over my bowl. I

wasn't crazy enough to get pulled into *that* conversation.

Harry got to his feet and picked up his bowl. "Your talents are not dinnertime conversation," he said. His father just laughed.

The gingerbread, topped with a small dollop of vanilla whipped cream, was delicious. After we'd eaten Harrison showed me the Christmas card he'd received that had been in the pile of found mail. A jolly Santa was on the front and a slightly naughty limerick was written inside in sharp angular writing. The card was signed, *Cyrus*.

"Cyrus was your older brother," I said.

Harrison nodded. "He was eight when I was born. The last thing he wanted was a baby brother. When I was about six months old the Edwards, who lived up the road a stretch, took in a dog somebody had just abandoned on our road. It had three puppies. Cyrus tried to trade me for one of the pups." He smiled at the memory. "When Mrs. Edwards turned him down he offered the contents of his piggy bank as well. He always said he figured if he'd had another twenty-five cents' worth of pennies in that thing they probably could have made a deal."

I laughed. "But you ended up being really close."

He stroked his beard and stared at something just beyond my right shoulder that only he could see. "We did. Cy was bossy as all get-out but he always had my back." His focus came back to me. "What about you, Kathleen? Do you boss around that younger brother and sister of yours?"

"Every chance I get," I said with a grin.

There was a knock on the door then. "Pops, are you here?" a voice called.

Mariah. She came into the room and stopped short when she caught sight of me. "Oh. Uh. Hi," she said. She looked at her grandfather. "I'm sorry, I didn't know you had company."

"It's okay," I said. "I was just about to head out anyway."

"How did you make out at the library?" Harrison asked his granddaughter. "Did you find any of those people we talked about in the old yearbooks?"

Mariah shrugged. "Some. I need to go back and look some more."

Harry came to the doorway. "There's gingerbread in the kitchen," he said to his daughter. "You can go get a piece."

"Okay. Thanks, Dad," she said.

"If you want some of the really old yearbooks, let me know," I said. "And I'll dig them out for you."

"Um, yeah, maybe," she said. "Thanks." She escaped to the kitchen.

Harrison had gotten to his feet and I wrapped my arms around him in a hug. "Thank you for dinner. And I'm sorry I stirred up something that was none of my business."

"You don't have to be sorry, girl," he said. "We cleared the air a little. No way that's bad."

"I'll walk Kathleen out and I'll be right back," Harry said. He narrowed his gaze at his father. "And you don't need another piece of that gingerbread."

"I didn't say I was going after another piece. I'm just going to the kitchen to keep my granddaughter company," the old man said. Then he winked at me.

Harry and I headed out, across the gravel driveway to my truck. "I was wrong to put you on the spot about Leo," I said. "I'm sorry."

"Mia's a good kid. You're trying to figure out who killed her grandfather. I can't fault you for that," Harry said. "Besides, I was acting like the hind end of a horse, as the old man would say. I think we're good."

We said good-bye and when I got to the bottom of the driveway I stopped and checked my phone. There was a text from Susan saying they had closed early because a squirrel on a power pole knocked out power to the library. I thought it was odd Mariah hadn't mentioned that, but it probably hadn't seemed like a big deal to her.

Maggie and I were standing in the computer area the next afternoon trying to decide exactly where and how we were going to display the framed photos from the post office, when Simon walked into the building. He looked in my direction.

"I think he wants to talk to you," Maggie said. She pulled a tape measure out of her pocket. "Go ahead. I need to check a couple of things."

"I'll only be a minute." I walked over to Simon. "Hi," I said.

He smiled. "Hi. I'm sorry to interrupt. I just wanted to ask if I can take you up on your offer to come with me when I talk to Celia Hunter?"

"Of course," I said.

"We're meeting at five thirty at the bar at the St. James. Will that work for you?"

I nodded. Owen and Hercules would be all right if I was a bit late getting home. "I'll meet you there."

"Thanks. Just put this on my tab."

He headed for the door and I rejoined Maggie.

She was measuring the width of the wall in front of her. "I think this is going to work," she said. "I'm going to do a sketch and try to figure out the layout." Maggie was meticulous bordering on obsessive when it came to displaying her work. I knew whatever she came up with for the display would show off the photos at their best.

"Before I forget, I'm going to miss class tonight," I said.

"Are you trying to get out of Push Hands?" she teased.

I shook my head. "No. I have to help Simon with something. Getting out of Push Hands is just a bonus."

Mags laughed. "We'll miss you." She made a tiny notation on the drawing of the wall she'd just made. "You'd make a great mom," she said.

I frowned at her. "How did you get from Push Hands to I'd make a great mom?"

"You're trying to figure out who killed Simon's father because you care about Mia. You've gotten really close with her."

I nodded. "I have. Leo and her father were all she had. Now all she has is Simon. My parents may have been a little out there but I always had them and Sara and Ethan. I can't imagine life without them."

Maggie folded the piece of paper. "That's because you've always had them. You'd miss your mother telling you to follow your heart but stand up straight while you're doing it. You'd miss your dad as the dancing raisin no matter how embarrassing it was."

Maggie's father had died when she was four. She almost never talked about him. She smiled. "It's good that Mia has you to talk to."

"You wouldn't believe the things she knows," I said. "It's like her head is a giant encyclopedia."

Maggie rolled her eyes. "Uh-huh. And I wouldn't have any experience with someone like that."

I got to the hotel just before five thirty. Simon was waiting for me just inside the lobby. Melanie Davis was at the front desk and lifted a hand in hello. We'd originally met just a few weeks after she'd taken the manager's job, when I'd had to collect an intoxicated Burtis and Marcus's father from the bar, where they were entertaining the customers with their vocal skills.

It was quiet in the bar. Simon chose a table near the windows. He ordered club soda with lime and I had the same. We'd been seated about five minutes when Celia Hunter arrived. She wore a long two-tone charcoal-and-dove-gray cardigan with a matching charcoal sweater underneath and black trousers. She seemed to hesitate for a moment but then she crossed the room to join us.

Simon got to his feet. "Mrs. Hunter, I'm Simon Janes," he said. "You already know Kathleen."

Celia took the hand he offered. "It's a pleasure to meet you." She turned to me and dipped her head in acknowledgment. "Hello, Kathleen," she said. "I wasn't expecting to see you."

"I asked her to join us," Simon said smoothly, holding a chair for the older woman. He had lovely manners. "I thought you'd feel more comfortable since we're strangers." He smiled.

"Well . . . thank you," Celia said. She took the seat and set a black leather purse on the table. Simon sat down as well. I'd brought Celia's scarf with me and I handed it across the table to her. "Thank you," she said. "I intended to get to the library yesterday but the day got away from me."

She set the scarf next to her purse and turned to Simon. "As I told you on the phone, I don't want to cause you any more grief, but this is probably one of the last letters your mother wrote and . . . and I thought you might like to see it."

Simon's face was unreadable. "I appreciate that," he said.

Celia opened her purse and pulled out a pale pink envelope. The paper had faded and the side folds were almost worn through. Even hidden behind the wall for so many years, time had taken its toll. The top of the envelope had been slit with a letter opener. Simon pulled out two sheets of folded paper and unfolded them. Silently he read what was written and then handed the two pages to me without a word.

I handled the paper carefully. It was dry and a little brittle, especially the right edge of the second page. I could see how the pages hadn't been folded evenly. The right edge of the second page hadn't lined up behind the first and because of the slit in the side of the envelope the edge was more faded and brittle than the rest of the paper.

> *Dear Celia,*
>
> *I hope you don't throw this letter away as soon as you see it's from me. You probably hate me for what I've done, but you couldn't hate me more than I hate myself. Victor and Leo may look the same but they're very different men. I thought Victor was exciting, and he seemed to know what I was thinking in a way Leo didn't, as if he could see into my heart somehow.*
>
> *I love him. I will see you soon.*
>
>   *Love, Merry*

My chest hurt. Nowhere in the letter was there a mention of Simon. I wasn't so sure this had been a good idea.

I handed the letter back to Simon, who returned it to the envelope and handed that across the table to Celia. "Thank you," he said.

The older woman pressed her lips together for a moment. She seemed to be struggling with some kind of emotion—sadness, perhaps—coupled with a bit of loyalty to an old friend. "She loved you very much," she said. "Please don't doubt that."

"Have a safe trip home," Simon said.

She had been dismissed and realized it. She got to her feet, nodded at both of us and made her way to the exit.

Simon turned to me. "Pizza?" he asked. A waiter was already making his way toward us.

"Excuse me?" I said.

"You couldn't have had time to have dinner before you got here. You must be hungry." He was all business. "So how about pizza?"

"Umm, all right. Yes," I said.

Simon gave our order to the waiter. Once the young man was on his way to the kitchen Simon turned his attention to me. "I know you're worried that . . ." He paused. "I'm all right, Kathleen. That letter didn't change my opinion of Victor or my mother. It changes nothing."

"Are you going to keep investigating?" I asked.

"Yes," he said. "I didn't kill my father. And I'm going to find out who did."

12

Harry showed up at the house about five to eight the next morning. He was going to do some repairs to Rebecca's gazebo and the raised flower beds at the back of my yard. One of the perks of my job at the library was my little farmhouse. Since Everett owned the property all the yard work was taken care of as well.

I'd pulled my truck out in front of the house so Harry could use the driveway.

"Thanks for letting me park here," he said. "Oren is still working at Rebecca's and I'd like to stay out of his way if I can."

Mariah came around the side of the house carrying a long extension cord and a tool box with a denim backpack that I recognized as being the same one she'd had with her at her grandfather's over her shoulder. "Hey, Kathleen," she said.

The high school kids had a day off due to teachers' meetings.

"Would you like a cup of coffee?" I said to Harry.

"I'm good, thanks," he said.

I looked at Mariah. "Would you like a cup of coffee?"

She nodded. "Please."

"C'mon in," I said beckoning at her. In the kitchen I got one of my stainless-steel travel mugs from the cupboard and poured her a cup. Then I indicated the cream and sugar so she could fix her coffee just the way she liked it.

She added three spoonfuls of sugar. "Dad got me up at six thirty," she said by way of explanation.

"Owen got me up at six thirty, too," I said.

Mariah smiled at me over the top of the mug as she took a drink. "Did he tell you getting up early builds character?"

"No," I said. "I'm pretty sure all he was interested in was breakfast."

She laughed and held up the cup. "Thank you. I'll make sure I bring this back," she said, and headed outside.

I'd just poured myself another cup of coffee when Owen came from the living room, walked purposefully through the kitchen and stopped in front of the door. He meowed loudly. I went over and opened it. He headed for the back door. I knew he wanted to see what Harry was doing. Both cats liked the gazebo. "Stay out of the way," I reminded him as I let him into the backyard.

"Mrr," he said, and then he was gone across the grass.

I stood for a moment on the steps, where I could see into Rebecca's backyard. Mariah had set her coffee on the gazebo railing and stowed her backpack on the seat below it. I watched as she unrolled the long yellow extension cord and went to plug it into the outside outlet.

When I stepped back into the porch I found Hercules sitting on the bench looking out the window. He followed me into the kitchen and I found myself telling him about the letter from Simon's mother as I gathered up the laundry. "I don't know what I was hoping for," I said. "Maybe I'm wrong. Maybe there is no connection between Meredith Janes's accident and Leo's death."

About ten thirty I washed my way across the kitchen floor to the back door. Hercules and I moved outside to sit on the steps, me with a cup of coffee—and him with a sardine cracker. We'd been sitting there about five minutes when I saw Owen coming across the grass. He had something in his mouth. What were the chances he *hadn't* taken something that belonged to Harry?

I held out my hand as he came up the stairs and Owen dropped what looked to be a tiny piece of molded plastic in my hand. He looked at me with a very self-satisfied look on his face.

"What did you do?" I said.

"Merow," he replied. He leaned over and nudged the small piece of orange plastic with his nose then looked at me.

Hercules leaned down and looked at my hand then looked at his brother. I'd had moments where it almost seemed like they could communicate without making a sound, and this was one of those times.

After a long moment, Hercules, like his brother, looked expectantly at me.

"Okay, you furry little kleptomaniac, what am I supposed to see here?" I picked up the piece of orange plastic by one end and held it up to study it. It was eight or nine inches long and at first I'd thought it was a disposable knife, but now I realized it wasn't.

"It looks like an airplane propeller," I said. I looked from Hercules to Owen, who both seemed to be waiting for me to make a connection.

A small airplane propeller.

Harry wasn't a model maker as far as I knew. I turned the strip of plastic over in my fingers. Owen continued to stare unblinkingly at me and one of his ears twitched. He was getting annoyed that it was taking me so long to make the connection.

"All I see is a little propeller for a little airplane." As I said the words aloud the last piece fell into place in my head. I looked from one cat to the other. "A drone is a little airplane."

Owen sat down on the step, seemingly satisfied that I'd figured things out.

I looked across the yard. I could see Harry and Mariah working on the gazebo steps. What had he said more than once about his daughter? *"She's good with anything mechanical."*

I knew there was no way Harry had a drone, but could Mariah have one? Could she be the person who'd been following cars on the highway? And if she was, why was she doing it?

I sat there trying to make sense of everything when

Harry came across the yard. "I'm just heading to the lumberyard for another one-by-six," he said. "We're just about finished with the gazebo and then we'll start on the end of that raised bed of yours."

"Thanks," I said. I waited until I heard his truck pull out of the driveway and then I started across the backyard. Owen came with me. Hercules stayed on the steps.

Mariah was sweeping up sawdust inside the gazebo. "Hi, Kathleen," she said. "Dad just went to get a couple of boards. He should be right back."

"I saw him," I said. "I wanted to ask you something." I held out the orange propeller. "Is this yours?"

Her face flooded with color. "I, umm, I don't know," she said. She couldn't quite keep her eyes on mine.

"It's a propeller," I said. "I'm pretty sure it's for a drone." I gestured at her backpack still lying on the wooden gazebo seat. "I'm sorry, I think Owen took it."

Her shoulders sagged. "Are you going to tell my dad?"

"Mariah, have you been following cars out on the highway and down by the marina with it?"

"A few . . . maybe," she said.

"That's really dangerous."

She shook her head. "No, it's not, because I didn't do it when there was a lot of traffic and I didn't get that close to the cars."

"But you were a distraction," I said, moving my hands around in frustration. "Those drivers were all paying attention to your drone, not the road. Someone could have been hurt."

She swallowed hard. "I never thought about that."

"What were you doing anyway?"

"I'm making a movie for my media studies class. There's a camera attached to the drone."

I suddenly knew why Mariah hadn't mentioned the power was off at the library. "You were out filming the other night when I had supper with your dad and your grandfather. You weren't at the library."

She shook her head. "I wasn't."

"How many other times?"

She listed off five other days.

"Where exactly were you filming?" I asked, an idea buzzing in the back of my brain.

"One time I was down by the marina. The others I was on the highway." She wrapped her arms around her body, hugging herself. "I'm in trouble, aren't I?"

I nodded. "I'm pretty sure you are, but it might not be as bad as you think."

When Harry came back Mariah confessed what she'd been doing. She didn't make any excuses. Harry pulled off his Twins caps and smoothed a hand over his scalp. "You could have caused an accident," he said. "What were you thinking? Somebody could have been hurt. Somebody could have been killed."

"I know," she said in a small voice, swallowing back tears that were threatening to fall.

"Mariah might be able to help someone with that footage she shot," I said.

Harry looked at me, frowning. "What are you talking about?"

I explained about Simon driving around the night

his father had been killed. "Mariah was flying her drone, filming up on the highway that night. I know it's a long shot, but she might have filmed Simon's car. She might be able to prove that he had nothing to do with Leo's death."

Harry looked at his daughter. "Do you have all the stuff you filmed?"

She nodded. "On my computer."

He turned to me. "Kathleen, would you call Marcus and see if he can meet us at the police station in"—he looked at his watch—"about forty-five minutes?"

"I will," I said.

"Let's get things cleaned up here," he said to his daughter. "Then we're going home to get your computer."

A chastened Mariah picked up the broom again. Owen had been sitting on the railing listening to the entire conversation. Now he tipped his head to one side, looked inquiringly at Mariah and meowed softly. "I said you could lie on my backpack, not go through it," she muttered.

Owen hung his head.

"It's not your fault," she said, her expression softening. "It's mine. I'm going to be grounded for the rest of my life."

"Or longer," Harry said darkly.

I picked up Owen and headed home to call Marcus.

Mary had an expression she'd use when it seemed like everything was going wrong at the library: *"Some days you eat the bear, some days the bear eats you."* This turned out to be one of those times when we ate the bear. The camera Mariah had attached to the drone produced excellent-quality video, and she was a skilled flyer. About a third of the way through the video she had shot the night Leo was killed she picked up Simon's car. The time stamp made it clear that he couldn't have been at the apartment killing his father.

"He's in the clear," Marcus said when he called me at the library. "What made you think Mariah might have video of his car in the first place?"

"I remembered Simon saying that he'd seen a drone flying over a field. I figured there was a chance he was on the same stretch of highway where Eddie had been followed. It was a long shot, but it was plausible."

I was sitting at my desk and I swiveled around so I could see out the window. Watching the water helped me focus my thoughts. "I'm sorry I ruined your case."

"Hey, don't apologize," Marcus said. "I don't want to arrest an innocent man. I want to catch the person who really killed Leo Janes."

"Any idea who that might be?" I asked.

Marcus exhaled softly. "I think I'll just say 'No comment' for now."

We said good-bye and I went downstairs to give Mary a break at the circulation desk. I had a quick meeting with Lita over at Henderson Holdings at two thirty. I told her about Maggie's idea to frame the photos from the post office for display along with some of the mail that had been found. Maggie was confident that at least some of the recipients would loan whatever card or letter they had received for our exhibit.

"I don't see why the board would have any problem with you doing that," Lita said.

"We're hoping to get the display done early in December," I said. "We have more people come into the library then anyway."

Lita and I spent another fifteen minutes on library business and then I bundled up to walk back to the library. The wind off the water was cold and very quickly I began to regret my decision not to bring the truck. When I came level with Eric's Place I decided to duck inside for a cup of coffee to go.

"I put on a fresh pot," Claire said. "It'll just be a couple of minutes."

"I don't mind," I said. I sat on a stool with my back to the counter. I was happy to have a chance to warm my hands. I'd left my gloves back at the library.

The front door of the restaurant opened and Rebecca came in. She smiled and came over to the counter. "I bet you're on your way back from your meeting with Lita," she said.

I nodded. "I came in to get warm and get a cup of coffee. I'm just waiting for a new pot."

"I'm meeting Patricia Queen for tea," Rebecca said. "I'm hoping she can repair an old quilt that Everett's mother made."

Claire came out of the kitchen then. "Would you like a table, Mrs. Henderson?" she asked.

"In just a moment I would," Rebecca said as she pulled off her gloves.

Claire smiled. "You can have the one in the window if you'd like or any other one along the back wall."

Rebecca smiled back at her. "Thank you," she said.

The door opened again and Elias Braeden and two other men came in.

"I'll just get these customers and then I'll get your coffee, Kathleen," Claire said.

"It's all right," I said. "Take your time."

Elias noticed me then. He gave a small smile and a nod of recognition, which I returned.

"Kathleen, who is that?" Rebecca asked, a frown forming between her eyebrows.

"His name is Elias Braeden. He's here on business. He's considering buying the Silver Casino."

"Oh, that explains it," she said, her expression clearing.

I turned to look at her. "Explains what?"

"Nothing, really," Rebecca said. "It's just the day before Leo died I saw him out in front of the house talking to that man. Did you know Leo liked to play blackjack?"

I nodded. "I did."

"That must be how he knew Mr. Braeden."

Claire came then with my coffee. Rebecca gave me a hug and headed toward the window table.

I headed out for the library. So Elias had talked to Leo the day before he was killed. Interesting.

Very interesting.

Oren Kenyon came into the library about four thirty. Oren was in his midfifties, tall and lean like a farmboy version of actor/director Clint Eastwood. He was quiet and thoughtful, a child musical prodigy who had chosen a quiet life working in Mayville Heights rather than the fame and fortune of a concert stage that certainly could have been his if he'd wanted it.

Mary was at the front desk. She beckoned Oren over. Some of the old photographs were spread across the counter.

"I think I've figured out where some of these were taken," she said as I joined them. "There used to be a summer day camp out at Long Lake when I was a girl." She held up one of the photos. "I think this one is some of the boys from the camp." She pointed at a little boy with a crew cut, sitting cross-legged on the ground with half a dozen other kids about the same age, all of them squinting at the camera. "Oren, isn't that your cousin Ira?"

Oren studied the old black-and-white image for a moment. Then he nodded slowly. "That's Ira," he said. "And I think that's Thorsten's brother behind him." A small frown creased his forehead.

Ira Kenyon was a little . . . eccentric. Back when Kingsley-Pearson had planned to develop the area around Long Lake, before the company's problems with the IRS and before Simon had bought the land, Ira had been camped out there, insisting the land really belonged to the Kenyons. One of the first things Simon had done was hire the man as a caretaker for the property, which seemed to settle the issue, at least for the moment.

Mary smiled. "Thank you." She looked at me. "I'll give Thorsten a call and get him to come take a look at these sometime in the next couple of days."

"Perfect," I said.

She looked over toward the computer area, where one of the older Justason boys was working at a terminal. He had one hand on top of the backward baseball cap on his head and he seemed to be squinting in confusion at the monitor.

Mary shook her head. "Excuse me," she said. "I think Perry is having more problems formatting his bibliography."

She made her way over to the computers and I turned to Oren. He was carrying a brown envelope and I hoped that meant he'd brought the drawings of the porch swing he was going to make as a wedding gift for Roma and Eddie from Marcus and me.

He had. He'd drawn a front view of the swing, a side perspective and a close-up of the detail along the arms. I spread the drawings out on the circulation desk.

"I hope you like it," he said shyly.

"It's beautiful," I said, tracing the lines of the sketch with one finger.

"Thank you," he said. "I think I have enough reclaimed black locust. It's beautiful wood."

"Whatever you decide will work is fine with me," I said. "I trust your judgment."

Abigail hung up the phone and leaned over to look at the drawing.

"It's for Roma and Eddie," I said. "Their wedding gift."

"They're going to love it," she said.

"The arms are based on a design my father did for a rocking chair," Oren said.

"Roma will love that," I said. Roma and Oren were distant cousins.

I put the drawing back in the envelope and offered it to Oren.

He shook his head. "Those are for you," he said. "I have another set." He tapped his temple with one hand. "And the idea is here anyway."

We started toward the entrance. Then Oren stopped and looked back over his shoulder at the circulation desk. "Kathleen, there's something I need to ask you," he said. His expression was serious.

"All right," I said. "What is it?"

"I saw you over at the hotel with Simon Janes and a woman named Celia Hunter?"

"Yes," I said, since he'd framed the sentence as a question.

Oren nodded. "I went to talk to the manager about restoring an old walnut desk that had been stored in the basement. It has some water damage. I thought it was her." He looked down at his feet for a moment, then his blue eyes met mine. "I wasn't sure if I should say anything or not, but maybe that old photo of Ira is a sign that I should."

I had no idea what he was talking about.

"I don't like to speak ill of people, but Celia is not someone who should be trusted."

I knew that Oren never spoke ill of anyone, so I knew I could trust what he was saying even as I was surprised by the comment. "How do you know this?" I asked.

He had taken off his cap when he'd stepped inside

the building and now he twisted the brim in his hands. "Ira and Celia went out when they were young. Celia broke up with him to go after Leo Janes, who had a lot more money."

"I didn't know that," I said.

"I don't think a lot of people do," Oren replied. "It didn't work. Leo was interested in Simon's mother, and Celia didn't get anywhere with him. She went after his brother, Victor, next but that didn't work out, either." Oren cleared his throat. "You're friends with Simon, so maybe you could tell him he shouldn't trust Celia. Before Leo Janes's marriage broke up Ira insisted that Celia was telling Victor things about Meredith. Private things."

I remembered Meredith Janes's letter: *He seemed to know what I was thinking in a way Leo didn't*, she had written. Could that have been because Celia Hunter had been feeding Victor information?

Oren's expression was serious. "Kathleen, sometimes the things Ira says are just things he's imagined, but sometimes, sometimes they aren't."

I thanked Oren for coming to talk to me, and he left. In the last two hours I'd learned that Elias Braeden had seen Leo the day before he died and Celia Hunter may not have been the friend to Leo's ex-wife that she'd seemed. The problem was I had no idea how any of that could help me figure out who had killed Leo.

13

I couldn't get what Oren had told me about Celia Hunter out of my mind. Was his cousin Ira right? Had Celia conspired with Victor Janes to end his brother's marriage so she could have Leo for herself? The whole thing reminded me of a gothic romance. All we needed was a lonely mansion and a dark and stormy night. I had no idea how this new piece of information fit into the puzzle. Based on the letter from Meredith it seemed as though she hadn't known about her best friend plotting to break up her marriage. Had Leo known? And did it have anything to do with his death?

I took the later supper break. I carried my bowl of vegetable soup back to my office instead of eating in the staff room. My mind was going in circles. I had all these pieces of information and no way to tie them all together or tie them to Leo's killer.

I wished I knew a little more about blackjack. I'd played poker before, but all I knew about blackjack was the basic rules. On the other hand, I did know someone who knew a lot more about casinos and gambling than I did. My mother. My mother was primarily a stage actor, but she did take on small film and TV roles if the part captured her fancy.

For the past month Mom and Dad had been in Los Angeles. They'd originally only planned to stay for two weeks while my mother did a brief guest stint on *The Wild and Wonderful*. She was incredibly popular with fans of the racy soap opera, who had been lobbying for a return performance since her last visit. On her second day on the set her visit had been extended by an additional three weeks.

Several years ago, Mom had had a small role in a movie set in a casino in Las Vegas. She'd flirted shamelessly—on camera—with Denzel Washington. The two of them had a chemistry that surprised everyone, except Dad and me. My mother had chemistry with everyone she worked with.

I checked the time. Los Angeles was two hours behind Mayville Heights. If I was lucky Mom was back from the set. If she wasn't I could try her when I got home. It was Dad who answered. "Hi, sweetie," he said. "It's wonderful to hear your voice."

"It's good to hear yours, too," I said. "How's Los Angeles?"

"Busy. They're using your mother as much as they can, because we'll be leaving in another week. And everywhere we go someone recognizes her. Not to mention men half my age are putting the moves on her right in front of me."

"He's exaggerating," I heard Mom call in the background.

I laughed. It didn't matter how many men tried to charm my mother. She only had eyes for my father. She told me once that being divorced from Dad showed her that she didn't need a man she could live with. She needed a man she couldn't live without.

"May I talk to her, please?" I said.

"Of course," he said. "I love you."

"Love you, too, Dad." I leaned back in my chair and my mother's voice came through the phone, just as full of warmth as if she'd been in the room with me.

"Hello, Katydid," she said. "How are you?"

The sound of my mom's voice always made me smile. She could be dramatic and aggravating and she'd never been the make-cookies or take-me-to-girl-scouts kind of parent, which I'd longed for at times growing up. But she loved me and Sara and Ethan with the ferocity of a mama grizzly bear and I knew no matter what any of us did in life, she always had our backs. "I'm fine," I said.

"And how are Owen and Hercules?"

"They're both all right now, but Owen did have a bit of an altercation with a stray dog last week."

"Is Owen all right?" she asked, and I could hear the concern in her voice. Mom and the cats had bonded the first time she came for a visit.

"He had to have stitches and wear a fabric collar for a few days, but he had Marcus feeding him things he probably shouldn't have had and me carrying him everywhere, so he survived. And for the record, according to Roma the dog looked worse."

Mom laughed. "That's probably the last cat he'll tangle with," she said. "And how's Marcus?" There was a teasing edge to her voice that made me blush even though she couldn't see me.

"Perfect as always," I said.

"You're happy." It wasn't a question.

"We are." I pictured her probably curled up in a big chair, elbow on the armrest and her head propped on her hand, and a wave of homesickness rolled over me.

"I have a feeling you didn't call just to tell me how terrific Marcus is," she said. "So what's up?"

"I'm hoping you can teach me about playing blackjack."

"Are you planning a career change you haven't told me about?"

I laughed and propped my feet on the edge of my desk. "No. Do you remember me telling you about Mia Janes, who works for me at the library, and her dad?"

"Simon," Mom said. "The developer."

"Yes."

"This has something to do with his father's death, doesn't it?" My mother read the *Mayville Heights Chronicle* every morning online. I should have guessed she'd make the connection.

"Leo—Simon's father—played blackjack. He was pretty good." The brownie I'd brought for dessert was still sitting on top of my desk next to a half-warm cup of coffee. I broke off a piece and popped it into my mouth.

"Did it get him killed?" she asked.

"I don't know," I said. "All I can tell you is that he won around a million dollars at one particular casino and no one seems to know for sure exactly how he did it."

"I'm surprised he wasn't banned from the tables."

"He was. And not just at that casino."

"How much do you know about the game?" Mom asked.

"I understand the rules," I said. "Players compete against the dealer but not against each other. The object of the game is to beat the dealer, by getting twenty-one points with your first two cards, say with an ace and a queen, or having your final score be more than the dealer's without going over twenty-one, or by the dealer going bust." I had another bite of my brownie.

"That's right," she said. "Face cards are worth ten and an ace can be worth one or eleven. The dealer deals two cards to everyone from the shoe."

"The shoe holds the cards, right?" I said.

"Yes." I could picture my mother nodding on the other end of the phone. "Invented, by the way, by John Scarne, one of the most incredible magicians I've ever seen. Before that the game was dealt from a single deck. The shoe can hold between two and eight decks of cards."

I did a little math in my head. "So, wait a minute; using more cards is going to give an advantage to the casino."

"Exactly," Mom said. "And it works against someone like Mr. Janes, who had to have been counting cards to have won that much money."

"He did have a PhD in math," I said.

"So he probably had math skills that were better than the average person."

"Yes." I checked my watch. I only had a few minutes left on my supper break.

"After those first two cards are dealt a player has several choices. 'Hit' means take another card from the dealer."

"And 'stand' means you don't want any more cards."

"That's right," Mom said. "'Double down' means you can increase your original bet. If your first two cards are worth the same you can split them into two hands. That's called a split."

"So if Leo was counting cards, what was he doing?" I said. "I'm guessing it means keeping track of what's been dealt and what cards are left to be played."

"Essentially that's it. A good card counter knows what the odds are of getting the card he needs. But keep in mind not only is the dealer watching, there are also cameras overhead watching. Card counters get in trouble when it's obvious what they're doing, for instance when everyone can see them looking around. I take it Mr. Janes didn't do anything to give himself away."

"I guess not," I said.

"Smart man," Mom said, and I caught a hint of approval in her voice. "Keep in mind," she continued, "it may be considered to be wrong by the casinos but card counting isn't illegal, not unless the player is using something other than his own mental acuity—some kind of computer for instance."

"So why was Simon banned from playing anymore?"

"Because a casino is private property. Just the way you can refuse to let someone in your house, a casino can refuse to let someone play. If I'm in your house after I've been told I'm not welcome, that's considered trespassing and that is a crime. The same would be true in a casino."

I checked my watch again. It was almost time to get back to work. "Thanks, Mom," I said. "This helps a lot."

"You're welcome, Katydid," she said. "Stay safe. Tell Marcus I said hello. And tell Maggie there's a surprise wedding coming on the show."

To my surprise Maggie had turned out to be a huge fan of *The Wild and Wonderful*. "Whose?" I asked. "Wait a minute, are you getting married? Is that why they wanted you for more shows?"

"You know I can't tell you that," she said. "I love you."

"I love you, too," I said. "I'll talk to you soon."

I ended the call and set my cell on top of the desk.

Card counting was a lot harder than I'd realized. Leo had been good enough that no one knew how he was doing whatever it was he'd been doing. I could see why Elias wanted to figure that out, why any casino owner would. Had Leo taught his technique to some of his students? He'd already cost Elias a million dollars. How much money had they, or could they, win as well?

I headed back downstairs and joined Mary at the

circulation desk. She was putting books to be reshelved on the cart while I sorted through the ones that had come in on reserve. The third book I picked was for Leo Janes.

"We can cancel this one," I said to Mary. "It was for Leo."

She took the book from me and turned it over to look at the back cover blurb. "I suggested this one," she said. "Leo came back in the morning he was . . . The morning he died. I got him set up with a temporary card and he asked me if I knew anything about theatrical makeup." She raised an eyebrow. "I told him I knew a few things about being onstage."

I was guessing that Mary had learned a lot of things from dancing at The Brick. I wasn't sure I wanted to know what they all were.

She handed the book back to me. "I suggested this book and requested it for him."

I put the book on the counter to be returned to the library it had been requested from. "Why was Leo interested in stage makeup?" I asked.

Mary shrugged. "He didn't say, but I know that Mia is thinking of getting involved in the spring production at the high school. It was probably just his way of staying involved in her life. According to Mia he was interested in whatever she was doing."

"From what I heard about the man, he was a good grandfather."

Mary nodded. "What happened to him wasn't fair."

I glanced at the makeup book that Leo would never

get to read with Mia. "Life really isn't fair sometimes," I said.

"I've always hated that," Mary said with a wry smile. She looked over her shoulder toward the computer room. "Change of subject. So, did Maggie figure out where she's going to display those old photos?"

"I think so," I said. I pointed at the side wall. "I think she's going to use that wall."

Mary was wearing her favorite fall-themed sweater— orange and brown with big embroidered yellow and red leaves. She brushed some bits of paper off the front. "I'm looking forward to seeing those old photos framed."

"Me too," I said. "And Maggie's convinced both Thorsten and Harrison to let her display the mail they received."

Mary laughed. "Well, in Thorsten's case I don't think it was the first card like that he received. He cut a pretty wide swath when he was younger."

Since rumor had it that Mary herself had been part of that swath I decided not to comment.

She was still staring across the room with a thoughtful look on her face. "You know, if this were a movie something dramatic would have happened because someone didn't get their mail when they were supposed to," she said.

"Mary Lowe, do you have a secret romantic side?" I teased.

"I like a good happily ever after once in a while," she said, her eyes gleaming.

"So have you heard of anything romantic happening because of a piece of that found mail?"

She shook her head. "Burtis got a note from the school about Brady. But I don't think there were any love letters found. I don't think there were that many pieces of mail behind the wall. You know about Thorsten and Harrison." She started ticking off names on her fingers. "One of Lita's cousins got something—another Christmas card, I think—and then there was Leo and maybe two or three other people and that's it." She'd started stacking books on the cart again.

"Wait a minute," I said. "*Leo* got one of those pieces of mail?"

Mary nodded but she didn't turn around, so she didn't see what had to be a shocked expression on my face. "He said it was nothing important."

Meredith Janes had written a letter to her best friend that had ended up behind that wall at the post office. Now I wondered, could she have written one to her husband as well?

Marcus had hockey practice so I headed home to Owen and Hercules when the library closed. Harry had left a note telling me that he'd fixed the side of the raised bed in the backyard and he'd be back on Monday with some topsoil and mulch to replace what had been lost.

I told the boys about my conversation with Oren. "And Leo Janes got one of those pieces of mail that were found at the post office," I said as I changed into yoga pants and a long-sleeved T-shirt. "Do you think it's possible it was from Meredith?"

Hercules made a face. It seemed he wasn't sure, either.

"You know, all we seem to have is a bunch of random facts and no way to connect them all together." I rubbed the space between my eyebrows. "This just gives me a headache."

"Mrr," Hercules said, heading for the door. He stopped and looked back over his shoulder before heading for the stairs, his way of saying a treat would probably make me feel better.

Who was I to argue?

By the time I'd finished half a mug of hot chocolate and two pumpkin-spice chocolate-chip cookies, I did feel better. I had about an hour before Marcus was going to be finished at hockey practice. I set my laptop on the table. "Right now we don't have any way of finding out what the piece of mail was that Leo got. But we could see what else we can find out about Celia Hunter."

Herc jumped up onto my lap and put one paw on the cover of the computer. We were in agreement.

Between my skill with a search engine and the serendipity of Hercules randomly touching the keyboard and somehow finding something useful, we learned quite a bit about Celia Hunter.

For one thing, she was in a relationship with a man named Edmund Holloway. Holloway was a successful businessman in his early seventies who owned, among other things, the largest organic baby food company in North America. He had seven children and twelve grandchildren. He and Celia had met at the 55+ Games, where both had been part of the dragon boat team. Celia, it seemed, had been a competitive rower in college. Edmund Holloway had taken up cross-country in college. I found a photo of the dragon boat in one of their races, crew straining as they sliced through the water toward the finish line, half a boat length ahead of their closest competitor.

Hercules seemed to study the image. He put his paw on the screen.

"Yes, I see that," I said. Celia Hunter had strong arms. Were they strong enough to have picked up that sculpture and killed Leo Janes?

14

Susan came hurrying down the sidewalk as I got out of my truck the next morning. As she got closer I saw that she had a pair of plastic scissors and an emerald-green pencil crayon stuck in her topknot, which just gave a bit more credence to my theory that her twins did her hair in the morning.

"Kathleen, do you remember seeing my car keys yesterday?" she asked.

I shook my head as I unlocked the doors and turned off the alarm system. "No," I said. Then I noticed she had a key ring in her hand. "What are those?" I asked.

"House keys," she said.

"You don't have them both on the same ring?"

She nudged her black cat's-eye glasses up her nose. "Thank goodness, no. Now I wouldn't have my house keys, either."

"Right," I said, thinking that I'd worked with Susan long enough that what she'd said actually made sense to me.

She moved inside and began flipping on the lights. Behind me I heard a soft knock on the outside door. I turned to let Mia in.

"Hi," she said. She was carrying a round metal cookie tin.

"What did you bring?" I asked.

"Coffee cake," she said with a smile. "I could go put the coffee on and you could try it before we open."

"That's an excellent idea," I said.

Susan was standing in the middle of the floor looking around the room as though she expected her missing car keys to suddenly fall at her feet.

"Susan lost her car keys," I said.

"What does the key ring look like?" Mia asked.

"It's a Troll doll with lime-green hair." She stopped and looked at us. "I think I know where they are. Kathleen, do you have the key for the cash drawer?"

"Right here," I said, pulling my own keys out of my pocket. I handed them over to her.

"Mike Justason was paying the boys' overdue- and damaged-book fines when Eric dropped off my car," she explained. She leaned over the counter, unlocked the cash drawer and after a moment triumphantly held up her keys.

"Yay!" I said.

Mia held up the tin with the coffee cake. "We should celebrate," she said.

We all headed up to the staff room, where I started the coffee machine and Mia cut us each a slice of her coffee cake.

"This is really good," Susan told her. "Seriously. If you ever want to work at the café, let me know."

I narrowed my eyes at her. "Hey, no stealing my favorite employee who also happens to bring coffee cake to work on Saturday morning."

"I brought you banana bread two weeks ago," Susan said.

"Which is why you were my favorite employee two weeks ago," I said with a grin.

Mia smiled. "I'm glad you both like it," she said. "It was my grandfather's favorite and I knew he'd hate it if I stopped making it. So I thought I'd make it for you guys."

"We're glad you did," I said.

Susan's keys were lying on the table.

"I like the Troll doll key ring," I said.

"Eric thought maybe it would help me stop losing my keys so often," Susan said. "He thought the hair might make them easier to notice."

"How's that working?" I asked.

"Not bad," she said with a completely straight face. Then she laughed.

I glanced over at Mia. She looked a little sad. "Are you all right?" I said. "The coffee cake really is good. I'm sure your grandfather would be happy you made it for us."

"I'm all right," Mia said. "I was remembering that Grandpa misplaced his car keys the day before he died. I'd made this cake and then we'd gone shopping and we were going to the cottage where Uncle Victor was staying for lunch. So he had to use my keys." She ducked her head. "Don't tell my dad."

Susan looked confused. "What?" she mouthed.

"Your grandfather let you drive his car," I said.

Mia looked up and nodded. "Dad would have a cow. You know how he is. He's always afraid someone is going to run me off the road. Grandpa gave me a set of keys to *his* car and said I could drive it as long as I was careful."

Susan patted her arm. "I used to drive my grandmother's car. It was this great big boat of a Buick. I sometimes wonder if my dad knew but just pretended that he didn't. Anyway, your secret is safe with us."

Mia reached over and combed the little Troll doll's green hair with two fingers. "Grandpa wanted me to go for a walk with Uncle Victor and get to know him a little but I tried to get out of it. I should have said yes because it was important to him."

"My great-uncle smells like licorice and has hair growing out of his ears," Susan said flatly. "It's the only hair on his head unless you count the hair that's growing out of his nose. And all he wants to talk about is things he and his friends have had cut out of their bodies."

Mia made a face. "Gross!"

"More than you can imagine," Susan said. Her top-knot bobbed as she nodded her head for emphasis and for a moment I was afraid the green pencil crayon was going to go flying across the room. "A lot of people don't want to hang out with their great-uncles, kiddo. It's okay." She looked at her watch and stood up. "I'll go open." She scooped her keys off the table, stopped at her locker and put them inside on the shelf before heading for the stairs.

Mia got to her feet as well. She took her cup and plate to the sink and then went over to her own locker and put her backpack inside. She hung up her jacket and, when she did, her own keys fell to the floor.

I picked them up. There was a red crayon attached to the ring.

Mia saw me looking at it and said, "It's not a real crayon. It's actually a memory stick. I have another one that looks like a little Hershey bar."

"That would make a great Christmas gift for my sister," I said. "Where did you get it?"

"Grandpa got both of them for me from the bookstore, I think," Mia said.

"Next time I'm down there I'll go take a look," I said. I got to my feet. It was time to get to work.

It turned out to be a busy morning. At least half of a grade-eleven English class came in looking for books on the reading list assigned by their teacher. Several of the quilters showed up to talk more about a possible quilt show in the new year.

I'd just helped a new mom find a copy of *Love You Forever* when I noticed Sandra Godfrey in the magazine section, one hand on her hip, studying the shelves. "Hi, Sandra, what can I help you find?" I asked.

"Oh, hi, Kathleen," she said. "What happened to *Scientific American*? It was right there." She gestured to a magazine shelf at waist level.

"One more shelf to the right," I said. "We added a

new magazine in the Ps and it bumped everything sideways."

Sandra tipped her head in the direction of the quilters, who were just heading out the door. "So are you going to hold the winter show here?"

"I hope so," I said. "I think we have enough space." I eyed her. "Do you quilt?"

She nodded and held up the copy of *Scientific American* she'd just lifted from the shelf. "You might say I'm a Renaissance woman," she said with a grin.

I smiled back at her. "I'm impressed."

"Have you made any progress on figuring out what to do with the photos from the post office?" Sandra asked.

"Yes. I should have called you," I said. I explained about Maggie's idea for framing everything and putting the photos and some of the mail that was found on display.

"I would like to see that since I was the one who delivered most of that mail." Her lips twitched. "You probably heard about the card Thorsten got."

I nodded. "I think the entire town has heard by now."

Sandra brushed a bit of lint, or maybe it was cat hair, off her red sweater. Did she have cats? I wondered.

"Ella King got a note from her grandmother and it had one of those chocolate coins wrapped in foil inside. The chocolate was still intact." Sandra rolled her eyes. "I don't want to think about how many preservatives were in that thing."

"Maggie's still rounding up more of the mail for

the exhibit," I said. "But that has to be the weirdest piece so far. I hope Ella still has the chocolate."

"Well, I don't think she ate it, if that's what you mean," Sandra said. She glanced down at the cover of the magazine in her hand.

I remembered what Mary had told me. "I heard that Leo Janes got something," I said. "Do you have any idea what?"

"That was odd," Sandra said, shaking her head.

The blood was rushing in my ears. "What makes you say that?" I asked.

"He got an envelope with a key inside."

"A key. You mean like a door key?"

Sandra shook her head. "I don't think it was a door key but I really didn't get a good look at it. All I know is it was a silver-colored key."

"Why on earth would someone have sent Leo Janes a key in the mail?" I asked.

"I don't know." She shrugged. "He didn't seem to know, either. And the funny thing is, it was the last piece of mail to be delivered."

I frowned at her. "Why?"

"There was an old change-of-address card from twenty years ago and somehow the letter ended up being sent there. Then it was rerouted a couple of times before it ended up back here. I heard Mr. Janes was in town, so when the letter came back I delivered it to him." She cleared her throat. "The day before he died."

"You're sure?" I said. I could hear my pulse thudding in my ears again.

"Positive," Sandra said. "It was my mother-in-law's birthday. My husband and I drove into Minneapolis after work to celebrate with the family."

Leo had received the mysterious key the day before he was killed. Was that important? Somehow I had the feeling it was.

Maggie called midmorning to see if we could have lunch so she could show me the proposed layout for the photo exhibit. We agreed to meet at Eric's at one thirty. She was already inside when I got to the café, seated at our favorite table, going through the little ritual she followed when she made her tea.

As soon as I sat down Nic appeared at my elbow seemingly as if by magic and poured me a cup of coffee without even asking if I wanted one because we both knew I did. "Do you need a menu?" he asked.

Maggie shook her head.

Nic grinned. He put two fingers to his temple like a sideshow psychic. "Let me see," he said. "I think you would both like a big bowl of . . . chili and . . . a plate of cornbread."

I smiled at his mind-reading routine. "Please," I said.

"It'll just be a few minutes."

"Are we getting too predictable?" Maggie asked.

"No," I said, slipping out of my jacket. "We're consistent."

"We've had chili the last three times we've been here for lunch."

"It's not our fault the chili is so good. If we didn't

order it we might hurt Eric's feelings and that would be wrong," I said solemnly.

"Well, I wouldn't want to hurt Eric's feelings," she said. Then she laughed.

"So show me what you came up with," I said.

Maggie pulled a brown envelope out of the messenger bag slung over the back of her chair. Inside were three sketches she'd made of three different layouts for the exhibit. We quickly settled on the second one and she spent the rest of the meal telling me what different people were doing with their frames.

"I have another idea, although I don't know if it's workable," she said as she pushed back her empty bowl.

"What is it?" I asked, scooping the last bit of cornbread from the bottom of my dish.

"The post office gave the library those photos, right?" Maggie asked.

I nodded. "We're becoming the repository for things people think the town needs to keep but that they don't want to be responsible for. That's how we got all the old yearbooks and the herbarium."

"So you don't have any obligation to keep all the photos?"

I leaned back in my chair. "No."

She smiled. "Great. Then why can't we auction off some of them to buy new books for the library? There are several gorgeous shots of the bluff."

"I'd have to run it by Everett and the board," I said slowly.

"We could put the framed photos up on the co-op's

website—I'm sure Ruby would agree. That would get you a wider audience."

"I like it," I said, grinning across the table at her.

We talked about the auction idea for a few more minutes and then Maggie looked at her watch. "I need to head for the store."

"Lunch is on me," I said.

She shook her head. "No."

"Yes," I said. "This was library business." I got to my feet and reached for my jacket.

"I'll get you photos of some of the frames that are already done, and I'll talk to Ruby."

I hugged her and she headed for the door while I went over to pay the bill. When I stepped outside I remembered what Mia had told me about her memory stick possibly coming from the bookstore. I had time. I decided I'd stop in and see if I could find one of the Hershey bar ones for Sara.

I was about to step inside the bookstore when the door opened and Victor Janes came out. He smiled when he caught sight of me. "Hello, Kathleen," he said. "How are you?"

"Hello, Victor," I said. "I'm well, how are you?"

"Under the circumstances I'm . . . I'm all right."

He looked so much like his brother and yet I never would have confused the two. Where all the lines on Leo's face had seemed to go up so that it looked as though he was smiling even when he hadn't been, Victor, I'd noticed, had a bit of a dissatisfied expression on his face, like a toddler who had just been told no. As soon as I had the thought I felt guilty. Victor seemed to bring out that emotion in me, guilt because I didn't like him, guilt because, for a moment I'd actually entertained the thought that he'd killed his brother. The man had a serious illness and had just lost his only sibling. Why wouldn't he feel unhappy with the world?

I was about to move past him into the store when he put a hand on my arm. "Kathleen, would you have a moment?" he asked.

"Of course," I said.

We moved away from the doorway.

"Simon told me you were the one who found my brother," Victor said.

An image of Leo Janes's body slumped on the floor flashed across my mind. I swallowed and nodded.

"I don't want to cause you any more distress than you've already been through, but I'm wondering if you can . . . tell me what you saw."

I hesitated. What was there to tell him? I'd seen Leo dead, blood on the back of his head.

Victor pressed his lips together for a moment. I noticed his complexion seemed pale. "Kathleen, I know it sounds gruesome, but Leo was my twin and we always had a connection, even during all the years we didn't speak. I had this feeling that something was wrong that night." He shook his head. "I keep thinking that if I hadn't ignored it . . . maybe Leo would still be alive. Please. Whatever you tell me can't be worse than what I've been imagining."

"There isn't really much to tell you," I said slowly, trying to choose my words with care. "Your brother was on the floor and I don't think he suffered. I think his death was . . . quick."

Victor exhaled slowly. "I was hoping that somehow he'd left me a message. I know that doesn't make sense."

I shook my head. The conversation was making me very uncomfortable and it was hard not to back away. "I'm sorry," I said. "I didn't see any kind of note or message."

"Well, you've put my mind at ease, at least," he said, reaching out to touch my arm again. "I wouldn't want Leo to have suffered. Thank you."

I nodded.

He headed down the sidewalk and I turned in the direction of the library. I didn't feel like going into the bookstore anymore. I felt bad for Victor Janes. I couldn't imagine what it would be like to lose Sara or Ethan. But it was hard to like him, unlike Leo, who had made me smile from the first moment I met him. I wondered if my opinion of Victor was colored by what I knew about his relationship with Simon's mother and how much pain that had caused Simon. I didn't like thinking I was that judgmental, but maybe I was.

When I got home after work Hercules was waiting for me on the back steps. "Hey, handsome," I said, leaning over to stroke his fur. The top of his head was warm from the afternoon sun. "What are you doing out here?"

He looked up at the sky. "Ah, yes, grackle patrol," I said. "Isn't that over for the season?"

Hercules looked at me as though he were surprised I was asking. I held up one hand. "Sorry," I said. "I just thought the grackle would have flown south by now. Though, now that I think about it, I'm not sure they do fly south."

I unlocked the door and Hercules followed me inside. "Where's your brother?" I asked. I glanced over at the basement door. "Down in his lair in the cellar?"

Hercules looked up at the ceiling.

Owen was upstairs somewhere, probably poking around in my closet. "I better not find a chicken head in my new boots," I said.

"Mrr," Hercules replied, which likely meant "Don't count on it."

By the time I'd changed into jeans and a long-sleeved T-shirt the chicken soup I'd left simmering in the slow cooker was done. I put it in the refrigerator after having a taste—and sharing it with the boys. I was going to have supper with Marcus but that wasn't for another hour and a half. I was restless, unsettled by what I'd learned from Sandra Godfrey and still a little uncomfortable about that encounter with Victor.

"I'm going to vacuum," I announced to Owen. He was headed for the basement but changed course and made his way toward the back door instead. I let him into the porch and then opened the door to the backyard.

Hercules was already sitting on the footstool in the living room, eyes fixed on my iPod dock. I got the vacuum cleaner out then slipped my iPod in the dock and started our favorite playlist.

Hercules bopped his head from side to side and I vacuumed as we sang along to the music of Mr. Barry Manilow, which always managed to put both of us in a good mood. Owen, not so much. We did rousing versions of "Copacabana" and "Daybreak" complete with a little choreography, and by the time we were halfway through "I Made It Through the Rain" I felt better.

Once the entire house had been vacuumed I shut off the iPod and made some hot chocolate. I sat at the table with Hercules on my lap and told him what I'd learned from Sandra. I'd set my messenger bag and my keys on the table when I'd come in and now Hercules reached up and batted the keys onto the floor. He looked at me.

"You're a little heavy-handed with the symbolism," I said. "But you're right. We need to find that key."

15

As she often was, Micah was waiting for me on Marcus's back deck. She seemed to share the same prescience that I'd seen in Owen. Her whiskers twitched and she sniffed at the canvas bag I was carrying.

"Chicken soup," I said. "He'll probably let you taste it."

She made a satisfied "Mrr," jumped down and led the way over to the back door.

Marcus was at the sink, washing lettuce. For a moment I just enjoyed looking at him. I thought about what Mary had once said about him: *"I know what really matters about a person is what's inside, and he is a good man inside, but that candy shell outside looks pretty dang delicious!"* I had to admit she was right.

Micah meowed loudly then, as if to announce me, and Marcus looked up and smiled. "Hi," he said. He dropped the lettuce into the strainer and wrapped me in a slightly wet hug. His mouth covered mine and I forgot all about his wet hand on the back of my neck.

I forgot about pretty much everything.

He finally let me go and I noticed that his face was as flushed as mine felt. "I have to stop doing that if we want supper," he said. "And we do want supper, right?"

"Yes?" I said. The fact that I'd answered as a question made him laugh. I set my bag on the chair, lifted out the two Mason jars of chicken soup and handed them to him. "For lunch next week," I said.

"Chicken noodle?" he asked with a raised eyebrow.

I nodded.

"Thanks." He dropped a kiss on the top of my head as he moved to put them in the fridge.

For the first time I noticed that the small table in the middle of the room had been set with extra care, a tablecloth instead of placemats, and four fat pillar candles. "This is beautiful," I said. "Is this for me?"

"It is," he said, moving back to the sink to finish washing the lettuce. "Given the past couple of weeks I thought maybe you could use a little romance."

"I definitely could," I said as I slipped out of my jacket.

"Good. We have about forty minutes until we eat, which means we have about forty minutes to talk about the case." He glanced at me. "I know that you want to."

"All right," I agreed, dropping onto the closest chair. Micah came to lean against my leg. "Did you know the day before he died Leo got one of those pieces of mail they found at the post office?"

Marcus hesitated for a moment. "Yes," he finally said.

"Did you know there was a key in the envelope?"

He looked over his shoulder at me. "A key?"

"Sandra Godfrey delivered the letter and Leo opened it in front of her. She said the only thing inside was a silver key."

"What kind of a key?" he asked. "A house key? A car key? One of those little keys for a diary?"

"I don't know. All Sandra said was that it was a silver key. Marcus, what if it was a car key?"

"Okay," he said. "Let's say it was." He grabbed a carrot from the counter. "What are you thinking? That another car caused the accident that killed Meredith Janes twenty years ago and that someone, *somehow* got the key to that car and instead of talking to the police put it in an envelope and mailed it to her estranged husband?"

"No," I said, reaching down to stroke Micah's soft fur. She seemed to be following the conversation, which didn't really surprise me. Like Owen and Hercules, Micah was a Wisteria Hill cat. "Even Owen wouldn't let me get away with a theory as far-fetched as that." I sighed. "It's just that I can't seem to let go of the idea that there's a connection between what happened to Meredith Janes all those years ago and Leo's murder."

Marcus turned to look at me. "Why?" He gestured with the carrot. "Go ahead. Make your case."

I tucked one leg up underneath me, getting a little more comfortable. Micah nuzzled my hand as if in encouragement. "All right," I said. "First of all, there's nothing that suggests what happened to Leo was some random act—a robbery gone wrong, for example." I leaned sideways for a moment so I was in his line of vision. "I'm assuming I'm right about that."

"Keep going," was all he said.

"So it was personal. Thanks to that video Mariah Taylor filmed, Simon has an alibi."

Marcus smiled as he chopped the carrot. "You can say 'I told you so' if you want."

I smiled back at him. "I thought that was implied," I teased. I was getting a kink in my back so I lifted Micah onto my lap. She immediately stretched across my legs. "Harry had a reason to kill Leo—at least in theory." I held up a hand before Marcus could object. "Yes, I know killing someone over an old watch is a pretty weak reason for murder, but people have been killed for less."

"Agreed," he said, dropping the chopped carrot into what I was guessing was our salad.

"More important, no one who knows Harry would ever believe he could kill anyone and he also has an alibi. That leaves two people: Elias Braeden and Leo's late wife's best friend, Celia Hunter."

Marcus turned to face me. "I don't see how Celia Hunter could have killed Leo. I doubt she has the upper-body strength to swing that piece of sculpture. As for Elias Braeden, he was on the road between Minneapolis and here."

I held up one finger. "Just because she's a woman doesn't mean Celia couldn't have the strength to have swung that sculpture. Look at Mary. People mistake her for just a sweet, cookie-baking grandma but she could probably take you down with just one round-house kick."

"Point taken," he said.

I held up a second finger. "And Elias's alibi is weak. He could have left a little bit earlier than he says he did or driven a lot faster. There's some wiggle room. I think we need to look at both of them anyway."

Micah meowed loudly.

"See? She agrees with me," I said, smiling at the little cat.

Marcus snapped on the oven light and bent down to look through the door. I was so busy watching him that I completely missed what he said. He turned and looked expectantly at me.

"I'm sorry, I got sidetracked. What did you say?"

"I said okay; let's start with Celia Hunter."

"All right," I said. "Didn't you think it was odd she came here just to show Leo that letter she received? I don't see why she thought it was so important."

He nodded. "I had the same thought."

"And she was at Leo's apartment no more than half an hour before his murder."

"The woman has an alibi, Kathleen," Marcus said. "Leo Janes got a phone call from a former colleague at the university where he used to teach just as she was leaving. He heard Leo say good-bye to her, not to mention Mrs. Hunter isn't tall enough or strong enough to have killed him."

"Are you sure?" I asked.

He set down the cast-iron frying pan he'd just picked up and gave me a puzzled look. "Unless she was wearing stilts, yes, I'm sure. So is the medical examiner. The murder weapon was that piece of abstract metal art. It's heavy. Too heavy for Celia Hunter to have picked up. And even if she happened to have a bionic arm that we didn't know about she was too short to have delivered the blow that killed Leo."

Micah sat up then and jumped down to the floor. She moved over to sit next to the stove, either to see what was going to be happening there next or because she'd decided to switch sides in the discussion.

I pulled my other leg up and rested my chin on my knee. "What if he was bending over?" I said.

Marcus picked up the pan again, set it on the burner and turned on the heat.

"Think about it. This wasn't a planned murder or the killer would have had a weapon with her—or him. What if Leo bent down to pick something up and Celia saw her opportunity?"

"Except that piece of artwork is solid metal." He frowned at the pan. "Could you swing a twenty-pound bag of potatoes at my head?" he asked without looking at me.

"No," I said. "But Maggie probably could."

Marcus did glance at me then. "Okay, but how about Rebecca?"

I shook my head. "No, but I think Celia's stronger than we both know. I found photos online of her from this past spring as part of a medal-winning dragon boat team." I put my hand around the upper part of my left arm. "She has actual muscles here. I don't think it's that unrealistic that she could have lifted that statue."

"So what's her motive?" He added a little butter and some olive oil to the pan.

"That's where I'm stuck," I said with a shrug.

"Okay, so what's your case for Elias Braeden?" He set two small bacon-wrapped filets into the pan. Micah's whiskers began to twitch as the smell of searing beef filled the kitchen.

"Leo took his casino for about a million dollars. And Elias doesn't know how he did that so it leaves him open for it to happen again, or at least it did while Leo was alive. Add to that he worked for Idris Black-thorne at one time. Idris had a reputation, and not all of that was just talk."

"So his motive is?"

"Money. Or in the heat of the moment, anger, especially if Leo wouldn't explain how he'd managed to win so much money."

"I've seen those motives before," Marcus agreed. He gave the pan a little shake and then turned the meat. "Do you happen to know if Celia or Elias are right-handed or left-handed?"

I closed my eyes for a moment and pictured Celia picking up things at the flea market. "It's possible that Celia is left-handed," I said. "I don't know about Elias."

"I think you need to give up on the idea that Celia Hunter is the killer," he said. "And I know you think there's some connection to what happened to Leo's former wife twenty years ago, but I think your connection is just a coincidence."

"Wait a minute, the killer is left-handed?"

Marcus held up both hands like he was surrendering. "I didn't say that."

I grinned at him. "You didn't have to."

He put our filets in the oven to finish cooking then pulled me up out of my chair so he could kiss me again, and for a while I forgot all about Elias Braeden and Celia Hunter.

Sunday dawned cold and wet. Eddie was coaching at hockey camp in Red Wing and Marcus was going along to help and to rub elbows with some former Wild players. I had been supposed to spend the afternoon with Roma but she called about ten to tell me a truck towing a trailer full of Angora show goats had gone off the road just outside of Lake City. She was on her way there to help with the injured animals.

I was at loose ends after lunch so I decided to go down to the library to repair some of the books that I knew had been piling up in the workroom. Neither Owen nor Hercules was willing to dash through the rain to the truck but I didn't mind having the library to myself. As much as I loved it when the hundred-year-old-plus building was full of life, I liked the occasional moment when I could walk through and appreciate all the beautiful details that made the library feel like my second home: Oren's carved sun over the doors, the mosaic tile floor, the intricate, wide woodwork that Oren had matched so well it was impossible to tell where old ended and new began, and of course shelf after shelf of books.

I pulled into the parking lot and when I got out of the truck a sleek silver Mercedes pulled in beside me. Elias Braeden was behind the wheel. He got out and came around the back of the car. "Kathleen, could I talk to you for a minute?" he asked.

"Were you following me?" I said.

"I'm sorry," he said. "I didn't mean to scare you. I just need to talk."

"What about?" I said. I was careful to keep some distance between us.

"Leo Janes."

I nodded. "All right." It was drizzling lightly, not enough to be called a shower, just enough to be annoying.

"Could we go inside?" Elias said. He was wearing a gray trench coat over dark pants. I had on my purple quilted jacket and a black-and-white scarf at my neck. Neither one of us would be cold staying outside.

"I'm good here," I said. I put one hand on the side of the truck. I didn't think Elias was stupid enough to try anything, but I had a couple of hockey sticks in the bed of the truck from a game of driveway hockey with Marcus. Maybe I couldn't swing a twenty-pound bag of potatoes at Elias's head, but I could swing a hockey stick if I had to.

"The woman you were with in the café on Friday. She told you she saw me with Leo." He stood with his feet apart, hands in his pockets.

"You lied to me," I said.

"No, I didn't. I told you I didn't see Leo the day he died. I didn't. I went to see him the day before, not to threaten him but to offer him a security job. He turned me down."

"Can you prove this?"

Elias nodded. "Leo turned me down but he suggested I hire one of his former grad students. I didn't tell you that because we were still negotiating her contract, but now that it's signed you and the police are welcome to talk to her. She'll confirm that Leo called her about my offer." He held out a piece of paper. "This is her name and her contact information."

I put the piece of paper in my pocket. "Thank you," I said. I hesitated. "I apologize for thinking the worst of you."

He smiled. "No apology necessary. I admire your loyalty and your tenacity. If you ever want to make a career change, please call me." He got back in his car and pulled out of the lot.

I headed for the front entrance. It seemed pretty clear that Elias wasn't Leo's killer. Was Marcus wrong about Celia Hunter, I wondered? Was I right? I didn't know what to think. I was glad for the distraction working on the books would give me.

Several of the repairs were minor and I breezed quickly through the first six books. I realized that the seventh was going to need Abigail's expertise. She'd taken a course on conservation and had been able to work on several of the old books in our reference section. That was where this book had come from. The stitching had come loose and several pages had fallen out. One page in particular seemed to have been sticking out beyond the book cover, unprotected by it, for some time. The edge was worn in several places and the paper was faded a lighter color about a quarter of an inch in from the edge the entire length of the page. I'd seen another page faded and damaged in the same way just recently. *I should put that book aside for Abigail as well*, I thought. I looked through the other books in the pile but I couldn't find it. Maybe Susan or Mary would know? I'd ask them both on Monday. Mia, too.

Mia.

Simon.

That was all it took to make the connection. The page I was remembering wasn't from a book, it was the second page of the letter Celia Hunter had shared with Simon. The outside edge of the paper had been faded and worn in exactly the same way as the book page in front of me. In the case of the book, the page had been loose and a small part of the edge had extended beyond the protection of the cover. So how had the second sheet of pink stationery gotten worn and faded?

I thought about it for a moment. Both sides of the envelope were worn almost through at the folds. If the two pages of the letter hadn't been folded evenly then that edge of the second page would have been exposed to changes in temperature and humidity inside that dusty wall, unprotected by the first page of the letter and by the envelope worn thin along the crease. But why didn't the first page of the letter show the same wear on the opposite edge of the page where that edge would have been exposed by an uneven fold of the pages?

Because there was a middle page, I realized. That wasn't a two-page letter, it was a three-page letter. Celia had shown Simon his mother's letter, she just hadn't shown him all of it.

I didn't stop to think whether it was a good idea or a bad idea; I closed up the workroom, got my purse and my jacket from my office and headed for the St. James Hotel to find Celia Hunter.

Sunday afternoons during the fall the St. James serves high tea in their dining room. That was where I found Celia. She was sitting at a table for two and I walked across the room as though I was supposed to be joining her, pulled out the second chair and sat down. She looked cool and elegant in a long purple heather sweater and black trousers.

"Hello, Celia," I said.

"What do you want?" she asked.

Since she had skipped the social niceties and gotten right to the point, so did I. "I want to know what it says on the page of Meredith's letter that you didn't show us."

The color drained from her face but it was the only sign that she was rattled. "I don't know what you're talking about," she said stiffly.

I leaned back in my seat, crossing one leg over the other to fake a confidence I didn't exactly feel. I had no way to make her show me the missing page of the letter.

At that moment a waiter made his way across to us.

"Ms. Paulson, hi," he said as he came level with the table.

"Hello, Levi," I said, smiling at the teen. He was a voracious reader, in the library at least once and often twice a week.

"I'll bring you a cup and a fresh pot," he said, smiling back at me.

"Thank you," I said.

Celia was far too polite to protest that I wasn't her guest. Levi moved to a nearby sideboard and returned with a larger pot of tea, wrapped in an old-fashioned quilted cozy, and a china cup and saucer. "Let me know if you need anything else," he said.

I poured myself a cup of tea and added a little milk and two lumps of sugar. My mouth was dry and getting the tea ready bought me a little more time to figure out what I was going to say next. I took a sip and looked at Celia across the table. "The letter you received from Meredith had three pages, not two. For some reason you didn't want Simon—or, I'm guessing, Leo—to see what was written on the middle page."

"You have a very . . . fanciful imagination, Kathleen," she said.

I may have rattled her a little when I'd first appeared at the table, but she seemed completely composed now. "What I don't understand is if there's something that you feel you need to hide in that letter then why show it to Leo or Simon at all?"

"And as I already said, I have no idea what you're talking about."

I studied her for a moment, hoping I seemed as unconcerned as she did, when I realized she wasn't quite as calm as she seemed at first glance. Her hands were folded in her lap, left over right, and I noticed she was fingering something in her right hand. I caught a flash of something round and purple and suddenly a lot of things began to make sense.

"You're working the twelve steps," I said.

Something shifted in Celia's face. She reached up and set the purple nine-month AA coin she had been fingering on the table. "Yes," she said. "I wanted to make amends with Leo."

I remembered what Oren had told me. "Because you helped break up his marriage."

Wordlessly, she nodded.

"But you didn't tell Leo or Simon the truth."

Celia took a deep breath and let it out. "Kathleen, do you know the twelve steps?"

"Yes," I said. Susan's husband, Eric, was in AA.

"Then you know that it's important to make amends but not if that will hurt the person or someone else." She picked up the purple token and set it down again. "I've been sober for ten months," she said. "I know what a cliché it is, but I really am a different person—a better person. What I did to Leo and Simon was unforgivable and forgiveness wasn't what I was looking for. I wanted them both to know that Meredith wouldn't have left them if it hadn't been for me. If I hadn't told Victor what to say to win her over."

She closed her eyes for a moment. When she opened them again I could see regret and shame in them. "I was all set to tell Leo the truth and let him read the letter from Meredith. Yes, there's another page. And then he told me that Victor was here and that he's sick."

I understood then. "And you knew if you told Leo the truth that any chance of the two of them reconciling would be gone."

She nodded. "He's sick, Kathleen. He could die. I couldn't do it. No matter what he did—what we did—I couldn't take away his chance to have a relationship with the only family he has left."

"But you'd already told Leo about the letter."

"Yes." She studied the purple token for a moment and set it on the table once more. "Then I realized I could just remove the middle page. The letter still made sense."

"Why did you push to show it to Simon?"

"A reporter who is doing an article about the mail that was found contacted me. I made the mistake of telling her that I had received a letter from an old friend. I was afraid Simon would put two and two together and figure out the friend was his mother. This way I could . . . control what he—what everyone—found out." She looked past me for a moment and then her gaze met mine again. "And because, selfishly, it made me feel a little better."

"What's on the missing page?" I asked.

She reached for her purse tucked next to her hip in the upholstered chair, removed the pink envelope and handed it across the table to me. I took out the three sheets of paper and read the letter, the whole letter, from the beginning.

Dear Celia,

I hope you don't throw this letter away as soon as you see it's from me. You probably hate me for what I've done, but you couldn't hate me more than I hate myself. Victor and Leo may look the same but they're very different men. I thought Victor was exciting, and he seemed to know what I was thinking in a way Leo didn't, as if he could see into my heart somehow. But I was wrong. I've learned that Victor is selfish, manipulative and cruel. He doesn't really care about me. He doesn't love me. I think the only reason he showed any interest in me at all was to hurt Leo. He's so jealous of his brother and I have proof of that now. I miss Simon so much. Victor is going out of town in a couple of weeks. I'll be able to leave then. I was a childish fool. I don't know if Leo will ever forgive me but I have to find out.

I love him. I will see you soon.

Love, Merry

I set the pages down on the cream tablecloth. I had to swallow down the lump in the back of my throat. "She was coming home to them."

Celia nodded. "And I know I have to let Simon read this. *Not* telling him leaves him with more pain than telling will cause Victor."

"I think so," I said. I put the pages back in the envelope and handed it back to her. "Thank you for telling me the truth."

"I should have told it from the beginning," she said.

"You were doing what you thought was right," I told her. "I can't fault you for that. I don't think anyone can. I do have one more question, though. Did you know Leo also received a piece of that lost mail?"

Celia shook her head. "He didn't say anything to me."

Nothing in her face or her body language made me think she wasn't telling the truth. "Was it from Meredith?" she asked.

"I don't know," I said. "Can you think of any reason she might have sent him a key?"

A frown formed between her perfectly groomed eyebrows. "A key?"

I nodded.

"No. That doesn't make any sense."

"I know," I said. I reached into my bag, pulled out a pen and a small notepad and wrote down my cell phone number. "If you think of anything, anything, please call me."

"I will," she said. "And I promise you I'll call Simon and let him read the letter."

"He's in Minneapolis with his daughter for a couple of days," I said. "They'll be back Tuesday. That's soon enough." I got up and made my way across the room.

Levi was at another table. I waited by the door and when he turned I raised a hand. He came right over to me. I gave him my credit card and paid for our tea with a generous tip. After what I'd learned from Celia it seemed the least I could do.

It was still raining when I stepped outside. I ran through the rain back to the truck, sliding onto the front seat, shaking the water off my hair. Then I pulled my cell phone out of my pocket. Marcus would be in Red Wing until late. There was nothing he could do with what I'd learned from Celia. At least not right now. I put my phone away.

I was glad Simon and Mia were in Minneapolis for a couple of days. Because as soon as Simon read that letter he was going to suspect what I was starting to strongly suspect—that Victor Janes had killed his own brother.

16

I called Marcus as soon as I got home. It went to voice mail but he called me back about half an hour later. I gave him the information I'd gotten from Elias and I told him about the missing page of the letter.

He stayed silent until I finished talking. "I agree that it doesn't make Victor Janes look good," he said.

"What's the but?" I asked, walking out into the porch with the phone.

"It doesn't change the fact that he has an alibi. And I saw him write his name in the guest book at Gunnerson's. He's *right*-handed. Whoever killed Leo Janes was left-handed, remember?"

"So what are you thinking?" I asked as I dropped down onto the bench under the porch window. "Do you think he hired someone to kill Leo?"

Marcus made an exasperated sound on the other end of the phone. "I don't know," he said. "Just promise me you'll stay away from the man until we figure this out."

"That's not a problem," I said. Victor Janes had made

me uncomfortable before I began to suspect he'd been involved in his brother's death. I wanted to be around him now even less.

Roma called after supper to say they'd managed to save all of the goats and both the driver and his passenger had walked away from the accident with nothing more than a few bruises. "I had planned to check Owen's ear when I came for dinner," she said. "Since I didn't get there do you think you could bring him into the clinic after you finish tomorrow? I'm sure he's fine, but I'd just like to take one more look."

"I can do that," I said. We settled on a time and I said good night.

The next morning was busy. Maggie dropped off the information for the board about her auction idea, two boxes of new books were delivered and a routine software update made all the public-access computers shut down at once.

I'd just gotten the computers up and running again when Abigail waved from the front desk to catch my attention. "Do you have a minute to talk to Lita?" she asked.

I nodded. "Cross everything," I said, gesturing at the computer where I was sitting. "I think I have things working again."

Abigail grinned. "You have the magical touch. The only thing I know to do is whack the side of the monitor with my hand."

I grinned back at her. "Hey, that's my Plan B." I

walked over to the desk and reached for the phone. "Hi, Lita," I said. "What can I do for you?"

"Good morning, Kathleen," she said. "I just have a quick question for you about Reading Buddies."

"Sure, what is it?" She was looking at an invoice and luckily her question was easily answered.

"Thank you. I wish every phone call this morning had worked out so well."

"Rough Monday?" I said.

"You're the only person I've been able to actually get to talk to in person. It isn't easy trying to change Everett's schedule around."

"Is everything all right?" I asked.

"You didn't hear about Rebecca?" she asked.

My heart began to pound and I put a hand down on the counter to steady myself. "No. Is she all right?"

"She's fine," Lita said. "I'm sorry, I didn't mean to scare you. She and Everett were at an auction on the weekend. Someone's dog got loose and knocked her down. She sprained her knee. She's probably going to have to be off it for a week." She cleared her throat. "Everett is hovering."

I struggled not to laugh. "You mean he's driving her crazy."

Lita did laugh. "Yes."

"He can't help it," I said. "He may be driving her crazy but it's because he's crazy about her."

"And Rebecca—"

"—is not the best patient," I finished. "I'll try to go see her tonight."

"Your good deed for the week," Lita said. "Thanks for the information, Kathleen."

I took a shorter lunch break so I could leave a bit earlier at the end of the day. Hercules was sitting out in the porch when I got home. I sat down beside him. "How was your day?" I asked.

"Mrr," he replied. Translation: "Good."

"Where's your brother?"

Herc turned toward the kitchen door.

"Roma wants to check his ear one more time," I said.

He put a paw over his face.

I laughed. "Yeah, I know how he's going to react."

I got up, unlocked the door and stepped into the kitchen. Owen was just making his way in from the living room. I set my things on the table and bent down to pick him up. "How would you like to go see Rebecca?" I asked. "She hurt her knee and she's housebound."

"Merow," he said.

"I thought we could take her some of those oatmeal cookies. There are a couple of dozen in the freezer."

He licked his whiskers. Okay, that was a yes.

"And we're going to stop and let Roma take a look at your ear," I said, running the words all together. It didn't matter how fast I said them, however; Owen knew exactly what I'd said. He immediately started to try to wiggle his way out of my arms.

I set him down on the floor. "No, it's all right," I said. "You don't have to go." I went over to the sink, washed my hands and then went to the freezer to get out the cookies.

Owen eyed me suspiciously.

I put the cookies in one of my canvas carryalls, picked up my purse and keys again and started for the door. "I'll give Rebecca your love," I said. As I stepped out into the porch Owen edged past me. He headed straight for the back door, making little grumbling sounds all the way. Apparently we were going to see Roma after all.

I stopped to give Hercules a scratch on the top of his head. He almost seemed to be smiling at me. "I'll see you later," I said.

Roma was waiting at the clinic. She quickly checked Owen's ear, and while he wasn't a model patient he wasn't any more difficult than usual.

"We're going to see Rebecca," I told Roma, explaining about Rebecca's injury.

"Give her a hug from me and tell her I'll be over to see her tomorrow," Roma said.

I'd called Rebecca before we'd left the house to see if she'd like a furry visitor. "I'd love one," she'd said. "I keep telling Everett that I'm fine but he's not listening." She'd raised her voice at the end of the sentence, I'm guessing because she intended her husband to hear what she'd said.

"She's stubborn, Kathleen," Everett had said in the background.

I'd laughed. "Owen and I will see you in a little while."

Victor Janes was just heading up the walkway when I got to Everett's big brick house. He stopped when he realized it was me and waited for me to join him. I had told Marcus I'd stay away from the man, but I didn't want to give him any hint that I suspected he was responsible for Leo's death. I wondered how he could stay in that apartment after what I thought he'd done.

"Hello, Kathleen," Victor said. He was bundled up in a heavy barn jacket with a navy-and-wine-colored wool scarf looped and knotted at his neck.

"Good evening, Victor," I said.

"You're here to see Rebecca, I'm guessing."

I nodded. "I brought her some cookies."

He held the door open for me and I stepped into the entryway. "Come in with me," he said, reaching in his pocket for his keys. "It'll save Everett a trip down the stairs."

I nodded. "Thank you."

He opened the door and once again indicated that I should go ahead of him. "Have a good evening," he said. He turned toward his brother's apartment.

"You too," I said.

Owen had stayed silent and out of sight during the entire encounter with Victor but once the apartment door closed he poked his head out of the top of the fabric bag and looked at me. He wrinkled his nose and then looked down the stairs.

"I know," I said softly. "Victor Janes smells like Biggie Burgers."

Back before Roma had gotten insistent that I stop

letting the cats eat people food, Owen had had half of his one and only Biggie Burger. When he heard the words he still got a blissed-out look on his face.

Rebecca was settled on the sofa in the living room with her knee resting on a pillow and a large cold pack wrapped around it. Owen jumped out of the bag and made a beeline across the room to her. "Hello, Kathleen," she said before leaning forward a little to talk to the cat.

"How is she?" I said to Everett.

"Stubborn and argumentative," he replied, rubbing his stubbled chin with one hand. "I wanted to hire a nurse but you'd think I was suggesting locking her up."

"I think for her it's the same thing," I said with a smile.

Owen and Rebecca had a great visit. She fussed over him; he sympathized with her. I left with a promise that I'd be back tomorrow after tai chi. Owen climbed into the bag without argument.

When we got to the bottom of the stairs he poked his head out for a look around but stayed put. It wasn't until I stepped outside that the bag wriggled against my leg. I moved to grab him but he was already half out. He jumped down to the walkway and disappeared around a large evergreen shrub.

"Owen!" I hissed.

No answer. Why was I wasting time? He wasn't going to answer and he wasn't going to come back. It would be faster to just go after him.

The yard of the big brick house wasn't very large, not a surprise given how close we were to the downtown. There was a small outbuilding by the back entrance. I found Owen pawing at the door.

"Okay, what are you doing?" I said, folding my arms over my chest and glaring at him.

He looked at the door and he looked at me.

"It's probably where they keep the garbage cans," I said. "There's nothing in there for you."

He continued to look at me unblinkingly.

"We shouldn't be doing this."

"Mrr," he said: Maybe we shouldn't be, but we're going to.

There was no sign of anyone else around. I opened the door. Owen squeezed inside and I slipped in as well. There was enough light from a nearby streetlight to see the three garbage cans stacked by the back wall. I lifted the lid of the first one. The empty package of bacon told me it was Everett and Rebecca's trash. The second can was empty. The third can held orange peels, an empty pomegranate juice container and at the very bottom a take-out bag from Biggie Burgers.

Owen sat on the top of the empty can and sniffed the air.

"You were right," I said. "Victor Janes had a Biggie Burger for supper." I pulled out the fast food bag. Underneath it, half hidden under another crumpled fast food bag, I saw the edge of something that looked familiar. Heart thumping in my chest, I reached into the garbage again and pulled out a small plastic container. It was empty but I'd seen many similar ones. I knew stage makeup well and I knew the container had held a tinted base. I rummaged in the bottom of the trash container and found another mostly empty tub of white crème color, a bruise-and-abrasions wheel and a half-used black pencil. I could only think of one reason Victor Janes had stage makeup. He wasn't sick. He was using it to create the illusion that he was.

I set the containers on top of the adjacent garbage can, pulled out my phone, took several pictures of the makeup and then put everything back. I used hand sanitizer to clean my hands and then I picked up Owen and made my way back to the truck.

I'd just set the cat on the seat when my phone rang. I climbed in next to him, took a deep breath and got my phone out of my pocket. I recognized the number as the library's. It was Mary.

"Bridget hit a deer up on the highway," she said. Her voice had a shaky edge. "She's all right but they're still taking her to the hospital as a precaution. I know she's a grown adult, but she's still my baby."

"Go," I said.

"Are you sure?"

"Go," I repeated. "I'm just leaving Rebecca and Everett's. Tell Abigail I'll be there soon."

I looked at Owen. "We have to get back to the library. And then we're going to have to call Marcus. I think Victor Janes has been lying about being sick, probably as a way to generate sympathy and work his way back into his brother's life. It was likely the only thing he thought would work after twenty years of estrangement. If he's lying about that then maybe he's lying about some other things, too."

I had the photos of the makeup on my phone,

makeup I felt certain Victor had been using to make himself look gaunt and pale. Would they be enough to convince Marcus that Victor had killed his brother? I started the truck. As soon as I got back to my office I'd find out.

The parking lot was almost empty when I got to the library. Monday nights were sometimes that way.

"Hi," I said to Abigail as I came in the front door. Owen poked his head out of the bag.

"Merow," he said.

She smiled. "Owen, it's so good of you to finish Mary's shift for her."

He tipped his head to one side and gave her his best cute cat look.

"You're such a hambone," I said. I took him up to my office, gave him a drink and a couple of crackers and went back down to help Abigail. I tried Marcus but the call went to voice mail. "Call me," I said. "It's important."

My phone rang about an hour later just as I was starting the walk through the building. I'd been expecting it to be Mary or Marcus, but it was Celia Hunter.

"Hello, Kathleen," she said. "Did I catch you at a bad time?"

"No," I said. "Is there something I can do for you?"

"I'm hoping there's something I can do for you," she said.

"All right."

"You mentioned that Leo got a key in the mail."

"Yes," I said, tucking a book back in place on its shelf.

"I think it's possible Meredith did send it."

"Do you know why?"

She exhaled softly. "Leo's father had a large metal strongbox in his house. He was a child of the Great Depression and he didn't really trust banks. The family didn't know for certain what was in it until he died. Meredith told me that Leo had suspected his father's lawyer may have taken things out of the box before it was opened with Leo, Victor and the lawyer present. There was only one key and the lawyer had taken charge of it as the executor when Leo's father died."

Celia paused and cleared her throat. "I keep thinking what if it was Victor, not the lawyer? What if he somehow made a copy of that key? What if Meredith found it? What if she figured out what it was for? Maybe Victor found out and . . ." She didn't finish the sentence. She didn't need to.

I thanked her for calling and hung up. I remembered what Sandra had said about *when* Leo had received the letter with the key. One day before he was killed. Victor Janes was looking more and more guilty. I tried Marcus again, and again all I got was voice mail.

Abigail was ready to go. "I can wait for you," she said.

I shook my head. "It's okay," I said. "I'll let you out now. I have to go upstairs and corral the furball."

I unlocked the door, watched Abigail walk to her car then relocked it again. Then I went upstairs to get Owen.

He trailed me as I shut off the remaining lights and double-checked windows. I wasn't really paying a lot of attention to what I was doing. I was putting together the case I was going to make to Marcus.

"Victor Janes doesn't have cancer," I said to Owen. "He's not sick and if he was faking that, maybe he also faked his alibi somehow. I think when Leo got the key in the mail he recognized it and he figured out that Victor stole something—money, probably, and maybe a lot of it—from their father, and I think he guessed that Victor had something to do with Meredith's death." I remembered the book on theatrical makeup Leo had requested. "In fact," I mused, "I think Leo was already getting suspicious that his brother's illness was just another scam."

I pulled out my phone again. I thought for a moment about trying Simon but he and Mia were still in Minneapolis. I put the phone back in my pocket and turned around.

Victor Janes was standing there.

17

"I'm sorry, Victor, the library is closed," I said. I looked down for Owen but he had disappeared. Literally.

"Yes, I know," Victor said.

I wrapped my fingers around my keys and began to move toward the door, making a wide path around him. "It's not a problem. I can let you out."

It took about three steps for him to plant himself in front of me. "Don't waste your time and mine, Kathleen," he said. "I saw you. You went through the garbage cans."

I didn't see any point in keeping up the pretense. "You killed Leo," I said. "You use your right hand but you're ambidextrous like he was. You used your left hand when you hit him even though most of the time you do things right-handed."

Victor laughed. It was a harsh sound in the empty library. He looked exactly like his brother but there was no way anyone who had met Leo could confuse the two.

"So we're going to play a game of Clue?" he said. "The killer was Uncle Victor in the foyer with a sculpture?"

"Yes, it was," I said. The only thing I could think was to stall, to keep him talking. "How did you fake your alibi? You weren't actually in that chat room."

He gave me a smile that made the hairs come up on the back of my neck. "The wonders of modern technology. I have this slick little app that lets me connect with my computer even when I'm somewhere else, like now, for instance. Makes it look like I'm there when I'm not."

"You had a second phone, a prepaid one that you got rid of." I studied his face, looking for even a hint of remorse. I didn't see any. "It wasn't a coincidence that the battery on what was supposed to be your only phone overheated that exact day, was it?" I remembered what Avis had said about her old tablet: *Heat isn't good for rechargeable batteries.*

Victor shrugged but didn't say anything. It was as close to an admission as I was going to get.

"I don't understand why you killed your own brother, though."

"You can call it sibling rivalry."

"You wanted his wife." I moved my left leg a little to the side. Was Owen still next to me? No.

Victor smiled. It just made his face more ugly. "I had his wife."

I shook my head. "No, you didn't. Meredith was

afraid of you, afraid enough that she was waiting for you to go out of town so she could get away from you. The night she died she was on her way home to her husband and her son. She didn't want you."

"Is this where I'm supposed to get angry and then you take advantage of my emotions to escape?"

"She was going to tell Leo what you'd done, how you'd stolen money from your own father. That's why you killed her," I said. I saw a flash of anger in his eyes.

"I didn't kill Meredith," he said emphatically. "I just wanted to talk to her. That's all. I wanted her to pull over so I could talk to her. It's not my fault that she wouldn't slow down."

"She found the key to your father's strongbox," I said. "She knew then what you'd done, what kind of person you really were. I'm guessing you almost caught her, so she dropped the key in an envelope and mailed it to Leo. She didn't want you to find it on her. And she knew she could explain everything when she finally saw him. Except she never did."

Victor took a deep breath and seemed to get his emotions under control again. "What I did was take what was mine. What I did was secure a future for the two of us. Which I could have made her understand if she'd just pulled the damn car over!"

"You must have wondered what happened to that key," I said. "She didn't have it on her. Then as the weeks went by you must have figured you were safe." I gave him a smile I didn't feel. "Then after all this time you saw the story about the mail found in the wall at the post office."

There had been a small story about it on the evening news, which had been picked up by the *Today* show. "You realized Meredith could have mailed the key to Leo and, if he got it, he'd know what you did—everything you did. That's why you came here. Not to reconcile with your brother. You came to see what he knew."

"He changed," Victor said, and for the briefest moment I thought I saw something—maybe a flash of regret—but it was gone and his face hardened again. He pulled a hand over the back of his neck. "He never used to be able to keep a secret. But he didn't let on that he'd hired someone to look into Meredith's accident. I thought . . . I thought we were actually going to be brothers." It was hard to miss the bitterness in his voice.

"Leo was trying," I said. "He invited you to come. He was urging Simon and Mia to give you a chance."

"He couldn't leave the past where it belonged."

"You mean that key." I glanced down at the floor. There was still no sign of Owen. "Your brother knew what it was for."

Victor nodded. "But he didn't know who'd sent it. Not at first. Then he looked at the damn postmark."

"And then he knew who had mailed the key. And when."

"Why couldn't he just let it be?" Anger gave his voice a hard edge. "Meredith's death was an accident and I didn't take anything from my father's strongbox that shouldn't have been mine."

He'd found a way to rationalize everything.

"What happened?" I asked. "I know you didn't go over there intending to kill Leo."

"I didn't." His jaw was tight, teeth clenched. "He told me that he was going to give me a choice. I could turn myself in to the police or he'd tell them what he knew." Victor gave me a long, searching look. "Do you have any siblings, Kathleen?" he asked.

"Yes," I said. "A brother and sister."

"Would you sell them out? Would you put them in jail?"

"Neither one of them would ever put me in the position to have to even think about that," I said. I made a mental promise that when I got out of this I was going to call both Sara and Ethan and tell them just how much I loved them. I imagined Ethan laughing and saying, "Yeah, yeah, big sister. I love you, too."

"Aren't you perfect," Victor said.

"No. I'm not," I said. "But I can promise you I would have made a different choice. And you still have the chance to make a different one now."

"You aren't leaving me any reasonable choice. Neither did Leo. I'm not going to jail. Leo backed me into a corner. I had to kill him. Don't think I won't kill you."

I heard a strangled sound behind me, like a half-choked-off sob. I turned to find Mia standing there. One hand was pressed over her mouth as tears ran down her face.

Victor was faster than I was. Even as I started to say, "Run," he grabbed her shoulder, yanked her body against his chest and snaked his arm around her neck.

I held up my hands. "Let her go," I said. "You have

me. You don't need her." I kept my eyes locked on Mia, trying to somehow let her know that we would get out of this. At the same time I took a couple of steps closer to them while I had the chance.

"Stop!" Victor said sharply.

I stopped moving. "Okay." I dropped my hands to my sides.

There was a large atlas of the world on the low shelf next to me and a wire rack of paperbacks level with my shoulder by the end. Behind Victor and Mia was a higher set of shelves. I noticed the end book on the shelf just above his head was moving. Now I knew where Owen was. And now I had a plan. All I needed was for Mia to move the right way when the time came, away from Victor, away from me and toward the door.

On the end of the low shelf beside me I caught a glimpse of a fire-safety poster and I knew what to do.

"Give me your cell phone," Victor said.

"Why?" I asked, trying to keep my tone even and neutral. At the same time I folded one arm across my midsection and laid my index finger against the arm of my sweater.

One.

Victor tightened his arm around Mia's neck. I added my middle finger.

Two.

"You don't need to hurt Mia," I said.

"Then give me the damn phone." I hoped Mia had noticed. I hoped she knew something was about to happen.

"All right," I said. And my ring finger.

Three.

I made a movement as though I was going to give him my phone, then I grabbed the wire book stand and swung it at him. At the same time I yelled, "Stop! Drop! And roll!" as loudly as I could.

The words echoed around the library. Mia went limp, dropping out of Victor's grasp onto the floor, where she rolled to the left just the way she had when we'd practiced with the kids. At the same time Owen materialized and launched himself onto Victor's back, digging in with four sets of claws. It was all the distraction I needed.

I picked up the heavy atlas and swung it with every ounce of strength I had. It made very satisfying contact with the side of Victor Janes's head, a little karmic justice. His eyes rolled back and he fell backward onto the floor.

"Run!" I yelled to Mia, pushing her toward the front entrance. Then I grabbed Owen and ran after her.

18

Once we were outside I put an arm around Mia and kept her moving toward my truck. As soon as we were next to it I called 911. Then I gave Mia the phone so she could call her father. I unlocked the driver's door of the truck and set Owen on the seat. He shook himself and gave me a self-satisfied look.

"You're my furry hero," I said, leaning my face close to his for a moment.

"Mrr," he said, nuzzling my cheek.

I straightened up and turned to Mia. Her face was streaked with tears and there was dirt on her sweater from rolling on the floor.

"You did great," I said, putting my hands on her shoulders. I had to stop and swallow back the surge of emotions that suddenly hit me. "What were you doing in the building? I thought you and your father were in Minneapolis?"

"We came back a bit early. I realized that I'd left my sociology textbook here. I came in to get it just before you closed and then I got a text and I got held up." She folded her arms over her chest. "I saw your fingers," she said.

I smiled. "I knew you would."

"And when you yelled, 'Stop, drop and roll,' I didn't even think. I just did it."

I nodded. "That's what I was hoping."

She looked over at the door. "He killed Grandpa."

I folded her into my arms. "I'm sorry," I said.

"What if he gets up before the police get here?" she asked.

I let go of her with one arm and reached into the bed of the truck to pull out one of the hockey sticks. Given how hard I'd hit Victor with that atlas I didn't think he was going to be getting up very quickly, but if he did, I was going to be ready.

"If he does," I said, "I'm going to show him my slap shot." I heard the sirens then. I kept Mia against my side with one arm and held my hockey stick with the other.

It was only minutes before the first police car pulled to a stop in front of the building. Marcus's SUV fishtailed to the curb right behind it. He got out, said something to the uniformed officer and then came striding across the grass to us.

"Are you all right?" he said, putting a hand on my arm and studying my face.

"I'm okay," I said, giving him a small smile. It was so good to see his face.

He turned to Mia. "What about you? You okay?"

She nodded. "Kathleen saved us," she said.

Owen meowed loudly from the seat behind us. He wasn't about to let his contribution not be acknowledged.

Mia turned and smiled at him. "And Owen, too."

"Victor . . . killed his brother," I said.

"I know," Marcus said. "I just got off the phone with his health insurance provider. We finally got a judge to give us a subpoena."

Suddenly I understood why Leo had wanted to talk to Harry's ex-wife. "He's not sick."

Marcus shook his head. "No, he isn't." He glanced over at the building. The paramedics had arrived and were on their way inside.

"Go," I said. "We're all right."

"We can take care of ourselves," Mia said, squaring her shoulders.

"I can see that," Marcus said. "Just stay here. I'll be back." He leaned over and kissed me and then started for the door.

Out of the corner of my eye I saw Simon's SUV pull to the curb. He got out and looked around. I raised a hand and he started toward us. "Your dad's here," I said to Mia.

Her face lit up. I kissed the top of her head and she ran to meet him. Owen walked his way over the seat to me and rubbed against my side. I leaned the hockey stick against the side of the truck and reached down to stroke his fur. My legs were trembling but I reminded myself that we were all safe and that was all that mattered.

Marcus came back out in a couple of minutes and had me walk him through what had happened from the moment Owen and I arrived at Everett's apartment. "I'm sorry," he said, shaking his head. "My phone died. That's why you couldn't get me."

I put a hand on his arm. "It's all right," I said. "I broke my own rule about staff leaving together."

I looked over at the building. Victor had already been taken to the hospital. I'd hit him pretty hard and I wasn't the slightest bit sorry. "I know where the key is," I said.

Marcus frowned. "You mean the one Leo got in the mail?"

I nodded. "At least I'm pretty sure I do. Send someone over to look at the clock in the hallway at Everett's building. My dad has a clock like it and he keeps the key to wind it in a little envelope taped to the back. Rebecca does the same thing. I think Leo slipped his key in as well when he realized his brother was on the way."

Marcus nodded. "I'll send a car over."

"Is it all right if I go home now?" I asked.

"Yes," he said. "I'll be there once I get things wrapped up here. It might be a while."

"I don't care," I said. I reached up to kiss him. "I love you."

"I love you, too," he said. I watched him walk over to Simon and Mia.

Mia kissed her father on the cheek and started back over to me. As she got closer I realized she was carrying two take-out cups. She handed one to me. "Hot chocolate from Eric's," she said. She shrugged. "I don't know how Dad got it delivered over here."

I took the cup from her. "And I don't think I really care." I took a sip. The hot chocolate was hot and rich and warmed me all the way down to my toes. "How are you really?" I said to Mia.

"I'm not sure," she said, shaking her head. "I mean, I'm glad Uncle Victor's been arrested, but Grandpa is still dead and it looks like Uncle Victor had something to do with my dad's mother being dead, too."

"I'm so sorry," I said. "I wish knowing the truth could somehow change things."

Mia turned and looked back over her shoulder at her father and Marcus still talking. "You really love him, don't you?" she asked.

I nodded. "I do." I couldn't help smiling.

She turned back to me. "I was kind of hoping if you spent enough time with my dad maybe you could fall in love with him instead and then"—she swallowed hard—"you could be my mom."

I couldn't speak for a moment, overcome with a wave of emotions. A tear slid down her cheek and I reached over and brushed it away, and then I pulled her into my arms again.

"It would be an honor to be your mom," I said. "But I promise you that no matter what, no matter where you are, I will always be your friend. You can call me anytime. You can show up at my door anytime. If you need me all you have to do is yell."

She nodded with her head against my shoulder and

I wished that there were some way to give her what she wanted, to at least give her part of a happy ending. But there wasn't.

I spent a few more minutes with Mia and then I walked her over to Simon.

"'Thank you' seems pretty damned inadequate," he said to me.

"I'm sorry," I said. I seemed to be saying that a lot. "I wish it hadn't been Victor."

"You and me both."

I took Mia's face in my hands. "Go home, soak in the bathtub, drink more hot chocolate and if you need to talk call me anytime, okay?"

"Okay," she said.

Simon gave her a hug. "Go sit in the car," he said. "I just want to talk to Kathleen a minute."

She nodded and started for the vehicle, both hands wrapped around her hot chocolate.

Simon turned to me. "That private investigator called on my way over here. He found the witness, the woman walking her dog the night of . . . of my mother's accident. She told him she saw a car following—chasing—my mother's car. She got a decent look at the driver."

"Victor," I said.

"Yes." His expression tightened. "Too little, too late."

"No," I said, shaking my head. "It'll help make the case against him. I know it doesn't make up for what you lost . . ." I didn't finish the sentence.

"It's something," Simon said.

I looked over at his car. "You should take Mia home."

Simon caught my hand and gave it a squeeze. "Thank you," he said.

I nodded wordlessly and walked back to the truck.

When we got home I opened a can of sardines and gave Owen the entire can. Hercules wandered in from somewhere. He gave me a puzzled look.

"Trust me, he earned it," I said.

I was sitting at the kitchen table with my second mug of hot chocolate when I heard a knock at the back door. It was Simon.

"Hi," I said.

He smiled. "Hi. I can't stay. Mia is with Denise. But I wanted to give you this."

He handed me a small cardboard box. I knew before I took the lid off what I was going to find inside. A man's gold watch. I'd told him about the poker game and Harrison's watch. I was surprised he'd shown up with it now.

"Thank you," I said. "I'll make sure Harrison gets this."

"You saved Mia's life," he said.

"She did a pretty good job of saving herself," I said. "She's smart and resilient and absolutely amazing."

"She's had some good role models." His eyes were locked on my face and I was suddenly aware of the small amount of space between us. "If I thought I had any shot with you . . . ," he said, letting the rest of the sentence trail away. "But I don't, do I?"

I shook my head slowly. "In a different place or time, but not this one. I'm sorry."

He nodded. "You ever need anything and Detective Gordon isn't around, you better call me," he said. "And if he's stupid enough to ever screw things up with you you'll find me camped on your doorstep." He leaned over and kissed my cheek and then he turned and left.

EPILOGUE

The exhibit, which Maggie simply named "Lost & Found," opened a week after Thanksgiving. Burtis donated the perfect Christmas tree, tall and straight and so perfectly symmetrical it had no "bad side" to tuck in the corner. Harry set the tree up near the main entrance and the scent of the huge fir filled the library, reminding me of hiking in the woods out at Turtle Lake with Marcus every time I stepped into the building. Once again, Ruby loaned us her collection of vintage ornaments to decorate with. Abigail and I hung twinkling white fairy lights all over the main floor, which transformed the space into a winter wonderland.

Mary and Peggy Sue from the diner had made dozens and dozens of holiday cookies. "If you want to get lots of people into the building you need food," Mary had proclaimed two days before the exhibit opened. Before I could say anything, she'd held up a hand.

"Don't worry. I'll take care of everything." I knew from the gleam in her eyes that she would.

Two hours before everyone was supposed to arrive, Mary and Peggy showed up with Mia and Taylor King in tow, and box after box of cookies. There were gingerbread men with icing smiles and candy bow ties; round sugar cookies with frosted snowman faces; and Swedish butter cookies, crisp, buttery rectangles dusted with powdered sugar. Mia and Taylor's job would be to circulate through the crowd, each with a tray of cookies, and I suspected our biggest problem was going to be running out before the evening was over.

"Thank you," I said to the two women. I put a hand on my chest and had to swallow down the lump of emotion that had formed because of their generosity.

Mary patted my arm. "We're family, Kathleen." She made a sweeping gesture with one hand that I knew meant she was including the whole library. "We may be a little odd from time to time and we may drive each other crazy once in a while, but when it's time to get the boat moving we all grab an oar and start rowing."

It was one of the strangest metaphors I'd ever heard, but I also knew exactly what she meant. As Leo Janes's death had shown me once again, family wasn't really about biology. It was about looking out for one another. Mary was right. We were family in the best sense of the word.

Maggie and I had temporarily rearranged our computer area, and the end wall of the space had been transformed into a gallery wall. The co-op artists had, as usual, done a spectacular job turning Maggie's flea-market frames into works of art. Nic had added reclaimed wood that came from one of the old warehouses by the waterfront to two frames. Ruby had put a selection of the pictures we thought came from the summer camp at Long Lake into small frames she had spray painted black and attached to a bicycle wheel. Several photos of the town, including one of Riverarts when it was still a school, were up for silent auction. And on the wall adjacent to the photos, Maggie had displayed all the letters and cards she'd persuaded the recipients to loan to us.

Thorsten took his share of gentle ribbing over the card from his old girlfriend and Brady was an equally good sport over the note Burtis had gotten from Brady's teacher explaining that the eleven-year-old spent too much time daydreaming and not enough concentrating on his schoolwork. He'd laughed and held out both hands as he stood with Maggie and me in front of the letter, protected in a shadowbox frame. "What can I say? She wasn't wrong."

Both Susan and Abigail were moving among the people, stopping to make notes whenever they heard an exclamation of recognition from someone looking at one of the photographs.

And it looked like we finally had an explanation of sorts for how the photos and pieces of mail had ended up behind the wall at the post office for all those years. Jon Larsen, grandson of the old postmaster, Campbell Larsen, who Harrison had mentioned, had turned up at the library just a day ago. It seemed likely the post-master had been the one to hide everything.

"My grandfather got a little obsessed about preserv-ing Mayville Heights's history," Jon had explained. "He'd been taking photographs his entire life and as his dementia got worse, he got a lot more secretive about where he put things he thought were important."

It turned out that Jon and his siblings had found a similar cache of old pictures and papers behind a wall when they had started to renovate their grandfather's house after his death.

I'd thanked him for coming in and giving me what felt like a logical ending to the story.

I was standing by the circulation desk, just taking everything in, when Marcus came up behind me, put-ting a hand on my shoulder. I turned to look up at him. He was incredibly handsome in a charcoal turtle-neck and black tweed jacket. I knew how corny it was, but the best part of him really was what was on the inside.

"I think we're going to figure out who's in most of those old photos by the end of the night," I said. "I've already heard some great stories, including one in-volving Everett and a panty raid."

"A panty raid?" Marcus said slowly.

"It's when a group of guys try to steal—"

He shook his head, a smile spreading across his face. "It's okay. I know what a panty raid is. And I'm thinking that story's going to be interesting."

"I could tell you over breakfast," I said, watching

his face. I felt a bit like Goldilocks, albeit a romance version, not the porridge-eating version. Too pushy? Not pushy enough?

"Sounds good," Marcus said, giving me a look that for a moment made me forget how to breathe.

It was just right.

If you love Sofie Kelly's
Magical Cats series, read on for a
sample of the first book in Sofie Ryan's
New York Times bestselling
Second Chance Cat Mystery series!

THE WHOLE CAT AND CABOODLE

is available wherever books are sold.

Elvis was sitting in the middle of my desk when I opened the door to my office. The cat, not the King of Rock and Roll, although the cat had an air of entitlement about him sometimes, as though he thought he was royalty. He had one jet-black paw on top of a small cardboard box—my new business cards, I was hoping.

"How did you get in here?" I asked.

His ears twitched but he didn't look at me. His green eyes were fixed on the vintage Wonder Woman lunch box in my hand. I was having an early lunch, and Elvis seemed to want one as well.

"No," I said firmly. I dropped onto the retro red womb chair I'd brought up from the shop downstairs, kicked off my sneakers, and propped my feet on the matching footstool. The chair was so comfortable. To me, the round shape was like being cupped in a soft, warm giant hand. I knew the chair had to go back down to the shop, but I was still trying to figure out a way to keep it for myself.

Before I could get my sandwich out of the yellow vinyl lunch box, the big black cat landed on my lap. He wiggled his back end, curled his tail around his feet and looked from the bag to me.

"No," I said again. Like that was going to stop him.

He tipped his head to one side and gave me a pitiful look made all the sadder because he had a fairly awesome scar cutting across the bridge of his nose.

I took my sandwich out of the lunch can. It was roast beef on a hard roll with mustard, tomatoes and dill pickles. The cat's whiskers quivered. "One bite," I said sternly. "Cats eat cat food. People eat people food. Do you want to end up looking like the real Elvis in his chunky days?"

He shook his head, as if to say, "Don't be ridiculous."

I pulled a tiny bit of meat out of the roll and held it out. Elvis ate it from my hand, licked two of my fingers and then made a rumbly noise in his throat that sounded a lot like a sigh of satisfaction. He jumped over to the footstool, settled himself next to my feet and began to wash his face. After a couple of passes over his fur with one paw he paused and looked at me, eyes narrowed—his way of saying, "Are you going to eat that or what?"

I ate.

By the time I'd finished my sandwich Elvis had finished his meticulous grooming of his face, paws and chest. I patted my legs. "C'mon over," I said.

He swiped a paw at my jeans. There was no way he

was going to hop onto my lap if he thought he might get a crumb on his inky black fur. I made an elaborate show of brushing off both legs. "Better?" I asked.

Elvis meowed his approval and walked his way up my legs, poking my thighs with his front paws—no claws, thankfully—and wiggling his back end until he was comfortable.

I reached for the box on my desk, keeping one hand on the cat. I'd guessed correctly. My new business cards were inside. I pulled one out and Elvis leaned sideways for a look. The cards were thick brown recycled card stock, with SECOND CHANCE, THE REPURPOSE SHOP, angled across the top in heavy red letters, and SARAH GRAYSON and my contact information, all in black, in the bottom right corner.

Second Chance was a cross between an antiques store and a thrift shop. We sold furniture and housewares—many things repurposed from their original use, like the tub chair that in its previous life had actually been a tub. As for the name, the business was sort of a second chance—for the cat and for me. We'd been open only a few months and I was amazed at how busy we already were.

The shop was in a redbrick building from the late 1800s on Mill Street, in downtown North Harbor, Maine, just where the street curved and began to climb uphill. We were about a twenty-minute walk from the harbor front and easily accessed from the highway—the best of both worlds. My grandmother held the mortgage on the property and I wanted to pay her back as quickly as I could.

"What do you think?" I said, scratching behind Elvis's right ear. He made a murping sound, cat-speak for "good," and lifted his chin. I switched to stroking the fur on his chest.

He started to purr, eyes closed. It sounded a lot like there was a gas-powered generator running in the room.

"Mac and I went to look at the Harrington house," I said to him. "I have to put together an offer, but there are some pieces I want to buy, and you're definitely going with me next time." Eighty-year-old Mabel Harrington was on a cruise with her new beau, a ninety-one-year-old retired doctor with a bad toupee and lots of money. They were moving to Florida when the cruise was over.

One green eye winked open and fixed on my face. Elvis's unofficial job at Second Chance was rodent wrangler.

"Given all the squeaks and scrambling sounds I heard when I poked my head through the trapdoor to the attic, I'm pretty sure the place is the hotel for some kind of mouse convention."

Elvis straightened up, opened his other eye, and licked his lips. Chasing mice, birds, bats and the occasional bug was his idea of a very good time.

I'd had Elvis for about four months. As far as I could find out, the cat had spent several weeks on his own, scrounging around downtown North Harbor.

The town sits on the midcoast of Maine. "Where the hills touch the sea" is the way it's been described for the past 250 years. North Harbor stretches from the Swift Hills in the north to the Atlantic Ocean in the south. It was settled by Alexander Swift in the late 1760s. It's full of beautiful historic buildings, award-winning restaurants and quirky little shops. Where else could you buy a blueberry muffin, a rare book and fishing gear all on the same street?

The town's population is about thirteen thousand, but that more than triples in the summer with tourists and summer residents. It grew by one black cat one evening in late May. Elvis just appeared at The Black Bear. Sam, who owns the pub, and his pickup band, The Hairy Bananas—long story on the name—were doing their Elvis Presley medley when Sam noticed a black cat sitting just inside the front door. He swore the cat stayed put through the entire set and left only when they launched into their version of the Stones' "Satisfaction."

The cat was back the next morning, in the narrow alley beside the shop, watching Sam as he took a pile of cardboard boxes to the recycling bin. "Hey, Elvis. Want some breakfast?" Sam had asked after tossing the last flattened box in the bin. To his surprise, the cat walked up to him and meowed a loud yes.

He showed up at the pub about every third day for the next couple of weeks. The cat clearly wasn't wild—he didn't run from people—but no one seemed to know whom Elvis (the name had stuck) belonged to. The scar on his nose wasn't new; neither were a couple of others on his back, hidden by his fur. Then someone remembered a guy in a van who had stayed two nights at the campgrounds up on Mount Batten.

He'd had a cat with him. It was black. Or black and white. Or possibly gray. But it definitely had had a scar on its nose. Or it had been missing an ear. Or maybe part of a tail.

Elvis was still perched on my lap, staring off into space, thinking about stalking rodents out at the old Harrington house, I was guessing.

I glanced over at the carton sitting on the walnut sideboard that I used for storage in the office. The fact that it was still there meant that Arthur Fenety hadn't come in while Mac and I had been gone. I was glad. I was hoping I'd be at the shop when Fenety came back for the silver tea service that was packed in the box.

A couple of days prior he had brought the tea set into my shop. Fenety had a charming story about the ornate pieces that he said had belonged to his mother. A bit too charming for my taste, like the man himself. Arthur Fenety was somewhere in his seventies, tall with a full head of white hair, a matching mustache and an engaging smile to go with his polished demeanor. He could have gotten a lot more for the tea set at an antiques store or an auction. Something about the whole transaction felt off.

Elvis had been sitting on the counter by the cash register and Fenety had reached over to stroke his fur. The cat didn't so much as twitch a whisker, but his ears had flattened and he'd looked at the older man with his green eyes half-lidded, pupils narrowed. He was the picture of skepticism.

The day after he'd brought the pieces in, Fenety had called to ask if he could buy them back. The more

I thought about it, the more suspicious the whole thing felt. The tea set hadn't been on the list of stolen items from the most recent police update, but I still had a niggling feeling about it and Arthur Fenety.

"Time to do some work," I said to Elvis. "Let's go downstairs and see what's happening in the store."

Sofie Kelly is a *New York Times* bestselling author and mixed-media artist who lives on the East Coast with her husband and daughter. She writes the *New York Times* bestselling Magical Cats Mysteries (*Paws and Effect, Faux Paw, A Midwinter's Tail*) and, as Sofie Ryan, writes the *New York Times* bestselling Second Chance Cat Mysteries (*The Fast and the Furriest, Telling Tails, A Whisker of Trouble*). Visit her online at sofiekelly.com.